I0556307

THIRD CHARM

A Reverse Harem Tale

Lovin' the Coven
Book 3

Jacquelyn Faye

∞ Untold Press ∞

Third Charm
A Reverse Harem Tale

Lovin' the Coven, book 3

All Rights Reserved
Copyright © 2019 by Jacquelyn Faye
Cover Design © 2019 by Sean Hayden
Cover Photo © 2019 by Depositphotos/sepavone
Cover Photo © 2019 by Depositphotos/ongap_
Cover Photo © 2019 by Depositphotos/raineralbiez
Cover Photo © 2019 by Shutterstock/Inara Prusakova

ISBN: 978-1-945893-09-4

All rights Reserved. This book or any portion thereof may not be reproduced or used in any manner whatsoever without the express written permission of the publisher except for the use of brief quotations in a book review.

Names, characters, places, and incidents are the products of the author's imagination and or used fictitiously. Any resemblance to actual events, locales or persons, living or dead, is entirely coincidental.

Published by Untold Press LLC
114 NE Estia Lane
Port St Lucie, FL 34983

www.untoldpress.com

PRODUCED IN THE UNITED STATES OF AMERICA

10 9 8 7 6 5 4 3 2 1

Dedication

To the person afraid to go to the ER because they don't want to explain the bruises

To the person who thinks maybe they deserved it

To the person too afraid to leave

To the person who thinks maybe they'll change

To the person lying on the ground, broken and bleeding

You have to, you didn't, you can, they won't, and it *will* happen again, no matter what they say.

National Domestic Violence Hotline

1-800-799-7233

Chapter 1

I was staring at my old boyfriend, currently sitting between Josie and Chief in the spot they had so graciously created for him. I don't know how he did it, but he made the simple act of forking small bits of turkey into his mouth seem erotic. I almost drooled in my cranberries.

He had instantly become the focus of our Thanksgiving meal. Everyone seemed to want to exchange a few words with him, probably just to hear his reply. The Irish accent he picked up over the past forty years could melt glass. Yeah. It was hot. I was restraining from fanning myself. He was already Mr. Popularity, but oddly enough, not with Chief *or* Jimmy. They both were just kind of oddly staring at him and pushing the food around on their plates.

I shrugged. I couldn't picture Jimmy having a problem with him, but Chief probably wanted to run a background check through Interpol before he invested so much as a hello.

Josie on the other hand kept flashing me grins and winks. I kicked her under the table.

"What do ye think, Dorothea?"

"It's Dot, actually," Chief said with a smile.

"Aye, so she tells me, but she'll always be sweet Dorothea to me, though."

"Don't be an ass, Derek. You know I hate Dorothea."

"Aye, but I like seeing your reaction when I do say it. It makes ye that much fairer."

"Cut the charm, too. We're not ready for dessert."

The table giggled. Most of them.

"So, what brings you to Cedar Falls?" Jimmy *finally* spoke to him.

"Madeline said Doro–Dot, was lookin' fer recruits. Said I should hop on the first plane out."

"And did she mention that we were flying to Ashville tomorrow morning?" His face told me she hadn't. He had that male stripper in a spotlight look, which is kind of like deer in headlights, but hotter. "Yes. I shall remember to mention her faux pas when I see her. I'm sure it just slipped her mind."

Like hell it did. What was she thinking?

"I don't mind. Lovely little town ye have here. I've already checked into the quaint motel. I shall be quite comfortable there until ye get back."

"I'm sorry to leave you so soon," I said, truly regretful in so many ways.

"Nay. I'll be fine. How long will ye be gone?"

"A few days. Chief and I have to get back pretty quickly."

"Oh, tis the chief that be going with you. Thought it might be a gentleman friend."

I blushed, knowing full well he was seeing if I was dating anyone. I had no idea how to tell him I was.

Chief took care of that pretty quick. "We are. Dot and I, I mean. We're seeing each other." He pointed at me and then himself.

I chuckled at his awkwardness.

"Oh. My apologies, Chief."

"It's okay. I don't mind dating her, but she has her moments."

I shot him a dirty look.

He smiled innocently, or a reasonable impersonation of innocence. He needed to work on it.

"We'll be back Sunday afternoon."

"I'll look forward to seeing ye."

I gave him a smile.

Dennis started asking him questions about Ireland while I pointedly ignored glances from both Chief and Jimmy. I would be spending quite a bit of time with Chief over the next few days. I could find out what crawled up his colon and made a nest. Jimmy I would talk to after everybody left.

The rest of dinner was joyful, in a sarcastic, I want to take some Xanax, kind of way. Derek remained the center of conversation for most, but everybody chatted amongst themselves, too. Jimmy was close enough to talk to, and I did. He didn't bring up Derek or our past relationship, he chatted about Ashville and the possible new members we would be interviewing, but there was an odd silence between us, even when we spoke.

Josie on the other hand, kept reminiscing on how much trouble Derek and I had gotten into in the past and how many times she caught us in compromising positions with an in-depth description of our clothing, or lack thereof. I kept kicking her, but she just wasn't getting the hint.

My fifth glass of wine found its way to my lips and we hadn't even made it to pie time. I seriously wanted to crawl in a hole and finally pushed my turkey away. I didn't finish my turkey. *Turkey...*

I sat and drank and ignored Josie. Candace looked like she wanted to hug me and finally reached over, grabbing Josie's arm, pulling her to her feet.

"Help me bring out the pie." Her tone left little room for Josie to argue and had an icy edge to it I'd never heard before. I kind of liked it.

"Want some help taking the food into the kitchen?"

I glanced at Jimmy. His smile looked strained and I didn't know why. Jealousy and Jimmy were like oil and water. Chief and laughter. Josie and savings accounts. "We probably should, I just don't know if I can stand right now," I answered and took another sip of wine.

"We can go get some fresh air, if you want."

"Nah."

"Please."

"Oh. Okay," I said and stood up, keeping my glass of wine. I had a feeling I was going to need it. Jimmy headed for the sliding glass door in the living room. I chugged my wine and grabbed a bottle off the table, pouring as I walked.

He held the door open for me and I handed him my adult beverages, grabbing somebody's coat off the couch. Had no clue whose it was. Didn't care. I took the wine and glass from him and stepped outside.

My porch wasn't covered, had no furniture, and was basically a concrete slab covered in snow on top of a layer of ice. I had no chance. I went down like Josie on a...never mind. I landed on my ass, but thankfully the snow stopped my head from smacking the concrete. The wine splashed whoever's jacket I'd grabbed, and the bottle smashed against the concrete. I stared at the neck of the bottle still clutched in my fingers. It had broken right above the label.

"Oh, my goddess. Are you okay, Dot?"

Dizzily, I looked up at Jimmy, pointing the broken end of the wine bottle at him. "I'ma shank you, bitch," managed to work its way out of my mouth, followed by me lying back in the snow and giggling.

Jimmy opened the slider with a sigh. "Guys, I need a hand."

Chief, Derek, and Dennis walked through after a moment or two. I had no idea how long it took. Time was moving very weirdly, and my porch was spinning. I must have hurt my brain when I fell on my ass. Or I was drunk. One of the two.

"What happened?" Chief didn't sound surprised.

"She slipped on the ice. Be careful and don't slip when you grab her," Jimmy warned.

"Be careful *where* you grab me, too. Make sure your hands are warm." I giggled as the four of them surrounded me, reaching down and hoisting me out of the snow.

"Is she drunk?" Dennis sounded confused.

"Aye, didn't ye see how she was sucking them down?"

"I hope you're talking about wine," I said with another giggle.

It was Derek's turn to look confused.

"She's gonna be fun on the plane tomorrow." Sarcasm from Chief. I was almost shocked.

I rolled my eyes. "I'll probably drink on the plane. Gotta do *something* to entertain myself with Captain Boyscout."

Chief dropped my leg. "She's a mean drunk." He pointed at me and walked back in the house. Derek lifted the dangling limb and held both of them in his arms.

"Were we takin' her, lads?"

"Bedroom. Through the door and back to the right."

"Aye."

At least Chief left the slider open. They managed to squeeze through it while holding me in their arms.

"Okay. You can set me down now. I can walk. No ice."

Derek looked at me dubiously, but gently set my feet on the floor while Dennis and Jimmy lifted me upright. They held on to me while I wobbled for a second and looked around for my wine. "Where's my wine?"

"That's enough." Jimmy spun me around to face him, bent down, putting his shoulder in my stomach and hoisting me up over his shoulder. He started walking me toward my room. My face was right by his butt. "Damn, you got a nice ass, Jimmy."

"Thanks, Dot. Means a lot when you're shitfaced."

"Oh, my goddess. Stop for a moment. Don't move."

"What?"

I lifted myself up enough to see the horrified stares of everyone at the dining tables. "Guys! I'm in a *fireman's carry,* on a freaking fireman! Woah."

"Goodnight, Dot," they all said in unison. I pouted as Jimmy started walking again.

There is no way to set somebody down on a bed gracefully when they're slung over your shoulder. Jimmy did an admirable job, but I felt the contents of my stomach slosh from the bouncing.

"Oh."

"You gonna puke?"

"Maybe. Gimme a bucket."

He walked into the bathroom and grabbed the trash can, setting it beside me on the floor. Luckily, I'd emptied it in the morning before guests came over. I'm weird like that. I can't stand trash in my trashcans when there's guests.

Jimmy sat down on the bed next to me. "How's your ass."

"I don't know. I can't feel it."

"I'll check for bruising when there are less eyes around."

"You mean Derek?"

"How'd you guess?"

"The way you and Chief were staring at him, I kind of feared for his safety. Why? What he do?"

"Not so much him as you, but he was looking at you all night."

"Well, I haven't seen him in forty years or so. What's that got to do with anything?"

"You gonna fuck him?"

Woah. Where'd that come from? "I wasn't going to, but I may now, asshole."

He sighed. "And I would deserve it. I'm sorry, Dot."

"I'll cut you some slack because I'm leaving tomorrow and really don't want to fight, because honestly, I may puke. Where the hell did that come from? You're uh...not usually the jealous type." He leaned back against the headboard by my head, unwisely blocking me from the trash can. "You better hand me that," I said and pointed over him.

He reached down and snagged it quickly, handing it over to me. "Sorry."

I sat up, stuffing the pillows behind me and holding it between my legs. "False alarm."

"I don't know where it came from, honestly, and you're right, jealous isn't me. Usually."

"So, why now?"

"A bunch of things, I think. He was your boyfriend when you were younger. Kind of hard to compete with that, and the thought of you running back to him kind of made me sick to my stomach. Then when he asked if you were dating anybody, Chief chimed in, but you didn't say anything about me... That kind of hurt."

Oops.

I reached over and gently touched his arm. "Yeah. I can see that. I just didn't think it was any of his business."

"No. You were worried about what he would think if he found out," he said angrily. *Very* angrily, with just a hint of sadness to heighten the flavor of the foot in my mouth.

Jimmy stood up and walked out of the room. I didn't blame him. I would have walked away from me, too. Looking down at the trash can between my legs, I started puking, and not because I was drunk.

The bedroom door opened, and I looked up as Candace walked in and slowly closed the door behind her. She took one look at my swollen, watery eyes and the snot hanging from my nose, and headed for the bathroom. The sink started running and she came out with a wet wash cloth. I reached for it, but she held on to it, setting the trash can on the floor and sitting in front of me on the bed. Tears were streaming down my face. She wiped them away before cleaning off the rest of my face and folding the cloth, pressing it against my forehead.

"I screwed up, Candace."

"It wasn't all your fault. I yelled at your partner in crime."

"Oh, my goddess. She wouldn't shut up."

"I know. And ignored your repeated attempts to quiet her. I do not think that was the entire reason for your troubles, though. Those two were on edge the moment your friend walked through the door."

"Which I can see with Chief, but not Jimmy. And now he's uber-pissed because I didn't introduce him as my boyfriend."

"Why didn't you?"

13

"I told him it was because it wasn't any of Derek's business. Jimmy says it's because I'm embarrassed for dating the two of them."

"Are you?"

I nodded.

She ran her fingers through my hair, leaned forward and kissed me on the forehead. "At least you admitted it. What are you going to do about it?"

"I suppose I should go back out there."

"If only to say goodbye to your guests. They should be leaving soon. They've been eating pie."

"I want pie."

"Come have some, and some coffee." She stood, offering me her hand.

I got up and the room didn't spin. It sucked how something so goddess awful as puking was good for you. Puking and kale.

I sidestepped into the bathroom and rinsed with my minty mouthwash. Pumpkin would mix better with mint than regurgitated turkey. Candace waited for me and took my hand, pulling me slowly into the dining room, much to the amusement of my guests. I smiled at Candace, grateful for her help. She nodded and headed for the kitchen while I turned to my house full of guests. "Sorry about that, folks. I should have eaten more before I started chugging the vino."

They made dismissive noise. I avoided the glances from Chief by shifting my attention to the kitchen as I sat down. Candace was getting me a slice of pie while Josie was by the coffee maker, looking at me apologetically.

Candace gave her an angry glare and walked back to the dining room, setting the pie down in front of me. The pumpkin pie was completely hidden beneath a dense shroud of whip cream. Just how the goddess intended it to be eaten. I grabbed my fork and scooped out a bite when my front door was kicked in.

For some reason, I expected a horde of SWAT team members to come trotting in chanting, "Hut, hut, hut, hut."

They didn't. But a purple streak shot from the door to my side as Yuki spun on my guests baring her claws, fangs, and hissing...

Chief stood, pulled out his gun, and pointed it at my vampire. I stood and pushed the chair out of the way with the back of my legs, grabbed her by the shoulders, and spun her behind me, putting myself between him and her.

"Calm down! What's wrong?"

"You're not being attacked?" She looked around me, looking for danger.

"Uh, no? Why?"

She leaned in closer and whispered, "I was asleep when I felt your pain, and then you were disoriented and sick and then very angry and sad..."

Oh. Shit.

"I couldn't leave the house because the sun was still up. It was driving me insane I couldn't get here sooner."

"Promise not to be mad?"

"No," she said and narrowed her eyes. "What happened?"

"Um... I got drunk, fell on my ass, had a fight with my boyfriends, and puked. You know, your normal Thanksgiving stuff."

"Are you fucking kidding me right now?"

"No."

"What the hell is going on?" Chief didn't sound too happy.

"All good," I said and turned around, making sure he wasn't still trying to shoot Yuki." He was. The gun was still pointing at us, but off to the left a little. I guess he didn't really want to shoot me. Yet.

He let out the breath he'd been holding and holstered the gun. I needed to make a rule about wearing weapons to the dinner table. Technically he was on duty, but... My life was too interesting to have armed people around me.

"She's okay," I told him. "She just had this horrible feeling I was in danger. Right, Yuki?" I looked at her to corroborate the story.

"Yeah. It was the darndest thing. Woke up and ran right over."

"You ran? Ten miles?" Chief sounded impressed.

That's when I noticed Herb and Marge looking like ghosts and shifting in their seats uncomfortably. I sincerely hoped I didn't need to have the upholstery cleaned...

"Um, I'm sorry to be late to the party... Did ye say, *boyfriends?*" Derek sounded incredulous.

I should have just stayed in my room.

Chapter 2

"Bye, Chief. Sorry again."

"Well, I'm sorry, too. Really."

"For dropping me or pulling a gun on my over-protective friend?" I smiled at him as we stood in the doorway saying goodbye. Almost everybody had left, and he needed to get home to pack. I noticed he stayed until Derek headed back to the hotel. I wasn't sorry to see him go, either. Once I had answered his polyamorous question, he started acting a little strangely.

"Little bit of both. Mostly for behaving like an ass to begin with."

"Sorry for having the ex-boyfriend drop by unannounced."

He sighed. "Yeah. That was a bit of a shock, but doesn't excuse my behavior, which probably wouldn't have happened if he wasn't so charming, funny, and witty."

"You forgot sexy and handsome."

"No, I didn't."

"Well, we can talk about it tomorrow."

"After you figure it out?"

"No. I already have. If it's going to bother you and Jimmy that much, I'll stay away from trouble. I'm lucky to have the two of you."

He leaned in and gave me a kiss. "We have no right to be jealous, though. We can talk about it tomorrow. I'll get to know the guy before I hate him."

"Oh, my gosh. That is the sweetest thing..." I laughed and watched him walk out the door and get in his car before I finally shut it and went to finish helping the girls clean up.

As I walked by Herb's chair, I let out a sigh of relief. It wasn't every day a human saw a snarling vampire. They had handled it better than I could have hoped. Herb even got close enough to ask her a few questions. Must have been the coroner in him.

Yuki and Jimmy were sitting on the couch watching the kick-off of the Christmas movie selection on the Hallmark Channel. I wanted to gag. Chief was the closest thing Cedar Falls had to a hometown hero here, but I couldn't exactly see him trying to teach me the true meaning of Christmas and I couldn't see Hallmark making Yule specials anytime soon. I slipped into the kitchen and put a cup of coffee on to brew.

Candace handed Josie one of the roasting pans and she started drying it. It looked like I had walked into the kitchen at the right time, they were almost done. "Need some help?" I asked even though I knew what the answer would be.

"No. We have this. Go sit, Lady."

"Anybody need anything before I walk all the way in there to sit?" I called to the living room from the kitchen.

"I'll take a beer if you're offering."

"Pie!"

"You can't eat pie, Yuki."

"You can."

I sighed, not really wanting another piece. For her I would, though. After the calamity had calmed down before, she had sat next to me almost moaning in ecstasy as I finished off my slice. Life without pie, wasn't.

I turned to grab a slice, but Candace was already cutting a piece for me. "Easy on the whip cream. I'm gonna get fat."

She grabbed the can and put about half the amount on it. You still couldn't see the pie, but I wouldn't have to dig for it, either.

"Thanks, sweetie."

"Welcome, Lady."

I was getting too used to her waiting on me hand and foot. It had been unsettling, and I tried to get her to stop, but she just seemed to enjoy doing it. I even stopped trying to get her to call me Dot. She'd do it once or twice, and then revert to the honorifics. She was the only one who called me that, too. Unless it was the boys when they were pissed off at me, so I heard it a lot.

I grabbed my stuff and walked into the living room. Yuki was on one end of the couch, and Jimmy sat on the other. I killed two birds with one hand-grenade and lobbed myself between them, careful not to spill anything on either of them. I leaned against Jimmy and tucked my feet underneath me. Yuki seized the opportunity to lean back against me and throw her tiny feet over the end of the couch, pressing as much of herself against me as she could. It wasn't a sexual thing, it was a power thing. She was soaking up as much of me as she could before I left for the weekend. I was pushing the limit of how long I could be away from her before she started feeling uncomfortable.

"Pie," she said and looked upward at me hopefully.

"Yeah, yeah. Let me set my coffee down."

"No beer?" Jimmy asked sadly.

"Shit." I sighed and leaned forward, putting the coffee and the pie on the table. "I forgot. I'll grab it."

"Nope. It's alright, I can live without it."

"Yeah, right."

"I'll grab it." Yuki shot off the couch and was back in a moment, handing it to him before resuming her spot. I was kind of shocked. She would do pretty much anything I asked of her, she didn't have a choice, but it was the first time she had volunteered to do anything for someone else in the house.

"Thanks, kid."

"I'm probably older than you." She scoffed.

"But I'm bigger."

They chuckled instead of carrying on. I had no clue. Maybe they'd bonded over the Hallmark movie. It probably wasn't the first time it happened in the history of Christmas.

"What are we watching?" I asked even though I didn't care.

"A Christmas movie," Jimmy answered sounding unimpressed. "She told me to leave it or she would bite my ankles."

"Gasp. The horror."

"I know. Skeeters always go for the ankles."

"You guys know I can hear you."

I took a bite of pie. That shut her up, word-wise. She still made *mmm* noises and practically rolled around on the couch. I was still mystified how it worked. She'd accidentally become my familiar, and she couldn't eat food, but she could taste whatever I put in my mouth. I sincerely hoped it pertained only to food. That could get pretty awkward, awfully fast. I hoped to test the theory tonight...

"You still staying the night?" I asked Jimmy.

"If you want me to."

"Do you still want to?"

"Yes."

"Oooh, that sounded heartfelt and enthusiastic." I took another bite of pie.

"Really? I was going for indifferent and sarcastic."

I elbowed him in the ribs. I could tell from his tone he was teasing. When I'd gone and accidentally mentioned the word boyfriends, plural, it had made him happy enough to forgive me. Jimmy was a simple man...

I finished my pie and adamantly refused to eat another piece, no matter how much Yuki begged.

"Please," she said for the thirteenth time.

"No. You get the taste, I get the calories," I said, adamantly. Jimmy, Candace, and Josie knew she had become my familiar. I hadn't told anybody else and planned on taking the secret to my grave. Not even Chief knew, but that was more out of fear on my part. I didn't know how he would react if he found out. I didn't *want* to find out.

The light shut off in the kitchen and Josie and Candace walked in. Josie made a beeline for the love seat, but Candace slipped between Jimmy and I, sitting half on my lap and half on his, but curling up against me. Yuki looked over her shoulder and rolled her eyes. She did that whenever Candace tried to snuggle with me.

We watched TV in silence, and I hated to admit it, but I got into the movie. I'd probably never watch another one again unless threatened under pain of torture, but it was cute.

"You ready for bed?" I asked Jimmy over Candace's head once it finished.

His eyes lit up like a Christmas tree.

I tapped Candace on her side, causing her to jump. I forgot how ticklish she was. "Sorry, Cand. I'm ready for bed."

She blinked at me with sleepy eyes and got up.

"You friggin' witches go to bed way too early. Shouldn't you be nocturnal or something?"

"Would you if you didn't have to be?" I asked Yuki seriously.

"No. Good point. Have fun on your vacation but let me know when you're home."

"I will. I'll text, since you'll be sleeping."

"Mind if I hang out a bit?"

I leaned over closer and patted her purple spiked hair. "*You* are always welcome. Come and go as you please. I'll get a key made for you."

She turned and blinked in surprise. "Dot...You're pretty cool. Way cooler than your mother."

"Yeah. That's not a hard thing to accomplish. Night, Yuki."

She leaned forward and let me slip out from behind her, taking up the whole couch when I got up. Candace looked at her, blinked, and moved to the loveseat with Josie.

Jimmy was already heading into the bedroom and I wasn't in a hurry to catch up. It had been a long day and a longer evening. He flipped the ceiling fan on and flipped on the light, motioning toward the bed. "Come on. I want to check out your ass before bed."

"You want to check out my ass all the time."

"True story. I have honest reasons this time. I want to see if you have a bruise."

I'd almost forgotten about my incident. I hoped I didn't, it didn't feel like I did and there hadn't been any discomfort sitting on the couch. "It doesn't feel like it."

"With as hard as you dropped, I'd be surprised if you didn't, witch constitution or not."

"Well, I want to brush my teeth. You sit, I'll stand. If I lie down now, I won't want to get back up."

"I'm good with that," he wiggled his eyebrows.

"You didn't yack up a turkey. I'm brushing my teeth. Rinsing with mouthwash just doesn't cut it."

He chuckled and sat on the edge of the bed. I walked over to him and turned around, lifting my shirt up and off. I took off my bra while he peeled my leggings over my butt. "Huh."

"No bruise?"

"No bruise. Snow must have padded your fall."

"Or my ass did."

He leaned forward and kissed me right at the base of my spine, sending a tingle up my back. "Save that thought. Toothpaste sounds heavenly right now."

"One more kiss." He turned me around so I was facing him, wearing nothing but pants and my fuzzy socks.

"I'm not kissing you until I brush my teeth."

"I'm kissing you." He tugged my leggings and my panties down, just below my happy patch.

"Mr. Duncan… *You*, sir, suck at waiting."

"Just one little kiss…" I expected him to dive in, but he pulled me closer, wedging me between his legs and rubbing his hands up my legs and onto my ass, pulling me toward his mouth. I leaned forward and he placed a single, solitary chaste kiss right above my hair. The tingles from the kiss on my spine were nothing compared to that gentle, tender moment. He looked up at me and smiled, running his lips up my stomach as he did. "Damn, you're hot."

"And horny. Now."

He chuckled as he squeezed my butt. "Does that hurt at all?"

"No."

"Wow."

"Yeah. I'm not looking the gift horse in the mouth."

"Maybe it's a drunk thing."

"Excuse me?"

"Like how when drunks get into accidents and the car gets totaled. They climb out of the wreckage and wonder what happened."

"Oh. Gotcha."

"Go brush your toofers."

"Aye, aye, cap'n."

Pulling off my leggings and socks, I tossed them in the hamper with my shirt and bra. I could see Jimmy watching me out of the corner of my eye. Trying not to smile, I stealthily watched him as he pulled off his shirt and jeans and set them on the floor by the bed. I looked over, toothbrush hanging from my mouth, as he began to stroke himself while he watched *me*. He was sticking out of the open part of his boxers.

I spit and rinsed, wanting some of that.

"You couldn't wait for me?"

"Not when you're in there looking like that. No man could resist."

I reached down and pulled his hand away, replacing it with mine. "Mmm. And is this for me?"

"All for you."

I bent down and gave it a little kiss.

"Yeah. You might not want to do that. I may not last too long."

"Geesh. Somebody is excited."

"Well, you *are* going away with Chief this weekend..."

I chuckled throatily. "You want me to text you updates, or tell you what happens when I get back?"

"Um… Both."

"Sick, sick man."

"You love it."

"I do."

"Ha! You just said I do. Are we married now?"

"You better be kidding."

"I am!"

I pushed him back on the bed and crawled on top of him.

"Would you like a back rub?"

"What?"

"Lie down across the bed."

"I'd rather just get right down to it, if you know what I mean…"

"Trust me. You'll like this back rub."

"Oh. Okay," I said, not fully trusting him. I looked around for video cameras but refrained from checking the closet to see if there was anybody hiding in there. With Jimmy, you never knew. I walked around the bed and slid across the comforter until my head was by the edge.

"Do you have any lotion?"

"Dresser."

He walked over and grabbed the bottle, moving to the side I had crawled across. He reached over and grabbed my panties and slid them down my legs, leaving my ass exposed to the cool air.

"Hurry up. It's cold."

He crawled over the bed, and his bare skin slid along mine as he scooted forward, straddling me. His naked butt sitting down on the back of my thighs. He must have pulled off his boxers. I sighed and turned my head, grabbing a pillow and putting it under my chest and head.

I heard the lotion bottle pump and his hands rub together. He at least had the sense not to squirt lotion straight on my back. I was definitely going to have to keep him. I moaned a little as he placed both hands down on the small of my back and immediately applied lots of pressure, sliding them up along my spine. "Holy shit, that feels good."

"I *almost* became a masseuse instead of a fireman."

"You missed your calling. Your hands are magical."

"You should feel the rest of me."

"Oh. I have."

He scooted forward a little, not quite being able to reach my shoulders. I moved my hair out of the way and let him at my neck. If he was going to go all out, I wasn't going to stop him. His fingers moved up, rubbing the tender muscles before using the edge of his hands to slide down my shoulders. He gripped my arms and massaged his way down to my elbows but couldn't reach any farther. I was using them to prop my head up under the pillow. When he pulled them back, he slid them down my sides and back up over my hips.

"You need to quit your job, I will pay you to follow me around and give me back rubs."

"I'd be good with that."

I chuckled while he paused for a moment to get more lotion. It was cold and dry outside, and my skin soaked it up way faster than it should have. I moisturized all the time, but my back wasn't exactly easy to reach.

He put his lotion covered hands on my hips, leaning forward to kiss the back of my neck as he used his weight to push down with his palms. I was enjoying the sensation of him moving them in circles when I felt his cock slide down my thigh and settle in between them. When he finished kissing my neck, he scooted forward just a tiny bit, pressing the tip of it against my lips and trapping it there.

He continued rubbing my back, stopping only to get more lotion. He worked his way up and then back down, not stopping until he was rubbing the muscles just above my ass. He almost put me into a massage induced coma until his hands moved a little lower, firmly gripping my ass. Kneading the flesh, he pulled me open and the head of his cock settled at my entrance, my well lubricated lips inviting him in. I sighed as he started massaging back up toward my shoulders again, the movement driving him forward agonizingly slowly. I could feel each millimeter of him as he slowly crept inside me.

"Can you do the front of my shoulders, too? They're kind of sore. You might need to scoot forward a bit." I, too, could play this game.

"Sure." He pumped some more lotion on his hands and used his knees to push himself forward a few inches.

I gasped as I stretched, accommodating him and squeezing him tight. He didn't move his hips, just used his hands to rock me. The motion was more than welcome, but I wanted more. I didn't know how he had the restraint.

His hands slid up my neck and back down my shoulders, fingertips squeezing the muscles. "Are you comfortable? I'm not hurting you, am I?"

"No, you're fine." I managed to get the words out, my breathy voice betraying me.

I started squeezing him inside me as much as I could, wanting to get some reaction out of him, and almost whimpering when I felt him throb inside me. My hips bucked on their own.

"You sure? You're awful twitchy. Your legs aren't falling asleep?"

"Nope. Just enjoying this massage. Inside and out."

That caused him to chuckle, the laughter causing some much-needed movement. I almost hissed at the sensation. I wanted more but wasn't willing to ruin the game.

Inspiration struck, I lowered myself off my elbows and used my movement to inadvertently push the pillow over the edge of the bed. "Oops. Clumsy me." I pulled myself forward, reaching for it. I even went so far as to pretend I couldn't quite reach it. The struggling sent quivers of delight all through me. "Got it!" I slammed myself back against him, and I swear I heard him groan above me.

"Next time I should tie you to the corners of the bed so you *can't* move."

The thought sent shivers racing through every nerve in my body. I shuddered beneath him and he noticed instantly.

He leaned forward and put his lips next to my ear, the movement causing him to dive that much deeper into me. I nearly came as he whispered, "Somebody likes that idea."

All I could do was nod, all capability of coherent speech leaving me. He sat back up but didn't continue his massage. Instead, he gripped my hips and jerked himself forward. I cried out. He wasn't pulling back either, just kept jerking his hips, bumping against me.

"Jimmy, fuck me, please..."

"You want me to? I thought I was just giving you a massage."

"If you don't pound yourself into me this minute, I'll do it my damn self. You win. Happy?"

His chuckle affirmed that much. He moved the bottle of lotion and slid his legs out behind him, lying over me and holding himself up with his arms. He used his knees to slide his cock back before driving it into me. I didn't even *try* to keep silent. I called out his name with every thrust.

"So fucking wet," he mumbled between thrusts.

I was going to come.

He knew. He doubled his efforts, slamming me against the bed with his hips as he drilled me from above. My cries of his name became a scream of pleasure. My orgasm washed over me, and I lifted my head and couldn't even cry out any more. My voice having completely left me. And then, just when I thought I couldn't take anymore, *he* cried out and emptied himself inside me.

The last thought I had as my face crashed into the pillow and I started panting was concern. I thought I heard someone scream from the other room...

Chapter 3

"Hello, Mother."

"Greetings, Child. Welcome home."

The chief and I slipped into the booth across from her, and I smiled as my eyes roamed the Five Star Diner. It felt like it had been ages since I sat in my mother's favorite booth, when it had literally been just over a month.

The trip from Cedar Falls had been mostly uneventful, unless you counted arguing with the rental kiosk girl at the airport and the forty-five-minute drive it took us to get to Ashville. Even Chief had been eerily quiet. Until we pulled into town and his jaw hit the floor. Ashville as it was prepping for Christmas was nothing short of miraculous.

"How was your trip?" She wore an evil grin on her face. Mother knew I hated flying. I was waiting for a charge to show up on my credit card for destroying the armrests of seat 15C. When white-knuckling them didn't alleviate the stress, I may have inadvertently made the metal a little malleable with magic...

"Uneventful."

"I'm sure." She grinned and looked at the chief. I'm sure mile-high-club thoughts were running through her over-sexed brain as she leered.

"Dot!"

I looked up and saw Jenny heading for our table. I waved frantically, grateful to see my most favorite waitress in the universe. Jenny had been seventeen when she started working at the diner. That was nearly forty-years ago. Her blonde ponytail had long turned gray, and her stick-thin figure had thickened, but she was still pretty, and I imagined would be for years to come. Jenny was human, but ageless in character. I got up from my seat on the edge of the booth and hugged her when she got close enough.

"I didn't think you'd be back this soon." She laughed as she pulled back, looking me up and down.

"Yeah. I'm stealing some Ashvillains to take back with me."

"They need any waitresses?" She winked to let me know she was joking. Had she been serious, I would have given her a job at the bookstore in a heartbeat. Jenny was more than a waitress. Jenny had been there for most of my life and when things got difficult, she was always there to lend an ear or a bit of advice.

"Sure. Call a moving truck, I have work for you."

"Nah. Dave wouldn't let me go alone and I don't want to move *with* him."

I sat back down. "Miss Blackwell, would you care for your usual tea?" Jenny went into full waitress mode, knowing better than to treat my mother familiarly. It made me want to slap her sometimes. Pretty sure someone had shoved the words prim and proper in the dictionary to describe my mother.

"Please, Jennifer."

"And who is this?" She turned her attention on Chief.

"This is my boyfriend, Bill. Bill, Jenny."

"Boyfriend, huh?" She reached out her hand and shook Chief's.

"He's the chief of police in the town I moved to. So, behave yourself," I told her with a laugh.

"He handcuff you, yet?"

"No. And we need to have a serious discussion about that." I turned to him and winked at him, enjoying the lovely shade of crimson his cheeks had turned. My mother even cackled.

"Hi, Jenny," he said shyly.

"What can I get you to drink?"

"What is a witches brew?" He pointed at the menu.

"Cream soda float."

"Huh. I'll try one."

"Usual, Dot?"

"Please."

"I'll be right back."

I smiled as she walked away.

"I swear, how you get so enamored with the help in these places."

"Relax, Mother. I've known her for forty years. It's your own fear of human interaction talking."

"I fear nothing, Child."

"Is that a spider on the booth behind you?"

She gasped and spun, tuning back toward me *very* slowly. I strengthened my shields just in case and perused the menu, trying not to chuckle.

"Daughter..."

"Yes, Mother?"

"You are an ungrateful, horrible child."

"Love you, too, Mother."

Chief just chuckled. "How's the food here? Any recommendations?"

"It's on par with Herb's. Stay away from the meatloaf, though."

"Not good?"

"*Really* good. Just think Nestor uses it as a front to get rid of bodies."

"Maybe a few centuries ago, dear. The health department regularly inspects his beef after the rumor mill refused to let that one go."

"Yeah. I'll stick to chicken." Chief looked a little green. "What are you getting?"

"Think I'm going to have the hot roast beef."

"Safe?"

I shrugged. "Worth the risk."

He sighed, but nodded, setting his menu down on top of mine.

"How has my daughter been treating you, Bill? It is good to see you two still together."

"She has her moments. Mostly when she's being reckless, but I'm trying to slowly teach her how to rely on others and not take everything onto herself."

"Good luck, young man."

"Thanks, Miss Blackwell."

"Madeline, please."

Chief nodded, and Jenny brought our drinks, took our order, and left us alone. There was the awkward moment of silence before Mother finally broke it. "I have two more names to add to your list of immigrants."

"Oh? You mean besides Derek? What were you thinking, Mother, sending him straight out? You knew we were coming here."

"Oh? Must have slipped my mind when I pictured the delight you would feel seeing him again. Should I not have?" She glanced at Chief to judge his reaction.

"It's fine," I said testily. "Who are the other two?"

Mother grinned evilly as one eyebrow arched almost enough to disappear into her hairline. "The first one is Miranda…"

"No. Not just no, but hell no. Now I know you've gone off the deep end."

"It would be almost a relief to have an older, *responsible* witch for you and Miranda's spawn to rely upon. She wishes to move closer to her daughter to help out, and she wants to move her floral business with her. I thought it might coincide with your thoughts."

"Hmmm. It's sound, but I'm afraid Josie might go spastic. If I agree to this, it would be a month before she spoke to me again."

"You say this as if that would be a bad thing…"

"Mother. Please." I sighed and made a note in my phone. "I'll at least think about it and talk to her. Will she be there tomorrow?"

My mother, in an effort to expedite things, had agreed to host an afternoon gathering and banquet at her house, having all the witches who wanted to move in attendance.

I'd blinked in surprise when she mentioned it over the phone.

"Yes."

"Okay. I'll talk to her, but no promises."

"That is all she asks."

"Who's the other addition?"

Mother froze and took a sip of her tea before looking at me sheepishly. I wasn't going to like this. "Your Grandmother."

"What?"

"Your–

"I heard you. Just trying to tell if you're joking or not. Why the hell would Grandmother want to move? She's nine-hundred-years-old..." Witches could, in theory, live forever. Grandmother was pushing the boundaries of reason. She looked as young as my mother, who looked as young as me, but the hair on her temples had started graying and the flesh around her eyes had begun darkening. The woman had seen knights battle upon horses, wars fought with swords, and lived through two out of three crusades. Why the hell she wanted to move to Cedar Falls was beyond me.

"I'm very serious. You may ask her yourself. I gave up trying to dissuade her."

"She'll be there tomorrow?"

"No. She's coming through the door now..."

I sighed and turned around. Grandmother nodded at Jenny behind the counter and turned her head, seeing me. A smile crept on her lips and she raised her hand in greeting as she walked slowly and confidently through the crowded diner.

"Nana?" I stood and made her name a question of a thousand words.

"Hello, Dearie." She leaned forward and kissed me twice, once gently on each cheek, before taking a seat next to my mother. Seeing them next to each other was quite a shock. I loved my nana dearly. The fights between the two of them had become legendary in Ashville, often wreaking damage and havoc upon the town.

"Nana, why?"

She shrugged. "Call it a calling. I had a dream and your Cedar Falls is where I need to be."

"If the goddess is pushing you, I don't even want to know what is coming," I said breathlessly. Fear slid down my spine like an oily hand. Witches did *not* lose power as they aged. They amassed it. I was a bazooka. Nana was a tactical nuke.

"Calm, Child. I sensed nothing from her, just a need to be with you. Maybe my time comes, and she wants me to live out the remainder of my days in peace." She held up a hand and pointed at my mother, rolling her eyes in the process.

"I'll shall make a large donation to the Cedar Falls Nursing Home prior to your arrival." My mother took another sip of her tea and smiled to herself.

"You just want my room after I leave this earth, Sweetling."

I sighed. It was like this every time they moved within five-hundred-yards of each other. Most of the time it was amusing, and it had yet to progress beyond that point, but I wanted to nip it in the bud before things got out of control. I was hungry.

"Nana, are you sure?"

She nodded once but didn't elaborate further. A calling from the goddess wasn't something she, or I, could ignore. I sighed heavily and took a sip of my coke. "Welcome to Cedar Falls." And just like that, we had one more witch in our coven. Chief didn't seem upset that I hadn't discussed it with him, either.

"Then I shall leave you to your dinner." She nodded at me and Chief and stood to leave.

"You're not staying?"

"Nay. I have much to do to put things in order here. I shall see you at our new home. I trust housing is fair?"

"Yes, Nana. You could probably buy one with your credit card."

"That cheap?"

I nodded solemnly. "Trying to fix all that."

"Do wait until after I purchase one. I shall see you in a week's time, possibly. Take care, my precious one." She bent over and kissed me on the forehead. Probably to annoy my mother. The women in my family were not the most affectionate of witches and kisses from Nana were rare.

"Coot," Mother said as soon as she was out of earshot.

"Mother!"

"Please, Daughter. I doubt all that driven by the goddess drivel. She just wishes to be far away from me."

"I don't blame her sometimes."

"What was that, dear?"

"Nothing, Mother."

∞ ∞ ∞

"You're absolutely sure about having your grandmother move in with you?"

I looked up at Bill wrapped in the hotel towel. He was drying his hair with one of the smaller hand towels and looking pretty damn hot. I could count the number of times I had seen him without a shirt on one hand, and it never failed to disappoint. He wasn't as chiseled as Jimmy, but he was still hot as hell. Distracted, I forgot to answer his question. "Um, what?"

"You're sure about your grandmother moving?"

"No, not really, but how can I say no?"

"True. At least you'll have some family in town." He set the hand towel on the back of the chair and crossed the room, settling on the other bed, wearing only the towel.

"You're going to get the bed wet if you lay on it in that."

He smirked across from me. "Would you prefer it if I weren't wearing it?"

I'd assumed he wasn't interested in playing at all, since he chose the other bed, rather than the one I was occupying. "Maybe, but I'm going to take a shower so wear whatever you want."

"Should have just taken one with me."

"The showers in the hotel aren't that big."

"True. But we could have made it work..." His smirk turned into a grin.

Memories of my shower with Jimmy made me blush and the room seemed to warm up a few degrees. "Yeah," I managed to mutter.

"You okay?"

I nodded and got up, wanting to wash the travel feeling from my body. It was cold, I hadn't even remotely worked up a sweat, despite having dinner with my mother, and I still felt grimy. It was something to do with airports and planes. Whenever I went *anywhere*, I always felt gross.

"I'll be out in a minute."

"Take your time."

Heading into the bathroom, I peeled off my shirt, dropping it by the closet door, and glancing over my shoulder. Chief had his eyes glued to me. I paused outside the door and reached behind me, unhooking my bra. I let it fall forward and caught it with my arms, sliding them through and stretching. I could almost feel his anticipation of me turning and getting a peek. I crossed one arm over me before turning and he groaned in disappointment. It was the little things that made me smile.

I hurried into the shower and let the pressure jet against my skin. Even without soap, I immediately felt cleaner. I reached over and grabbed the tiny bottle of hotel shampoo and dumped it into my hand. Chief had killed half the bottle, but there was more than enough left. I scrubbed my scalp and stepped under the water.

When I opened my eyes, Chief was standing there with the curtain open. I hadn't even heard him come in. "What?"

"Just wanted to see if you needed any help." He seemed so shy, asking. His eyes told a different story as they soaked in the view.

"Bullshit. You just wanted to see me naked."

"That I did."

Looking down at the towel around his waist, I noticed he was definitely enjoying the view. "You coming in? You're getting water all over the floor."

"Do you want me to?"

"I wouldn't have asked if I didn't."

He nodded, pulling the towel from his waist and running it through the bar on the wall. "I really wanted to ask you to join *me*, but I was too afraid to ask."

"But you had no problem sneaking in while I was in here?"

He stepped over the side of the tub and grabbed the bottle of conditioner, squirting some in his hands and rubbing them together. "I figured I better or I might miss the show. The thought of you in here, all wet and soapy, kind of made up my mind for me."

I turned around, letting him run the conditioner through my hair. "Well, I'm not soapy yet."

He didn't have to be asked twice. Rinsing the conditioner off him, he grabbed the small bar of soap and used it to work up a nice lather before rubbing his hands across my back. Their roughness sent shivers of pleasure all through me. I may have even moaned softly as I leaned my head forward just outside of reach of the water.

"You are amazingly beautiful, have I mentioned that before?" His voice gave a little quiver as he asked.

"Once or twice, but I don't think you're in danger of me getting tired of hearing it."

His hands slid down to my hips and pulled me closer to him. I gasped, feeling the length of him press against me as his face brushed gently against mine. Soapy hands glided around me and rubbed my stomach before cupping my breasts. I turned my head and my mouth awkwardly found his. His tongue gently probed my mouth as he began kneading my breasts. I began to breathe heavily into the kiss, wanting and needing more.

One hand snaked its way down my front and washed me, parting me and teasing me. My tiny moans grew into something a lot bigger as I continued to pant into our kiss.

"Not yet. I want you, but not in the shower," I managed to say before pushing his hand away. His chuckle let me know he wasn't too disappointed.

I quickly turned and rinsed the conditioner out of my hair while his fingers teased me, gliding lightly across my flesh. My knees nearly gave out when his mouth found one of my nipples.

I gently pushed him away, turned back around and shut the water off, anxious to get out of the slippery, hard shower and into a warm, firm bed.

"Let me grab you a towel."

He slid open the curtain and stepped out, returning a second later and offering me a steadying hand. After all the teasing, I needed it, not trusting my legs in the least. Stepping out onto the cold tile floor, he wrapped me in a large white towel and used its edges to pull me against him. I lay my head against his chest as he dried the water from my back. He pulled away and let me turn around before he did the same to my front. By the time he finished, my skin tingled everywhere and was begging for even more attention.

I pulled back, grabbing a smaller towel off the rack and wrapping it around my hair before walking out the bathroom door, stark naked. The room was warm enough not to be uncomfortable, but cool enough to tighten my skin in a myriad of tiny bumps. I walked toward my bed and sat in the edge, leaning back on my arms and opening my legs widely for him to enjoy the view or do whatever he wanted.

He didn't have to be invited twice. I watched, mesmerized, as his cock bounced as he walked. I'd never had him inside me, but tonight I was going to try, damn it.

We'd never gone all the way, and the anticipation of it was driving me insane. I wanted him, completely.

He knelt in front of me and didn't waste a moment as his mouth found me. Reaching up with one hand, he gently pushed me back on the bed, giving him the angle he wanted, as he lifted my legs over his shoulders. His tongue snaked its way inside me as his nose rubbed me gently. Within seconds my back arched, and my hips began to quake.

"Slowly. You're going to make me come."

His tongue slowly pulled out and glided up my channel until he found my sweet spot. I whimpered, my legs opening even further as my ankles pulled him closer. Gently, he licked me, swirling around me before his lips fastened to me and suctioned me between them.

"Chief..."

He sucked harder, his tongue flicking across me.

The room faded away as I came on his mouth and tightened my grip on his head, pushing myself against him even harder. When it was over, I groaned and gently ran my hands up my stomach and over my head, stretching as I released my grip on him. He looked up, a soft, adoring smile on his face.

"What ride do you want to go on next?" He chuckled.

"That," I said, pointing at his throbbing cock and smiling. "Just go *slow*, please."

"Are you sure?" He knew I'd been hesitant.

"Not a doubt in my head." I quivered in anticipation.

He nodded, and his smile faded into seriousness and need. Standing back up, he lifted my legs off the floor. Miraculously, the tall hotel beds put me *almost* in the perfect position for him. He merely had to spread his legs a bit to align himself at my entrance. I gulped in anticipation *and* fear. I had no idea how he was going to fit in me.

True to his word, he started very slow, merely rubbing the head against my very wet opening and pushing the flesh around my clit upward. He repeated this motion, spreading my wetness all around before reaching with one hand and parting me with two of his fingers. I felt the tip enter me and pull back before diving in a little deeper and retreating over and over again. He slowly worked his head inside me and paused a moment while I caught my breath.

"Holy fuck that feels good," I whimpered, turning my head to the side and closing my eyes.

"Yes, you do."

He began his slow, steady movements as he worked more of himself inside me. *Finally*, he stopped pushing. I was almost afraid to look down, but I did. "You fit."

"Did you really think I wouldn't?"

"I'm still not convinced you would in a different position. If I were riding you, I don't think you would have."

"Hey, Dot?"

"What?"

"Shhh." He pulled himself out slowly and then thrust his hips forward, impaling me on his flesh.

I came again. One thrust and I grabbed two handfuls of comforter and began panting and calling out his name. He immediately stopped moving, letting me calm down, staring at him through half-lidded eyes. "What the fuck."

"Did you just…?"

I nodded. "You couldn't tell? Goddess, give me a minute. Don't you dare move."

"I won't. Want me to pull out?"

"Don't you fucking dare." I hooked my ankles around his hips, to make sure. I just needed a minute.

I felt him throbbing inside me and it almost sent me over the edge again. I concentrated on the sound of the electric heater under the window and ran through some multiplication tables in my head, ignoring the feel of him, the length of him, and the heat of him burning me from the inside out. When I had calmed enough, I opened my eyes and saw him grinning mischievously at me.

"Chief…"

"Yes?"

"Fuck me."

He needed no further encouragement as he *slowly* worked himself back and pushed in again, each thrust filling me completely. My voice started as a groan and built in pitch and volume as the feel of him became the only thing I could focus on. Even he began grunting with every thrust. I came once more and he didn't stop. I had just come down when the third one started. I could only imagine the faces of our neighbors if we had any. In my orgasm clouded mind, their ears pressed against the wall tickled my love of being watched and I exploded in pleasure. I hadn't even finished when Chief grunted and thrust against me, bottoming out as he came.

Still joined, he collapsed on top of me. I wrapped my arms around him and held him against me while we both caught our breath.

"Wow," I managed to whisper in his ear before giving it a gentle kiss.

"Did you like that?"

"Why does every man feel the need to ask that stupid question whenever they finish?"

"Insecurity probably. I know I ask to see if there was anything I could do differently to make you happy. Happier. Whatever."

"Nope. That was amazing enough."

He just sighed happily in my arms. It was kind of cute and I found my fingertips gently gliding through his hair as we lay there. Eventually, he rolled over, arms wrapped around me and pulling me over on top of him. He still hadn't softened and was still inside me. There was no way I could take any more, though.

"Don't you dare," I whispered.

"Do what?"

"Anything. I'm done. I'm tapping out. Don't you dare move that thing inside me."

He just chuckled and nodded his head. "Fine. But that's not fair. You came like four times and I only came once."

"I don't care. Any more and I won't be able to walk for a few days. I may be walking a little funny *now*."

"Then my work here is done."

Chapter 4

*W*e did it.

I hit the send button after staring at the small, three-word sentence I had typed on my phone for several minutes. I couldn't believe I was telling him through a text, but I did. I could almost picture Jimmy's face as he read it. He was going to be sporting wood for a few hours, wanting nothing more than the sordid little details.

I was sitting on the toilet in our hotel bathroom, Chief still sound asleep in the bed we had passed out in. Staring at my phone, I waited for the delivered notification to turn to read. I had just about given up on him being awake when it did.

Was it what you imagined?

I smiled as my fingers danced over the keyboard. *And then some. Holy shit.*

Did he fit? Did he come inside you?

Barely and yes.

He didn't reply for a few minutes and the fear that I had shared too much started to fill me with dread. This was Jimmy I was talking to. He wasn't supposed to get jealous...

I'm stroking myself right now. Tell me more.

I laughed, my fears driven away by his not so subtle charm. I upped his request and took a picture of me, naked on the toilet. A closeup shot of my nether regions. Without so much as a second thought, I sent him the picture.

I'm sore. Would you kiss it and make it feel better?

I kind of wanted to know how far Jimmy would go, and wanted to torment him a little. Without thinking about it, I'd just asked away.

It took almost three minutes for the picture of his orgasm-splashed chest to come back to me. I wasn't kidding when I told him I was sore. If I hadn't been, I might be the one masturbating next.

I'll take that as a yes, you sick little monkey. I laughed. He truly was, but he was *my* sick little monkey.

Bet your ass. That was fucking hot. Have fun! See you tomorrow.

See you tomorrow, I replied, thought about it, and sent, *Miss you.*

Miss you, too.

I got off the toilet and set my phone on the bathroom counter before jumping into the shower and giving myself a quick wash. I walked out of the bathroom wearing a towel and blinking at the sight of an empty room. Chief had managed to get up, dressed, and left without me hearing a sound.

I was getting dressed when the door opened, and he walked in with a tray of muffins and coffee.

"You do room service, too?"

"Well, I did service you in this room, so I guess that would be a yes. Morning, Dot."

"Morning, Chief," I said with a smile, giving him a kiss for being sweet.

He sighed. "Could you not call me Chief for once? Feels kind of weird after...you know."

I had lifted my coffee to take a sip, but set it back down. I wrapped my arms around him and put my head against his shoulder. "I don't say it to be impersonal, you know. I just like calling you that. You're my chief."

"Really?"

"Yes, really. Think of it like this, when I call you Chief, it's like me calling you sweetie. Or snookums. It's a term of endearment, not a job title. But, if it bothers you, I'll call you by your name."

There was a moment of silence while he rolled the thought around in his head. "No. If that's how you feel, I'm okay with it. I won't bitch about it anymore."

"Sweet." I gave him a smile and another kiss, with a *lot* more feeling.

"I'm calling you snookums, though." He laughed.

"Go ahead. I may gut you."

"Fine. Lady, it is then." He got down on his knee and pulled me closer, rubbing his face over my still naked stomach. I had gotten my leggings and bra on before he came back in the room or it might have turned into something more.

"Lady is kind of...reverent. Pick something else," I said, pulling him to his feet.

"Yes. But, you *are* my lady and I do worship you..." He smiled and gave me a peck on the lips.

"I drive you insane. You don't worship me."

"You do, but I still feel that way."

"Whatever." Reaching down, I picked up my coffee, pausing a moment to try and wipe away the smile that seemed to have gotten stuck on my lips. At least I managed to take a sip without drooling coffee all over my chest.

"So, what's the plan for today?"

"We're free until this afternoon. I figured I'd show you around town before we head to Mother's and get this over with."

"You anxious to get back home? Your new home, I mean."

I thought about it for a moment while I sipped my coffee and tore a hunk of sugar-coated blueberry muffin off, popping it in my mouth. "Yes. Actually, I am."

"Good. I like that you get homesick for this place, I don't blame you. It is beautiful and everything you said. But I'm ecstatic that you think of Cedar Falls as your home. If that makes any sense."

"Perfect sense, and yes I do."

That just made his smile light up all the brighter. He was handsome enough as it was, but when he smiled, I melted. I sat down at the small table where he had set the tray and sipped my coffee, nibbling on my muffin. He joined me and we ate breakfast in companionable silence.

I finished getting dressed and we headed out into the bustling streets of Ashville. We had, at least, been spared the craziness of Black Friday. Ashville was no different from the rest of the country when it came the insanity of holiday shopping, which reminded me, I needed to pick up a few things for Mother to open for Yule. I might not be around when she opened them, but it would be more personable than shipping them to her.

"It's definitely warmer here," Chief said, looking up at the sky.

"Well, we are a bit farther south."

"True. When do you usually get snow?"

"Christmas if we're lucky. Or unlucky. Depends on your tastes. Most we see in November is usually a bit of freezing rain. Too warm for even that much right now."

"We've had a few green Yules, but they are *few* and far between."

"Good," I answered. "I'm not a fan of snow most of the year, but it just seems wrong without it during the holidays."

We stopped in front of Wilson's Jewelry. I wore a couple of rings, but never understood the appeal of wearing too much. I even hated wearing *anything* around my neck, let alone a metal chain. My Mother on the other hand...

"What do you think of that?" I pointed at a braided gold chain with a caged pearl, larger than I had ever seen, on a padded neck display.

"Pretty, but I don't see you wearing it."

"Not for me. Mother."

He leaned forward, I assumed to inspect the pearl, but he stood up rigidly and slowly turned to me. "Dot, that costs more than I make in a month..."

"Do you think she'd like it?"

"You're not even going to blink at the price?"

I sighed. I hated discussing money, but I wasn't shy about it. "Yeah. Not too worried about that. Is it pretty?"

"Very."

"Come on," I said and grabbed his hand, dragging him inside.

"Dot!" Mr. Wilson called my name and waved as I walked through the door.

"Hey, Mr. Wilson. Merry Christmas."

"Happy Yule."

I'd been shopping at his jewelry store since he opened it in the eighties. Most of the jewelry my mother wore had been purchased from him at one holiday or another. She loved her sparklies. "Thank you. That caged pearl in the window…"

"Want to see it?"

"I did. I'll take it, please."

He simply nodded and retrieved it from the window, placing it in a long box and wrapping it neatly for me. I handed him my card and we were out the door in a few minutes, Chief insisting on carrying it and glancing around nervously.

"Relax, Chief. Nobody is going to try and steal it. Crime in this town is almost unheard of…" My voice trailed off as a police car sped by us with its lights and sirens going.

"You were saying?" He chuckled softly.

"There's probably a two-for-one sale at the donut shop."

"Hundred bucks says there's a robbery."

"No way. I'm not taking that bet. You probably have some secret cop code with the sirens to tell what's going on."

"Do you honestly believe that?"

"Maybe." I started walking the opposite direction the cop car had gone.

Chief wasn't moving, just staring after the cop car, almost longingly. "They stopped."

"How do you know?"

"The siren isn't getting farther away. Can we check it out?"

"Seriously? We're on vacation."

"Technically this is a working vacation. I'm just curious. They don't sound far away…"

"Fine." I started trudging toward the siren, but it cut off. "Guess they caught them."

"I doubt it. Call it a hunch, but I have a feeling this might be bad."

"That's where you're wrong. Nothing *bad* ever happens here. Some kids were probably graffitiing a bridge or something. Or Mother shrank the Mayor's limbs again."

"We'll see."

We rounded the corner and all three of Ashville's police cars were parked in the street in front of the Ashville Historical Museum.

"Well, that's odd." I started walking a little faster, my curiosity officially piqued.

"Museum?"

I nodded without looking at him. "Historical Museum. Mostly bits and pieces of our town's heritage."

"Anything of value?"

"A few artifacts, but nothing monetarily significant. Just a lot of family heritage put on display."

"Your family?"

"Yes, Chief. Old books, heirlooms, et cetera."

"Come on. Let's check it out."

I followed him up to the front door and one of the police officers, Haven, if I remembered his name correctly, moved to stop us. Or at least he did until he saw it was me. "Miss Blackwell," he stuttered, making my name a greeting.

"What happened?"

"The Chief is inside, go ahead in."

I nodded, and he opened the front door of the museum for Bill and me. The lights hadn't been turned on as the museum still had a few hours before opening. Even in the dimly lit hall, it was easy to spot the chief standing in front of the broken display case with a look of utter shock etched on his face.

"Chief Blakeslee, what happened?"

"Dot, is that you?"

I nodded when we got close enough for him to see us. "Long time no see."

"I just hung up with your mother. She didn't mention you were in town."

"She avoids mentioning me when she can. What was stolen?"

"Three of the books she personally put on display."

My eyebrows disappeared into my hairline. "That's not good."

"Well, they'd be useless to a human, but in a witch's hands... You and your friend here wouldn't have needed them for anything, would you?"

I felt the hair on the back of my neck stand on end. I didn't like being accused of anything. Especially things I didn't do. "*Had* I needed them, I would have simply asked for them back, *Chief* Blakeslee. They are Blackwell heirlooms."

He nodded but didn't seem entirely convinced. "And what about your friend. Who is he?"

Chief opened his mouth to answer, but I beat him to the punch. "This is Chief William Jonah Bates. The police *chief* of Cedar Falls."

"And what are the two of you doing in town?"

"Last time I checked, coven matters fell out of your jurisdiction. At least, that's what Mother tells me you agreed upon."

"Your mother failed to mention that, as well." He gave me a sneer.

"Are you accusing me of something?"

"No. Now if you'll excuse me, I have a robbery to solve."

The other officer broke away from Blakeslee and motioned us toward the door. Opening my mouth to curse him, I changed my mind and smiled. I turned and headed for the exit but whispered, "*A bheith ina phortach*," as I ran my hand over the wooden frame of the door.

"What was that?" Chief asked as we exited the dark museum into the bright sunlight.

I blinked a few times, letting my eyes adjust before answering him. "Turn around."

He did. I didn't need to turn to know Blakeslee and the other cop would be pouring themselves out the front door. I heard them and some coughing before he shouted, "Dorothea Blackwell!"

"I turned the museum into a bog. Complete with mired floor and rotting vegetation. I assume the smell became unbearable quickly."

"You're evil."

"I have my moments. He should have known better than to accuse me of stealing my family's things."

"He was just doing his job."

"No. He's banging my mother and thinks that gives him leverage over me. He just needed a little reminder. That and he's probably pissed I let my mother know about our police files. I'm sure that didn't go well for him."

"Oh. You should have turned it into a fire swamp then."

"That would have been inconceivable. Plus, destroyed the rest of the things in the museum. Want some coffee?"

"Sure. Diner?"

I nodded. We still had some time to kill before heading to Mother's. For all I knew, she was heading to the museum. If priceless family heirlooms had just been stolen, that's where I would be going if I were her. She donated them, it was her problem. Not mine.

It didn't take long to get to the Five Star, and I could tell Chief had a thousand questions on his mind. I opened the door for him and let him lead the way. He chose a booth close to the door and sat facing the entrance. I put my back to the door and sighed.

"So, what exactly was stolen. I'm hoping not spell books?"

I nodded and held up my coffee cup at Jenny. She nodded and grabbed the pot, coming over and filling our mugs. "Morning. Need anything other than coffee?"

"I'll have some fries, too. Thanks, Jenny."

She nodded and looked at Chief, who shook his head. "Just coffee, thanks."

"Be out in a minute."

"Thanks."

I watched her walk toward the kitchen before elaborating to Chief. "Yes. My grandmother's spell books and the Blackwell Grimoire. The one that had been handed down through the generations since the beginning of the written word. Half the Irish in it was so archaic, I couldn't even decipher it."

"What's in it?"

"Ritualistic magic for just about anything and everything. My grandmother's spell book is scary enough in the wrong hands, the Blackwell Grimoire could be potentially devastating if they could read it."

"Don't take this the wrong way, but what the hell was it doing in a museum?"

"Mother being Mother. Figured it was safer than in my grandmother's hands."

"You don't think your grandmother…"

"No. She's powerful enough without them. I can't imagine what she would need them for. Not to mention, she *is* a Blackwell. She could have just asked for them back, too."

"So, one of the witches in town?"

"Or one of the ones moving with us? That's what you're thinking."

"Maybe."

"Don't worry. I was, too."

With my vantage point of having my back to the door, I couldn't see the gathering storm, but I could feel it. Chief's face gave me a pretty good warning, too.

"My mother is coming this way, isn't she?"

"Yeah."

"She looks pretty pissed off, too, doesn't she?"

"How can you tell?"

"I can feel it." I picked up my coffee and took a sip when the chime over the door rattled instead of ringing. "Hello, Mother."

"Don't hello me. What did you do?"

"Turned the museum into a bog. Chief Blakeslee was being a douche."

"That's not what I am referring to." She stood next to our table, arms crossed and foot tapping impatiently against the linoleum beneath it.

I blinked in surprise. "Don't tell me you think I stole the grimoires."

"Who else would? I don't see why you didn't just *ask* me for them. I would have gladly given them to you."

"Gee, thanks, but I didn't take them."

"You did not?"

"That's what I just said. If I had, I would have told you."

That gave her pause for thinking. When she finally nodded, she slid into the booth next to Chief. Jenny ran over with a cup of tea and set it down in front of her. "Thank you, Child."

"Any idea who could have taken them?"

She shook her head. "If it wasn't you, I'm at a loss."

"Are you sure it wasn't *your* mother?" Chief stressed the word at my mother.

"She couldn't have. I have alarms in place to warn me if she draws too near the museum."

"Why?"

"Because, with her spell book, she has a tendency to blow things up. I tired of paying to have the damages fixed."

"And you want her to move to Cedar Falls with us?" I didn't even attempt to keep the snarky tone from my voice.

"Without her books, she is mostly containable. And it was not my idea, Daughter."

I sighed and nodded, wondering what I had agreed to, and what other troubles we were inviting.

Chapter 5

"Hi, Alister," I said and smiled at Alista's twin as he strode into my mother's study.

"Greetings, Lady." He bowed low and took the seat across from me. Only then did he greet Chief with a small nod.

"Alister, this is Chief of Police William Bates of Cedar Falls, a member of our coven."

"Pleased to meet you, sir."

"Just call me Bill."

"Bill." He nodded.

"Your sister tells me you wish to pack up the bakery and move to our little town. I'm all for it, I just wanted to make sure you both were happy with the idea of moving?"

He gave me a smile I had seen a hundred times over the past few weeks. They might be fraternal, but their smiles were identical. "Alista might be a little more excited about the move than I, but yes. I definitely think a change in scenery would do us both a world of good."

"Great. I have a spot in mind for your shop, if you trust me. I'd be making the land purchase and leasing it to you, with a grace period until you get business going. Your sister seemed okay with the idea, I just wanted your input."

"Not necessary, but I'm grateful for your assistance. She probably told you we have a buyer in mind for the location here."

"She did. I told her to use that money to handle equipment and housing."

"Then we accept. You have our thanks."

"I don't know if she told you, but the bookstore I am opening will also be selling your baked goods? Hopefully."

"Yes. I've been in contact with her nightly. She seems very excited, and I'll be honest. If it weren't for the nervous butterflies in my stomach, I might be just as excited. Change never comes easy for our kind, I thank you for assisting with the transition."

"I wish to make the town as much as a sanctuary for our kind as Ashville. I can't do it alone," I answered with a smile. The interview with Alister had been a formality. He already had a place in Cedar Falls. I just wanted to make sure he wasn't reluctantly following his sister's whims. Alister had the business sense, and his sister the artistic touch that made their goods almost magical in quality. I couldn't wait to sample them on a regular basis. "You and your sister are both more than welcome to Cedar Falls."

"Thank you, Lady."

I nodded as he stood. "Send in the next person, please."

He exited the room and I looked up at Chief, a smile on my face.

"You didn't ask him about the grimoires."

"No. Nor shall I. That is between my mother and the police. They have until we leave to find the thief."

"But what if it is one of the witches moving to Cedar Falls?"

"*Then* it becomes our problem."

He didn't look too happy but nodded as another witch walked into the study. I smiled at the familiar face. "Trevon! Good to see you."

"Dot, always a pleasure. I apologize, as it is Lady now, is it not?"

"It is, but call me Dot. This is Bill," I said and pointed beside me. It was time to shorten the introductions and get through the interviews. I had little patience for them, and they were more to assuage Bill than pass any judgement. Of course, he didn't know that. "I was surprised to see your name on the list."

"Surely not as surprised as I to write it."

"What?"

Trevon sighed and leaned forward in his seat. "Call it what you will, a drive, a whim, the guiding hand of the goddess... I felt the need to move."

"But your move will leave Ashville without a...pharmacist."

"No. My daughter, Aliya, will remain here. I'm opening a second apothecary."

"Oh. I had wondered at her absence from the list."

"Would you rather have her make the move?"

"Not at all. You are more than welcome. Chief?" I looked up over my shoulder.

"Pharmacist?"

"Yes. I am a purveyor of rare herbs and components. Do you not have an apothecary in your town?"

"Uh. We have a drug store?"

"Spell components, medicinal herbs for potions, the odd magical implements," I explained. I was never big on potion making or charms, but Mother and Grandmother were experts.

"Oh. I see. I shall trust your judgement then, Lady."

"Trevon, welcome to Cedar Falls. My assistant Jason will be contacting you in the next few days to expedite your move. We shall eagerly await your arrival."

"My thanks, Lady." He bowed low and left the office.

"Potions? We have some references to them, but nobody in our coven remembers how they work. Won't that alert the humans?"

"As I said, things are getting ready to make a major change. The coven is healed, but we still need a good education. I'm even nothing when compared to my mother and grandmother. As for the normal folk, they usually buy medicinal herbs and the odd love potion or two," I said with a smile, not letting him know some of the more interesting things that had happened...

He just nodded and went to get the next candidate. He came back leading a cloaked figure hidden in the shadows of their hood. The cloak alone was enough to let me know who had sat down in front of me. While I had never seen his face, the elegant nature of his movements, his slight frame, and the almost nonexistent presence couldn't have been hidden under ten cloaks.

"Greetings, Shea."

"Greetings, Lady." The cowl of the cloak dipped slightly.

"You wish to move?"

Again, nothing more than a slight nod and a shrug.

"Why?"

I could see the chest of the cloak lift slightly as he sighed even though not a wisp of sound escaped his lips. "Change. I've always been an outsider in the coven. I wish to...grow. Become more active."

"Do you think you can do that by moving with us to a smaller coven?"

Again, nothing but a nod answered our question.

"I mean no disrespect, but are you a man or a woman?" Curiosity colored Chief's question. Shea, when he wasn't blending in the shadows, often evoked that from the people who finally paid attention to him. It was almost as if they couldn't stand not knowing what lie beneath the cloak. I'd known Shea for fifty years, had spoken to him less than a dozen times, and *never* seen his face other than a quick glance as he turned.

"I am male." He spoke, but hearing his soprano voice wasn't very reassuring, I'm sure.

"What do you do?" Chief asked, trying to keep the conversation going.

"Pardon?"

"He is the chief librarian for both the town and the coven. I guess you could call him a scholar of sorts."

"Oh. We do have a library, but I don't know if there are any positions available..." Chief almost sounded sad. I was surprised by his reaction.

"But I am opening a *book* store. I'm sure I can find a position for Shea."

"That's true."

58

"So, what are you thinking, Chief?"

"It's a yes from me, on one condition."

"You wish to see my face," Shea answered, almost expecting the response.

"Call it the cop in me, but I don't like not knowing what a person looks like."

"That is fair, but it might be a deal breaker for you."

"Why?"

Instead of answering, he pulled his hood back and I couldn't help it, I gasped. Shea was beautiful, not handsome. There wasn't a masculine bone in his body. Long brown hair swept back from a prominent widow's peak, waves cascading back into the depths of his hood. Large, almost too large, green eyes blinked at us in the unaccustomed light of the study. He had no facial hair, I truly doubted he could grow any, and his ears tapered up into slight points. He wasn't an elf, but he had fae blood, like Candace. It was for that reason and that reason alone, he kept his features hidden. Many people, witches included, would either naturally shy away from his otherworldly features, or become so enamored with him, they would resort to stalking. And then there was those who would hunt him simply for the blood he carried. I didn't blame him for staying hidden, even among the coven.

"Wow." That was all the speech Chief was capable of.

"You wish to have me?"

"Excuse me?" Chief sounded a little strange.

"I think he means in Cedar Falls, Chief." I chuckled a little.

"Oh. Yes."

I sighed, thinking of Candace. She had lived all those years in Cedar Falls without resorting to cloaks or magic to hide what she was. She didn't have any human friends that I knew of, but I did know that the people she worked with shied away from her. Maybe she could teach Shea a few things. "We have another witch with fae blood. You might not be as alone there as you were here."

"Another?"

"Yes. Candace. I'll introduce her to you when you move."

"I am ready whenever you are."

"What about your house, your things?"

"I am keeping my home here. I shall purchase another. I can have my things boxed and shipped."

I hadn't been expecting that. Most of the witches planning the move would slowly trickle in over the next few months. Even my grandmother would need time to make the transition. "Then book a flight for tomorrow at ten in the morning. We are leaving then. Unless you need me to arrange transportation."

"I dislike human transportation. May I ride your shadow?"

"Pardon me?"

"Your mother did not share my particular talents?"

"Um, my mother isn't exactly a sharing type of person."

"My apologies." He stood and motioned to the other side of the desk. I nodded and stood as he walked around. The desk lamp cast my shadow behind me. I turned, following his movements as he stood between me and the wall and stepped back until his back brushed against the wood and plaster. He then melted into the shadow until his cloak blended perfectly and he faded from view.

"Where'd he go?" Chief reached out and touched the wall, feeling around.

"He's a shadow walker. I've read about them, but never seen one. You won't find him."

"What's a shadow walker?" He turned and stared at me in disbelief.

I smiled as Shea stepped forward, back into the light and solidified behind Chief, reaching out and touching his arm.

To Chief's credit, he didn't scream. He did, however, let out a yelp and jumped. "Don't do that!"

I laughed and the faint etchings of a smile graced Shea's lips. "A shadow walker. I can step between this world and the shadow realm. Time and movement are much different there. I can ride someone's shadow or jump from shadow to shadow there if I know where I'm going. Since I've never been to Cedar Falls, I will be forced to be by Lady's side until we arrive."

"That's pretty cool," Chief said, dumbfounded.

"It has its uses. Especially since I will be able to travel from Cedar Falls to Ashville at any time. If there is nothing else, I shall make ready to depart."

"Welcome to Cedar Falls, Shea."

"Thank you, Lady."

The rest of the interviews were more mundane, including our brief interview with Josie's mom, Miranda. She basically marched into the study imperiously and told us she would be joining us as soon as possible. The rest just seemed to want to get away from my mother, not that I could blame them. Chief didn't say no to one of them, either. I think he realized about halfway through that this had been a waste of time on his part. Anyone not worthy of moving to Cedar Falls would not have had a place in Mother's coven to begin with. However, if it set his mind at ease, then so be it. It was nice to visit, but I was definitely looking forward to getting on the plane and going home in the morning.

The food was set up by the time the interviews were over, and we ate and mingled, getting the additions to our new coven to become more acquainted with each other and discuss plans for moving. Those with less could share the cost of moving trucks and hammer out timelines. By the time I had forked the last of my pulled pork into my mouth, I felt the change in the air. Something or someone was coming, full bore. They had just hit the edge of town.

I set my fork down and glanced at Chief, who didn't seem to be sensing anything out of the ordinary. Even my mother was at the head of the table, sipping her wine as if a rocket wasn't bearing down on all of us like a thermonuclear warhead. I barely had time to stand and turn toward the front door when it burst open in a blast of shards and glass.

Everyone spun, defensive spells flaming in their hands when the vampire latched itself to my chest and we both landed on the floor in a heap. I knew in an instant who it was. I felt the bond between us flare and I could feel her shaking in my arms.

The group around us calmed down when I lifted my hand above us, signaling them everything was okay. The only sound echoing in the dining room was my mother, slowly walking to where Yuki and I were lying in a crumbled heap.

"Daughter, who is this?"

"Um. My friend, Yuki."

"Is Yuki a skilled carpenter?"

I looked over at the shattered remains of my mother's front door and sighed. "I'll fix it as soon as we get up."

"Hmm. Yes, you will. After the both of you follow me to my study and explain what is going on."

She turned and walked away, heading to the depths of the office.

"You okay?" I whispered into Yuki's ear.

"Now. I couldn't bear it anymore. I'm sorry. I almost made it here last night. As soon as the sun went down, I finished my journey."

"You ran?"

I felt her nod against my chest.

"I'm sorry. I didn't realize it would have been that much of a problem. Next time, we'll just figure out how to bring you with us."

She lifted her head and looked into my eyes, seeing the sincerity. I felt horrible. I thought she could have handled just a few short days away from me. I guessed wrong.

"It was the single most horrible feeling in the world. Don't ever do that to me again, please."

"I won't. But you might want to rethink your words. We need to go speak to my mother. That might be worse."

"I doubt it."

She crawled off me and helped me to stand. I took a deep breath, nodded at a very confused looking Chief, and led Yuki into my mother's study. She was sitting in the chair I'd been using all day. I took one of the seats in front of her and Yuki slinked into the other.

"Now then, what is all this about?"

I didn't even entertain the thought of lying to her. She would have seen through it in a minute. I'd never been able to be anything but truthful with the woman and I hated it. Especially growing up.

"I was too long away from my familiar."

To Mother's credit, she didn't even blink. "I see. Would you care to explain how this happened?"

"I gave her some of my blood to heal her wounds." Yuki sounded apologetic and wondered if it was the bond forcing her to defend me, even to my mother. Either way it was me my mother looked to for further explanation.

"She's not lying. That was all that happened. No ritual, no magic, nothing. I merely drank some of her blood and the bond was complete."

"I did not think you would do something as foolish as *trying* to bring a vampire to your side as a familiar. My shock comes from the fact that you did not, and had planned on not, telling me."

"Oh. Well. I didn't think of it until I found my arms full of vampire in your living room."

"That is a lie."

"Maybe. If you were me would you have told Grandmother?"

"I see your point. Do you want things to remain the same, or do you wish the bond to be broken?"

"Leave it," Yuki squeaked at the same moment I said, "Break it."

"Well? Which is it?"

"Yuki?" I made her name a question.

"Leave it, please."

"Why?" It was my mother's and my turn to speak simultaneously.

"My powers have increased dramatically. That...and..."

"What?"

"I can taste food again through you. And also..."

"What?" I had a feeling I knew, but I wanted her to say it. The scream from the living room when Jimmy and I had been having sex had been all but forgotten by me. Until I saw the blush on the vampire's cheeks.

"I'm asexual. I rarely, if ever, have the desire to have intercourse or anything. When Lady Dorothea plays with her lovers... I can't even begin to describe how much joy it brings me."

"It would almost seem you two were made for each other," my mother interjected, dryly. "What about you, Daughter? Any gain to your power?"

"Not that I've noticed. I can't hear her thoughts even if I concentrate. She can hear mine, and at first it was uncontrollable, but that might have been the bond."

Mother sighed. "She didn't drink your blood."

"No, she didn't."

"Why? What would happen?" Yuki sounded curious.

"Dorothea would have gained some unique abilities."

"Why didn't you tell me?" Yuki asked me.

"I didn't want to bind you to me in the first place. Why would I have?"

"To gain power. No offense, but if the vampires ever find out about this..."

"I have a feeling Mr. Abernathy already knows. Don't forget, he is the lord of your clan. He is your sire, but now you belong to my daughter. Don't think for a moment that there is any way you could have hidden that from him. Before you leave, Daughter, you need to reach out to him."

"He did sound a little odd the last time I spoke to him on the phone."

"Exactly," my mother added.

"Yuki and I will go there from here. If things go badly..."

"They will not. He will understand, but if he does not, please use his sanctuary in our humble town as a bargaining chip."

I could see the fire in her eye and knew without a doubt she was not joking. My mother had her moments, they were few and far between, but when they were there, they were epic. "Thank you, Mother."

"Visitations from the goddess, vampire familiars. Should anything else unusual befall you...please do let your poor mother know as soon as it happens, please?"

"Yes, Mother."

"Also, complete your bond with the child before you leave. I am curious as to what will happen, and you may need the boost in power before you visit Lord Abernathy."

"Are you sure?"

"Do not doubt me, Daughter. Ever."

"Yes, Mother," I said doubtfully.

She cackled and left Yuki and me sitting alone in her study. Yuki was staring at me almost hopefully.

"I thought you said the bond could never be broken. Why did she ask if we wanted it to be?"

"As far as I know, it can't. My grandmother and mother are both ancient, and maybe they know of some archaic way that might leave one or both of us dead."

"'Til death do us part?"

"Exactly."

She shuddered next to me. "I made the right decision then."

I nodded, sorry she had to make the decision at all. "So. Where do you want to bite me?"

"Are you sure you want to go through with this?"

"You heard her. There is little room for argument."

She nodded and motioned to my wrist. I handed it over to her, grateful it wasn't my neck she'd chosen. I watched with morbid curiosity as she brought my flesh up to her lips and let her fangs settle just above the vein running through my wrist. I could almost hear the skin as it snapped under their sharp tips. I winced just as the fireworks exploded in my head.

Chapter 6

The limo that Mr. Abernathy sent for us pulled into the large circular drive in front of the pristine stone mansion. It wasn't my first visit, but I'd never been as nervous on any other visit as I was at that moment. My jitters were even setting Yuki on edge. She sat forward on the leather seat, nearly trembling in fear. I took a deep breath, settled my nerves and watched her visibly relax.

She looked up at me.

"Sorry," I said, trying to maintain my calm.

"Don't be. I'm afraid, too. I feel as though I've done something wrong, even if it wasn't intentional."

I nodded in understanding. "Like you borrowed the car to get him a present and crashed it on the highway."

"Something like that."

The limo rolled to a stop and we waited for the driver to get out and open it for us. I'd pulled the door open when he arrived at my mother's house and he seemed perturbed I'd touched the door handle. I wasn't making that mistake again.

"Thank you," I said to him as we walked up the stone walkway leading to the front door. Before we could even ring the bell, it opened and a butler, complete in the standard black butler attire, greeted us.

"Good evening. Please come in. Lord Abernathy will join you shortly." He led us to a small waiting alcove right off the foyer.

"Thank you." I had a feeling I was going to be repeating myself a lot.

He nodded and wandered off to butler somewhere else. I shook my head at the pretentiousness of the whole idea of butlers. We probably had twenty times the Abernathy's fortune. My mother would die before hiring a butler or a maid. She could use a maid, I'd seen the dust on her shelves, but a butler...not so much.

"Lady Dorothea?"

I looked up at a lovely Asian woman in a full kimono standing at the entrance to the alcove.

"Yes?"

"Please, come with me. Philippe will see you now."

She turned without waiting and I heard Yuki gulp next to me as we stood and hurried to catch up to her.

"Hello, Mother," Yuki said quietly as we fell into step behind her.

"Greetings, my child."

"This is your mother?"

Yuki nodded somberly, not elaborating further. The kimono-clad woman led us up the stairs and stopped at a heavy wooden door on the second floor, rapping softly with her knuckles.

"Come," echoed through the door.

"Husband, your guests are here." She opened the door and we followed her into the dimly lit room.

I blinked in confusion. If the woman was married to Philippe, then she had to be June Abernathy and that would make Yuki his...

"Hello, Daughter."

"Greetings, Father," she whispered reverently and bowed low.

I chose to remain silent, not liking surprises. While I wasn't exactly angry, happy wasn't very high up on the list of emotions warring inside me. When Mother had said he had sired her, I assumed she had incorrectly thought Mr. Abernathy had made her into a vampire. Yuki winced as she felt my surprise.

Sorry. I should have told you. I'm his second child and he sent me to you as a punishment. I didn't even think he still considered me a daughter.

We will discuss this later, I thought at her as hard as I could. I doubted she would be able to hear me, since she never had before, but I hoped with the exchange of blood, she would.

That is fair. I'm sorry.

You can hear me?

Yes.

Good. I don't like surprises. Ever.

Yes, my Lady.

"Are you two done conversing?"

I gasped in surprise. "You could hear us?"

"No, but if you're going to converse privately, be sure in the future to control your expressions. You were both gazing at the floor and more than once my daughter winced. Which answers my question of who is the master in your relationship."

"So, you know why we are here then?"

"I had suspected as much when I could no longer feel Yuki through our clan ties. At first, I assumed they had formed a clan with your two wayward vampires, but George's bond is still there. Then I assumed she had perished, and you were afraid to tell me, but again, George alleviated my fears."

"I'm sorry, Mr. Abernathy. I wanted to tell you in person."

"Do not lie to me, Lady Blackwell. I know my daughter, she probably feared for her life and you both intended to take this secret to your graves. Before I get angrier, would you care to explain to me how you stole my daughter from me?"

I cleared my throat nervously and attempted to gather my thoughts. "You know witches may call a familiar?"

He nodded and narrowed his eyes.

"Well, it is a complicated ritual involving both spells and magic. It also has an extraordinarily high rate of failure, especially with the more developed...familiars."

"Go on."

"Another component is the sharing of blood..."

"You did all this to entrap my daughter as a familiar?" His eyes flared, and he stood, nearly frothing in anger.

"No. I was badly injured and your daughter, out of the kindness of her heart, gave me a drink of her blood to save my life. Without even remotely trying, and without the ritualistic magic, spells, or me giving her my blood, she became my familiar. I can't explain how or why it happened, but I swear upon the goddess herself, it was *not* my intention."

He transferred his angry stare to his daughter for confirmation. She nodded, meekly and bowed low again in contrition.

Then his visage softened and became almost afraid as he slowly turned and regarded me with a look. I just didn't know what it meant. "You *swear* all you have told me is true?"

"Yes."

"And I am sure there is no way this bond can be broken?" he asked sarcastically.

"Yes."

"Then I must ask you one more thing, Lady Blackwell. What are your intentions?"

"As far as?"

"My daughter"

"She is my familiar. She draws strength from me, as I draw strength from her. I'll always be there for her."

He nodded before I finished, either expecting my answer or happy with my decision. "And what of the other vampires in your care?"

"They are welcome to stay or go as they please?"

"You do not intend to bind them to you as well?"

"Oh, hell no. I didn't even mean to bind Yuki. You have to believe me."

"I do. Now. But, faced with the opportunity to almost endlessly increase your power... You're not tempted?"

"No, Mr. Abernathy. I am not."

"You swear?"

"Of course."

"And I may let the vampires in Cedar Falls know to never share blood with you and why?"

"Please do. I wouldn't want any accidents, even if I were near death or unconscious."

He shifted his attention over our heads, to his wife, still standing by the door we had entered. "June. Contact your nephew. Let him know of everything we have discussed."

"Yes, my husband." She opened the door and quickly exited.

"Do you know why this has happened?" I had nobody else to ask and he seemed to know more than he was letting on.

"I have a few theories, but I will say this. Never before has a vampire been bound to a witch as a familiar. Husband or wife on occasion, but never bound magically."

"Has a witch ever been turned into a vampire?"

"No. The magic which gives us life does not work on a witch. Nor can our two species interbreed. It is rare enough for vampires to give birth. Our two children are almost unheard of. We evolved to reproduce through our bite, not our loins."

"What are vampires?"

"None of us know. The oldest of us have even forgotten the tale of our birth."

"Would you even tell me if you knew?"

"I do not know. I will tell you I'm leaning toward no, right now. You should *not* have been able to do what you have done. I feel that the less you know of what we are, the better off we would be. I do, however, know that you do see us as equals and would do anything in your power to protect those of us you consider friends. That fact alone is cutting you much slack in my dealings with you and your family right now."

71

"I thank you for that. I also promise not to let this happen again and to treat Yuki as my friend."

He nodded. "Since she did not feel inclined to obey me, maybe it is good that she has a master she cannot disobey."

I nodded, not knowing or wanting to know what she did to get banished to Upstate New York.

"Well, I thank you for your time," he said and stood. We were clearly being dismissed.

"Thank you for your understanding."

"Not that I had a choice. I'm sure your mother instructed you to threaten our peaceful existence in Ashville if things had not ended on a friendly note."

"You know my mother well. Rest assured, I am nothing like her."

"Yet, young Lady Blackwell. I remember your mother in her youth, you are more alike than you know."

"Now that thought scares me more than anything."

His chuckle slithered across my skin. "Then maybe you shall avoid the heady drug of power. I wish you luck."

"And I thank you. It feels awkward to ask with everything that has transpired, but we are trying to grow our supernatural population. Should you have any other vampires who wish to spread their wings and move, they would be more than welcome. Even ones you send to keep an eye on me."

"George is good enough for that. June trusts him completely, as do I. But I shall keep your offer in mind for some of the younger ones of our clan."

"Thank you."

"No, thank you."

He walked us to the front door and instructed the driver to return us to my hotel. I had to pack and figure out a way to get Yuki back to Cedar Falls. She had literally run the entire way, the thought boggled my mind, but I couldn't ask her to do it again.

∞ ∞ ∞

Main Street in Cedar Falls had been completely decked out in Christmas decorations. They had sprung from every store front, and even the empty ones had garland and painted images of snowmen and Santas. "Wow. We were literally gone for two days."

"Um, yeah. I've never seen it looking so festive," Chief said with the sound of awe coloring his voice.

He was sitting next to me in my SUV after having driven back from Syracuse. Our flight was short and sweet, but I wanted to get home as soon as possible to check on our stowaways.

"It's like Christmas threw up everywhere. It's beautiful," I rambled and headed toward my house.

Thankfully, our arrival had put us in town just after lunch. I was starving, but my stomach could wait. At least the timing had kept traffic to a minimum. Getting from the edge of town to pulling in my driveway took less than ten minutes.

I left the luggage and practically ran into the house. Josie waved and yelled, "Hi," as I ran past her and into the spare room. I had texted her to make it sun-proof again. Closing the bedroom door, I plunged the room into darkness, which wouldn't work either. Reaching over, I flicked on the light switch and stared at my shadow on the wall.

Moments later, a hand reached out and grabbed the wall, Shea pulling himself from the shadow and dragging a very comatose vampire behind him.

"Is she okay?"

"Yes. You knew she would be, Lady. It's not as if we did not test it before travelling."

"I know, I know, but you can't blame a girl from worrying. Thank you, Shea," I reached down and picked her up off the floor. Our travel solution had worked perfectly. The only thing lacking had been Shea's inability to lift the vampire on his own. I gingerly set her down on the spare bed and motioned him for the door. Just as a precaution, I grabbed the blanket off the foot of the bed and covered her before we left the room.

Josie was waiting for me with a cup of coffee.

"Bless your face." I gratefully took it from her.

"Bless yours. Missed you!" She squealed and hugged me as I tried not to spill the mug of heavenly goodness on the floor.

The front door opened, and Chief plowed through with my luggage. "Shit." I rushed over and grabbed my bags. "Thanks."

"No problem. I shut the trunk, but your car is still unlocked." He wasn't exactly happy I hadn't told him I had a vampire familiar. It took me a while to convince him that it was Yuki's wish to not let anybody know. I even made up a little white lie about Jimmy "finding out" so he wouldn't get even more pissed off. But he was being civil, for which I was extremely grateful.

"I'll lock it later."

"Everything okay?" He looked over at Shea standing nervously in the doorway. You couldn't see his face, but he was fidgeting.

"Yep. She's in bed. Worked perfectly," I answered.

"Good. I'm heading out. I want a shower and I need to check in down at the station. Let the guys know I'm back."

Setting my bag down on the floor and my coffee on the table, I wrapped my arms around him and kissed him gently. "Thanks for going with me."

"Yeah. That was fun, but unnecessary. In the future, I'll trust your judgement a bit more. At least on coven members," he added dryly.

"Thank you. I'm just glad you realized it." I ignored his little jab.

"See ya, Josie. Bye, Shea." The fae gave Chief a half wave. Josie wasn't even paying attention, just staring at Shea.

"Where did he come from?" She looked over at me and pointed at Shea.

"Long story. He brought Yuki. That's why I had you sun-proof the room for her."

"Okay. Fill me in later. How'd it go back home?"

"Better than I expected. Everybody who wanted to move, will be. Chief didn't have one objection."

"You knew that would be the case," she said with a little snort. "Shea? You want some coffee or anything?"

"Would you happen to have any wine?"

Josie nodded and headed toward the kitchen, I followed her. I had some seriously bad news for her, and while I would have preferred to deliver it in a room devoid of sharp objects, sooner, rather than later, would be best. She had pulled a bottle of chardonnay out of the wine fridge and was peeling the foil off the top when I put my hand on her arm. "Chief didn't have any objections, but you might…"

"Excuse me?" She set the corkscrew down and looked over at me, suspicion plainly etched on her delicate features.

"We had a couple of surprise additions to the immigrant list…"

"Who?"

"My grandmother."

Relief spread across her face, softening the lines that had formed. "Oh, jeez. You scared the shit out of me. I love your nana. Her moving here would be kind of cool, add a little spice to the mix."

"Yeah. I kind of thought that, too. Just wasn't sure how'd you'd react."

"Don't be silly. There isn't a single person in Ashville I wouldn't object to moving here."

"Even your mother?"

"Okay. Maybe my mother."

I laughed and opened the wine for her, pouring three glasses and dumping my coffee. I was going to need something a little stronger. "What if I wasn't joking."

"About what?"

I took a sip and handed one of the other glasses to her. "Your mother."

"What about her?"

"Moving."

"What?"

"What."

"Huh?"

"Your mother."

"What about her?"

"She's moving."

"Where?"

"Here."

"When?"

"Soon."

"How soon?"

"Very soon."

"Fuck me."

"No."

Josie downed the contents of her glass of wine and poured another. She didn't even look over at Shea as he approached the kitchen counter. I started to fear for her sanity when she lifted his glass of wine and set it down neatly in front of him while she slowly looked up at me. I could feel the storm brewing and I was fresh out of umbrellas.

"Do you hate me?"

"Josie, I swear, I didn't even get a say in the matter. She basically waltzed in and told me when she would be here. She's moving the floral shop and everything."

"Where's she going to live?"

"I'll buy her a fucking house on the outskirts of town if I have to. On the opposite side of town. In the woods or something."

"You didn't offer her a place here, did you?"

"At our house?"

"Yes."

"Oh, hell no."

"And you're not going to kick me out and make me live with her?"

That kind of broke my heart. I set down my glass of wine and wrapped my arms around my friend. "Oh, Josie. Don't be ridiculous. This is *our* house. Not mine. Ours."

"Okay. I'll let you live."

"Bless your face."

She giggled and pulled away, downing the second glass of wine. I had a feeling I was going to be peeling her off the floor and carrying her to her bed within the hour.

"Is everything okay?"

I looked up at Shea. He had picked up his glass of wine and took a worried sip. "Yes. Josie's mother is moving here."

"Ah. Yes. I can see that would be cause for worry."

"You know her?"

"Miranda? Yes. She often comes to the library. Much to my dismay, I know most of your escapades. She even tried to get me to date you." He looked at Josie and smiled from the depths of his hood.

"She did not!" Josie poured more wine and stared, wide-eyed as she nursed it a bit slower.

"She did."

"What did you say?"

"That a woman of your beauty would not be interested in a recluse such as I." He even bowed, the slick little thing.

I chuckled into my wine. "Be grateful the offer never made it to her. She probably would have eaten you up."

Shea took a step back from her.

"I'm kidding, Shea."

A little bob of his hood was all the acknowledgement he gave.

"You know you can take that off here, right?"

"What?"

"Your hood and cloak."

"Oh, my apologies. I'm sensitive to the light."

I hadn't thought about that, but it made sense. He was a shadow walker after all. "Ahh. I'm sorry, I didn't know."

"We have much to learn about each other. The benefits of a smaller coven. I have spoken to the two of you but a few times. I look forward to rectifying that."

"Me, too." I raised my glass at him and blinked in surprise as Josie clinked hers against mine and then his.

Chapter 7

"Seriously?"

Chief nodded.

"I'm hungry, damnit."

"Sorry. You can eat if you want, but I need to run."

"No. I'll wait. Want me to tag along with you?"

"Sure, but don't blame me if you lose your appetite. Marcus said it's pretty gruesome."

I sighed. A murder scene was hardly a good idea before dinner, but I didn't feel like being alone. I was feeling a little off and I couldn't quite put my finger on why.

"Don't worry. I won't puke on your crime scene."

I'd met him at Bunyan's Steakhouse after offering to buy him dinner as sort of an apology for not telling him about Yuki. We'd made it to the front door when his phone started ringing. I sighed, at least we hadn't ordered yet.

We hopped into his Jeep and I punched the lock button on my remote, making sure I had locked my Sportage. It beeped and the hazard lights blinked as we were pulling away. He took us to the edge of town and didn't stop until we were in the woods out by Jason's trailer. A lump of fear formed in the pit of my stomach.

"It's not Jason. It's Frank Dunbar."

"Who's Frank Dunbar?"

"A friend of Dwight's who's just about as sociable. He lives in a trailer on ten acres, pretty close to Jason."

"Survivalist?"

"No. Convicted felon. Robbed a bank twenty years ago. Did ten years in prison and then moved out here, trying to make ends meet, not meet his end." Chief sounded upset.

"You know him?"

"I kept tabs on him. Nice guy. Made a mistake in his youth, but never started any other trouble. Dwight got him a job at the factory, even with the conviction."

I nodded, not knowing what to say.

Chief pulled off the road and onto another dirt drive. Jason's trailer was relatively close to Branner Parkway. This one was set another five minutes back. He must have parked the trailer pretty damn close to the back of the property.

"Is that Marcus?" I pointed at the police officer leaning against his squad car.

"Yeah. Call him Officer Brown though."

"Roger." I even gave him a small salute.

"You're a dork."

"Yep."

He pulled the Jeep up to the squad car and shut the engine off. It immediately began ticking in the cold November air. "Come on. Let's get this over with."

He got out of the vehicle and I did the same, nodding at Officer Brown as we walked up.

"Hey, Chief." Marcus had a nice speaking voice, smooth like silk but deep enough to still sound very masculine. He should have a job on the radio, not police work. He definitely didn't have a face for television, though. He wasn't ugly, but his skin was scarred and pitted. From what, I had no idea.

"Marcus. This is Dot. Dot, this is Officer Brown."

"Nice to meet you," I said and offered him my hand, which he accepted with a firm, but not overbearing, shake.

"Call me, Marcus. I've heard a lot about you…"

"I'm sure it was all sugar-coated."

His chuckle told me all I needed to know. I probably should have been flattered Chief talked about me at work. Marcus' reaction told me it was more ranting than talking.

Oh, well. We all need a place to vent.

"Where's the body?" Chief asked to either change the subject or get the ball rolling. I was happy with either.

"Out back, what's left of it. Looks like he was grilling when he got mauled."

"Did you say mauled?" Chief had told me there'd been a death, and that it was gruesome. I'd assumed it was a murder because he left out the fact that it had been caused by an animal.

"Yeah. Looks like a bear or wolf chewed him up pretty good."

Chief flipped on his flashlight, heading around the trailer. The sun wasn't completely down, and a chill ran down my spine that had absolutely nothing to do with the frigid temperature. Officer Brown followed behind Chief, and not wanting to be left alone, I quickly caught up to the two of them before they disappeared out of sight.

I almost ran into the back of Chief. He'd come to a complete standstill as soon as he rounded the corner. Letting out a little squawk of surprise, I stopped just in time. He gave me a look over his shoulder.

"What?"

"You...um. You might want to stay here." He strode forward and that's when I saw the blood. Blood and bits and pieces. For the first time in our very brief relationship, I did *exactly* as he said. I was no stranger to gore, but it looked like someone threw Frank into a woodchipper. For good measure, I turned around and put my back to the grizzly scene.

I could hear their muffled conversation and they mentioned wolves and bears, again. My eyes began darting around and I slowly started to back up closer to the two guys with guns. Whatever ate Frank might still be around. I raised my hands up, just in case I needed to make a wildlife flambé.

"You okay?"

I shrieked and spun around. Chief had one hand in his pocket and the other was shining the flashlight at me.

"Yeah. Just don't want to get eaten."

He flashed me a mischievous grin. I sighed. A guy had just been torn to shreds, but something like that never stopped little boy humor. Hell, if the ground didn't look like someone had just busted open a fifty-gallon drum of Spaghettios, I might have giggled a little.

"Whatever did this is probably *long* gone, Dot. You can relax." He turned back to continue inspecting the carnage. I sighed and did the same.

Long gone or not, my eyes still darted all around, scanning the edge of the trees. When I saw the two large eyes staring back at me, I screamed like a little girl. The German Shepherd stepped out from its hiding place and gave me a scared look. I felt bad for screaming at the exact moment the gun went off behind me as Chief shouted my name.

I watched in slow motion as the red splotch appeared on its chest and it fell over to the ground, yipping in pain. My heart broke. Ignoring the shouts behind me, I ran to it and dropped down beside it, already calling the words for my healing spell. I put my hands over the wound and sent out a tendril of power, trying to find the bullet in the deep wound. The poor dog was thrashing, crying, and growling. Blood splashed across my arms as it moved. Whoever pulled the trigger must have hit an artery. Insane from the pain, he bit down on my forearm. I cried out but didn't pull my hands from the wound. I had just found the bullet and was slowly working it out in reverse, using my magic to pull it. I would heal it after it was free.

After what felt like an hour, the slick feel of metal touched my palm. I tossed it away and changed spells, sending healing magic into the wound. It was working or the dog was dying. His grip on my arm lessened and the pain started. My arm was on fire as Chief's hands settled on my shoulders, steadying me.

"I sent Marcus for a first aid kit. Bind the wound, even if it's healed. That way he won't ask questions."

"Grab it from him, don't let him see."

"Sorry, Dot. I thought it was a wolf."

I let go of the wound and ran my fingers over it. I could feel the bump of a scar, but no hole. I'd healed him, hopefully in time. He let go of my arm and looked up at me with his ears back against his head.

"I'm sorry, puppy. You okay?" I asked, soothingly.

His eyes widened and he started scooting back away from me. I let him go and he stood, unable to get his legs under him for a moment but finally succeeding.

"Tell Marcus you only nicked him." There was no way the dog was going to let me get close enough to wrap an unnecessary bandage around a healed wound. If I were the dog, I'd be pissed off as all hell.

"You're turning into quite the healer."

"Tell me about it. I'm just tired of having to practice."

I turned and gave Chief a tired look. He tilted his head. "You have blood all over your face. There's a bunch on your lips."

I wiped my mouth off on the back of my arm and instinctively ran my tongue over them. The metallic taste of iron made me almost gag. I hated the taste of blood, and dog was no better. "Ick. I didn't get it all."

"No. You're covered."

Marcus returned with the first aid kit. "No need. I just nicked him. He seems to be fine."

Marcus looked at the dog and shook his head, then his gaze drifted over to my arm. "Glad you're worried about the dog and not your girlfriend."

He quickly strode forward and opened the case, setting it on the ground by my feet. Chief shined the light on my arm. A German Shepherd dental impression completely covered my forearm, halfway between my wrist and elbow. You could see every puncture wound from every tooth in the dog's mouth. I looked down at him, surprised he hadn't run.

"Bad puppy."

The dog cowered and lay down on the grass.

Sorry. It hurt.

I blinked at looked up at Chief. "Did you say something?"

"No?"

"Never mind."

"Let me wrap it for you," Marcus said and did just that.

I sat patiently and let him bind the wounds. I'd have Josie heal it up when I got home. I didn't have any strength left. Marcus expertly finished, closed the kit, and headed back to his car.

"Are we almost done here? I want to go get these," I motioned at my punctured arm, "healed up. And, I'm hungry."

"Yeah. It's not a murder investigation. Poor Frank just picked the wrong night to grill a steak. That must be his dog."

The Shepherd was lying there with his head between his paws, blinking at us as Chief shined the light at him. I walked back over to him and squatted down, moving slowly to not spook him anymore than he already was. "Good boy," I said and reached for his neck. "No collar. I don't know, maybe?"

"Well, we can drop him at the pound."

"Yeah. I hate to, he's beautiful, but a dog is the *last* thing I need right now. I already have a Josie."

The dog sat up straight. *Yours. No pound.*

I blinked at him again and my mouth fell open. My mind flashed to him chomping down on my arm, my blood filling his mouth, and me licking my lips and making a face at the disgusting flavor of his blood...

"Shit." *Can you hear me?*

The shepherd barked.

"What?" Chief asked suspiciously.

"Guess he's going home with me."

"Why?"

"Well, I can't exactly send my familiar to the pound now, can I?"

∞ ∞ ∞

"What's his name?" Josie was leaning against the open door of the bathroom, impatiently tapping her foot. She was waiting to pet the damn dog. I told her she had to wait until I gave him a bath.

"I don't know," I said and scrubbed the last of the blood from his fur. The water in the tub was still pink as it slid down the open drain. I just prayed the old pipes didn't clog with all the dog fur.

"Well, ask him."

"What's your name?"

The dog stopped enjoying the feeling of the brush against its fur and looked up at me, tongue lolling to the side of its mouth.

Dar.

"Why on earth would somebody name a dog Dar?"

He gave me a German Shepherd shrug. I didn't know there was such a thing, but there was no doubt that's what he did. Josie started laughing.

"Are you done yet?"

"Yes! Oh, impatient one. Grab a towel, you can dry him."

Josie squealed in joy and grabbed the towel out of the linen closet by the bathroom door. I shut the water off and let the last of it drain. Dar tensed and twisted, getting ready to pelt me with a deluge of shake-water...

"No!"

He stopped. I could see the fur rippling over his tensed muscles.

I hate being wet.

Wait until I leave, and Josie comes in, I said conspiratorially.

He gave me a wink and I scratched his head before getting up off my knees and opening the shower curtain as far as it would go. Josie was walking in as I was walking out. By the time I got into the living room she was screaming, and I was smiling. Maybe having a dog around would be fun...

Dar ran past me and into my bedroom, Joie chasing after him and swinging the towel over her head like a helicopter.

"You friggin' ungrateful *mutt*!"

I laughed, went to the fridge, and poured myself a large glass of wine, wanting nothing more than to get the taste of fast food out of my mouth. Chief's and my dinner had gone from steak to hamburgers. The rim of the glass was at my lips when the doorbell rang. Taking one quick sip, I set it down on the counter and headed for the front door, unlocking it when I got close enough, and pulling it open.

Yuki was standing on my porch, ignoring the snow falling on her as tears ran down her face.

"What's wrong?" I stepped outside and tried to pull her into a hug when she stepped back.

"How could you? After everything you promised? Was I not good enough?"

"Hold on. Slow down. Come inside and tell me what the hell you're talking about." I turned around and walked back in the house, my fluffy socks no match for the cold concrete I'd been standing on. I almost half-expected her to stand there defiantly, but she was my familiar. She didn't have a choice.

I walked back into the kitchen and she followed. I pointed at the couch in the living room and followed her, letting her choose a seat. Once she had sat down, I took one on the opposite couch, so I could face her.

"Want to start over, slowly?"

"You took another familiar? Was I not good enough? Is it because I can't guard you during the day?"

And just like that, it all made a little more sense.

"Dar!" I shouted over my shoulder, toward my bedroom.

The shepherd came trotting out and sat down in front of me, staring at me intently. His fur was still damp, but not dripping wet. Hopefully my bed wasn't soaked.

"Yuki, this is Dar. Dar, this is my other familiar, Yuki."

Yuki was blushing horribly. "He's a dog."

"Yep."

"But... I could have sworn you took a powerful familiar. I felt the bond form and the strength of it almost hurt. He's a dog?"

"Yep." I cocked my eyebrow at her.

"I was jealous...of a dog?"

"Yep. And how does that make you feel?"

"Kind of stupid. I'm *so* sorry, master."

"First of all, never call me that again. Ever. Second, never ever jump the gun again like that. I promised you I would never do anything to hurt you, and I meant that. Didn't you believe me?"

"When you said it, yes. But then the sun went down, and I woke up, and then *bam*. I felt another familiar. I'm truly sorry," she said and bowed her head.

"That's okay. I'll tell you something else. Dar was another accident. I didn't mean to do it. He was shot and there was a lot of blood. It got everywhere."

"Oh."

"Feel better now?"

"Yes. Are you mad at me?"

I shook my head and gave her a small smile. "Sad that you didn't trust me, but not angry."

She got up from the couch and crossed over to me, leaning over and giving me a short hug. She wasn't the affectionate type, so I let her pull away as soon as she was done.

"I won't ever not trust you again." She plopped down on the couch next to me. Dar gave a little snort and put his head on my leg. I scratched behind his ear.

"What's going on?" Josie stood in the doorway of my bedroom, staring at the three of us.

"Just a little family bonding."

"Well, I'm going to use your shower. I smell like wet dog."

"You can go after me. I smell like wet dog blood."

Yes. You do.

"Go lie down. I'll be back shortly," I said to Dar before turning to Yuki. "You watch a movie or something. You going to hang out here tonight or with the vampires?"

"I need to run home and feed. I'll be back after that, if that's okay."

"I gave you a key for a reason. My house is yours."

She nodded, still a little remorseful.

"I'll be back later." She got up and almost skulked out the front door. I hadn't lied, I wasn't angry with her, but she needed to stop being so damn sulky. Sighing, I got up and headed for a much-needed shower.

Not wanting to get into the shower with my arm all bandaged, I tugged at the tape holding the gauze and pads against my wounds. It was already wet from giving Dar a bath, but I still winced as it pulled the hair on my arm. I couldn't see anything, so I moved over to the sink and turned the water on, grabbing the antibacterial soap. A good cleaning before having Josie heal the puncture wounds was probably a good idea.

Running my arm under the water, I scrubbed it, the blood foaming pink in the soap. At least it stopped hurting on the ride home. In fact, I couldn't feel anything at all…

Staring, I rinsed my arm off under the hot water and gasped. The wounds were completely gone. I couldn't believe my eyes. It was like it never even happened. I had no clue what was going on with me, but my natural healing ability had been amped up exponentially. Not that I was complaining, just confused. I decided not to think about it while I took a shower.

I shut the water off, dried myself, and put on a pair of sweatpants and an oversized hoodie. It was a pajama kind of night. Maybe I could find a half decent movie to watch while I did absolutely nothing. I deserved the rest of the night off.

Grabbing my wine off the counter as I passed by, I did just that, parking my ass next to Josie. Dar even came over and lay on top of my feet, keeping them warm.

Thanks, I thought at him.

Don't get used to it. I'm drained. Stealing some of your energy.

Works for me.

Your other familiar...she's moody.

She's a vampire. They're supposed to be.

Instead of answering, he harrumphed.

I blinked in surprise. He was very *articulate* for a dog. Sure, German Shepherds were smart, but this was...strange. I'd never had a familiar before Yuki, so I wasn't an expert, but my understanding was that all animals could speak on some level once the bond was formed. I'd never heard of one being able to handle complex conversations, though.

Dar, what's four plus eight?

I'm not a calculator. I believe you have one of those on your phone.

Just seeing if you knew the answer.

Fourteen.

I gave up. Apparently, it was a night for weirdness. Trying not to let my shock show, I picked up the remote and flipped to the movie channels, stopping when I saw a mindless, comic hero movie. Some guy in a red suit that was pretty funny and totally scrummy. Until I saw him without the mask...

"Ew. Shower time." Josie got up and headed for her room.

"Where's Candace?" I hadn't seen her since I got home, but knew she was still on her leave of absence from work. It was unusual for Josie and I to be home alone. Shea had shadow walked back to Ashville to start the process of moving. He'd only come with us to get familiar with the area so he could come and go as he pleased. Jimmy and Dennis were both working, and Chief had called it a night.

"She's sleeping."

"Still not on normal hours, eh?"

"Doubt she ever will be."

Dar picked his head up and started watching the movie. I could have sworn I heard him chuckle a few times. It was beyond creepy. Ignoring it harder seemed like a prudent choice. I'd take a smart dog over a dumb dog, any day.

The movie was just getting interesting when a sudden drop in pressure made my ears pop. Even Dar dropped his head to the ground and covered it with his paws. I began yawning frantically, trying to get my ears to equalize. Static popping erupted behind me. Springing from the couch, I turned and froze as Dar started growling next to me.

Josie and Candace poured out of the hallway, stopping and blinking.

"Get back!"

They moved back into the room and I could barely hear the sound of their door slamming over the cacophony of the electrical discharge. I backed slowly out of the room and into the kitchen, ducking behind the counter and watching the lightshow by the sliding glass door.

"Dar!"

He turned and ran, joining me in the kitchen.

Something is coming, he shouted into my brain. I winced.

Hopefully it's not wicked.

The wall next to the sliding glass door had lightning crackling up the surface. Mini cracks of thunder pounded my senses. After a few moments, the wall began to darken as the blight took a rectangular shape when the plaster turned to wood. A flash of lightning and a pound of thunder later, a door had formed just off my living room.

"What the fuck?"

The door rattled and the ancient knob slowly turned, the door creaking open and grating on my last nerve. I lifted my hands and called forth some fire with a whispered word, poised to blast whatever the hell had the nerve to somehow create a portal into my home.

White smoke, smelling of sage, bellowed out from the open door. I heard the clacking of heels as a shrouded figure stepped out through the cloud. It began waving its arms around frantically, dispelling the smoke. I slowly lowered my arms as the figure became more visible.

"Hello, Child."

"Nana?"

Chapter 8

*D*_{ing.}

Herb needed to change the chime over the door, but that just might have been me being picky. I'd heard it so many times, I was getting sick of it. I made a mental note to look for an electronic one on Amazon that made random noises. I'd give it to Herb as a Christmas present.

"How quaint," Nana muttered as she passed by me through the open door.

"It's just as good as the Five Star back home," I said defensively.

"And how many times have you seen me dining there?"

"Uh…" I stopped and thought about it. "Twice?"

"If that many," she replied and took a seat in the closest booth, which just happened to be the one with my name on it.

I breathed a sigh of relief and sat down across from her. She had taken my usual seat, but at least I got to sit in my booth.

Nana took one look at the placard on the table and gave a little roll of her eyes. "Eat here often?"

"Once or twice."

"Mornin, hon. Usual?"

Glancing up at Marge, I willed her to be polite to Nana with a look. From her return stare, I'm sure I came across as constipated. "Yes, please."

"Welcome back," she said to Nana with a smile.

"Back?"

"Aren't you Dot's mother?"

"No."

Marge looked at me in confusion. I should have known she would get the two mixed up. Nana and Mother looked more alike that either would care to admit, and while I shared a resemblance, it was nowhere close. I figured I had too much of my father mixed in. Almost giggling out loud, I had an image of Nana cloning herself and begetting my mother. It might have even explained why they didn't get along. At all.

"Marge, this is my grandmother, Cathleen Blackwell. Nana, this is Marge. Her husband owns the diner and will hopefully be selling you a house. Soon." I hadn't meant to add the word, but after one night with my grandmother, I was ready for her to move. Back to Ashville preferably.

Marge's face was priceless. She knew better than to make a scene or even say anything about how young my grandmother appeared. "My apologies. What can I get you to drink?"

"Tea, please."

She nodded and practically ran away. I didn't even get a chance to ask her to have Herb come talk to us. I sighed and picked up the menus she'd left. Handing one to Nana, I decided to go for something different and opened mine.

We were an hour or so from lunch, so I had no idea which way I wanted to swing. Breakfast sounded good, but so did a burger. That's when I noticed the sticker on the inside of the menu. Due to popular demand, Herb had added the Dot to the menu, and the bright yellow, star-shaped sticker proudly announced it. Rolling my eyes, I prayed silently to the Lady that Nana didn't notice it.

Her short bark of laughter squashed my dreams.

"You have a sandwich named after you?"

"Yes, Nana. I eat here quite often," I said with a resolved sigh.

"No shame in being unable to cook for yourself."

"Good thing, or Mother would spend the rest of her days in the box of shame."

That caused her to cackle merrily and took some of the heat off me. My grandmother was a conundrum. Aloof, beautiful, wise. When she was scrutinizing you, it almost felt like being under a heat lamp. Even the force of her gaze was withering. While I regretted sacrificing my mother's honor to escape the spotlight, I was grateful for the respite.

"The woman burned water, once," my grandmother said wistfully, reminiscing in the joys of my mother's flaws.

"I remember." My mother had been determined to make pasta for me in my youth. She had set a pot of water on to boil and poured oil in it to keep the pasta from sticking together. Then, in typical motherly fashion, forgot about dinner. The water boiled away, and the oil caught on fire. It only took her a few moments to magic the kitchen back together, but about a week get rid of the smell. I do believe it was the last time she attempted to cook dinner in my lifetime. Thankfully.

Marge returned with our drinks. "Here you are, ladies. What can I get you to eat?"

"Actually, I think we need a few moments. Could you ask Herb to join us when he has a moment? Need to look at some properties."

"You keep it up and you're gonna own half the town."

"Yes, but I need your husband to make sure I buy the good half."

"I'll send him out, darlin'."

I let Nana peruse the menu while we waited. I knew what I wanted and had settled on the best of both worlds. The hangover burger. It had an egg on it and was smothered in hollandaise sauce. I hadn't tried it yet, but it sounded like the perfect answer to my brunch desire.

"Hey, Dot."

Herb smiled when I looked up. "Hey yourself. Herb, this is my grandmother. She needs a house. Quickly."

"Well, I can show you a couple after the lunch rush... Miguel can handle the diner until dinner. How big of a house?"

"Around the same size as mine."

"Let me check the listings. Call you after lunch if you're around."

Nana lowered her menu, gazed at Herb and actually said, "Thank you."

"Thanks, Herb."

He gave a quick nod and headed back to the kitchen, wiping off a couple of tables with the rag he'd been carrying.

"The cook is also the real estate agent?"

"He isn't a cook. He owns the diner."

"How quaint," she reiterated.

I decided not to tell her about the whole coroner situation. I somehow doubted she would find that as quaint. "What are you going to eat?"

"I think I shall have the Salisbury steak."

"Good choice. It's yummers."

"Yummers?"

"Delicious."

Marge came back around, we placed our order, and she was about to put it in when the door chimed behind her. I glanced over her shoulder and my day brightened in the form of a six-foot hunky police chief walking through the entrance. The sunlight was filtering through the glass around him and illuminated him in a swath of light. My heart began fluttering, and I was pretty sure it had nothing to do with the illumination. His face lit up when he saw me sitting there.

"Hey sexy," I said with a little giggle. Leave it to Chief to reduce my mannerisms to that of a teenage girl.

"Ditto."

"You eating in or taking out?" Leave it to Marge to ruin the mood.

"Mind if I join you?" He looked unsure if I wanted the interruption with Nana.

"Please." *For the love of the goddess, interrupt.*

I scooted over, letting him slide into the booth next to me. He must have sensed my agitation and simply placed his hand on my leg as he leaned over and gave me a quick kiss.

"So, what are you two beautiful ladies up to today?"

"Lunch and house hunting," I answered before Nana could say anything snide or condescending. It wasn't that she didn't like Chief. It was like she didn't like anybody. She marginally tolerated me.

"Herb finding you something, Miss Blackwell?" He actually tried instigating a conversation with her.

"Call me Cathleen, please. But, yes, he is. After he makes our lunch, apparently."

Chief chuckled. "He is a man of many talents."

"What about you? Is the chief talented, Dot?"

I felt the heat rise to my cheeks. Maybe having Chief join us wasn't the brightest idea I'd ever had…

"Yep," I managed to stammer.

"Well, he certainly has no issues tying your tongue."

I took a sip of my Coke and looked anywhere but at him. His throaty chuckle told me all I needed to know about how much he was enjoying watching me squirm.

My round in the torture chamber was unexpectedly cut short by an explosion. The boom rattled the plate glass windows in the diner as a plume of smoke and the billow of flames shot over the building across the street.

Chief shot out of the booth and was out the door before I stopped rubbing my ears. "Wait here," I shouted at Nana and raced out the door after him.

People were huddled on the ground up and down Main Street. A few of the older storefront windows didn't survive the shockwave of the blast. Thankfully, the diner had been renovated within the last thirty years and had newer glass. Being showered in shards would have been the icing on my cake day.

I saw Chief round the corner of the building, heading down the alley between. Looking both ways, I ran after him. A secondary explosion, much smaller than the first, sent another cloud of smoke close to the other. The sound of sirens in the distance offered a ray of hope.

I nearly slipped on some spilled garbage when I hit the alley. The putrid smell made me gag as I righted myself and tried to run a little faster. I blinked in the sunlight as I emerged behind the building.

The source of the explosion was quite clear. A small tanker truck carrying gray cylinders of propane had gone up. The bed of the truck was obliterated. The few remaining unexploded fuel tanks littered the ground around it. One had rolled away and caught fire, explaining the second explosion. The roof of the building above it added to the growing predicament, flaming and smoking merrily.

Chief stood there, surveying the damage. "Well, fuck."

"What happened?" I felt stupid after the question came flying out of my mouth, right about the same time I saw the driver lying half-through the windshield. His blood was pouring over the hood of the truck. Wanting to help, I started jogging toward him. Chief stopped me with his hand as I moved to pass him.

"Don't. The rest of the truck could go up in any minute." He pointed at the truck's fuel tanks under the cab.

Looking up, I sighed at the cloudless blue sky. If there were clouds, I could have caused them to swell and drop rain. Cloudless was hopeless. I couldn't call something from nothing.

Luckily, the fire engine pulled up behind the flaming bomb about to go off again. Jimmy gave a quick wave as he and two others poured out of the doors. Dennis was driving. Two of the other firemen I had never met grabbed the hose as Dennis pulled forward, dragging the heavy hose off the rack on top of the truck. It was almost mesmerizing watching their coordinated movements as they hooked everything up. When the spray started, Jimmy slowly approached the hood of the vehicle, checking on the driver. As soon as he touched him, he began shaking his head.

Then the fuel tank Chief had warned me about exploded.

My world blew up with it...

My mouth opened as a primal scream of despair tore from my throat as the fireball expanded, engulfing Jimmy and a portion of the rear of the fire engine. The scene quickly disappeared as Chief tackled me, covering me with his body as the heat from the flames blasted over us.

"No, no, no," I chanted as I frantically pushed him off me. Wide-eyed, I scrambled off the already wet asphalt beneath me and ran to where I had last seen one of the two men I loved.

"Fuck me," Chief yelled as he staggered closer while the smoke cleared. "Fuck, fuck, fuck." He sounded almost as desperate as me to find him. I feared the worst, but until I saw his body...I would continue to hope.

I saw the dent in the side of the fire engine as my eyes slowly lowered. Then I saw him. Crumpled in a heap beside the tire was Jimmy, my Jimmy. His arms had been thrown over his face and weren't moving. I cried out as I ran to him, everything else around me fading away to nothing.

I skidded to a stop and dropped to my knees, praying softly to my goddess as I reached out to touch him, tears steadily rolling off my chin.

"Jimmy! Jimmy, you fuck, don't you be dead! I'll fucking kill you!"

My fingers touched his jacket and his flesh was rock solid beneath it. With a hopeful gasp, I frantically tried to pull his arms away from his face, wanting nothing more than to see it, but they wouldn't budge. I felt the magic as it left him, his flesh once again becoming supple...

He sucked in lungsful of air, coughing and gagging from the heat and smoke he had sucked in, but he was alive. It was the most beautiful sound I had ever heard.

"Jimmy?"

"Yeah?"

"You alive?"

99

"Yeah."

"Good," I said and slapped him before I threw my arms around him, burying my face in his wet, smoky neck.

"Dot?"

"Yeah?"

"That hurt. But not as bad as the hunk of metal you're driving deeper into my leg..."

I gasped and pulled away. There was a footlong shard of metal sticking out of his leg that must have hit him before he triggered his stoneskin spell. There hadn't been any blood until he released it, and then it had started gushing.

"Artery!" Dennis shouted behind me.

He tried to pull me away, but I wasn't going to lose Jimmy after just getting him back. I shot him an apologetic look as I reached down and tried to pull it from his leg. It was stuck in the bone and wouldn't budge.

"Fuck," I said as he screamed. "Sorry!"

"I'll pull it out, you heal him," Dennis said beside me as he squatted down.

"It's really in there."

He just nodded and grabbed it with both hands, looking at me and nodding. "On three."

"Guys, maybe we should just get me to the hospital?"

"One."

"I'm ready," I said determinedly.

"Guys?"

"Two."

"Clench your teeth," I said to Jimmy in warning.

"Guys?"

"Three," Dennis hissed and pulled, lifting Jimmy's leg off the ground as he yanked the shard free in a spray of blood. Jimmy screamed and punched Dennis in the shoulder. He fell backward and I clamped my hand over the wound.

"*Leigheas*," I said through clenched teeth as Jimmy grabbed my wrists, struggling to get my hand from the wound. I poured as much power as I could into it and his grip immediately lessened as the pain ebbed.

"Lord and Lady, that fucking hurt."

"Big baby. 'Twas a mere flesh wound."

He didn't even giggle. I sighed as I continued healing him. He let go of my arm and dropped back against the wheel, letting me do my work.

When I felt the last of it close and heal, I let go, looking over my shoulder to make sure I hadn't drawn an audience. The other two firemen finally put the blaze on the vehicle out and were working on the building.

"You're not very popular."

Jimmy gave me a quizzical glance. "What?"

"You get blown up and they keep going with the hose?"

Dennis started chuckling behind me.

"What?"

"You can thank Chief. They were dropping everything when Chief told them to get the fire out first."

"Oh. Good Chief."

"You should thank him later," Jimmy said with a wink.

"You get blown up and you're going there. Dennis, give me that hunk of metal, I'm putting it back in his leg."

He chuckled and held his hand out to Dennis. His friend reached down and helped hoist him up to his feet. He gingerly put some weight on his leg and nodded in approval at my healing work. He took a step forward and nearly collapsed.

"It's still bad?"

"Not my leg. My back."

"Not surprised with the dent you put in the truck," Dennis said and helped steady him. "I'll radio for an ambulance. Let's get you back down on the ground."

"Let me heal it," I said concernedly.

"I can't come out of this *totally* unscathed. Let me go to the hospital and see how bad it is. Probably just bruised a muscle. Just set me against the truck. It doesn't hurt to stand, just to move."

Dennis leaned him against the truck, and I slid in beside him, giving him another anchor. The last thing he needed was to fall over.

"Thanks, Dot."

"You're welcome." I leaned in and kissed him gently on the side of the head, the tears falling freely again. This time they were out of relief. I hadn't lost him, but I'd come too close. Way too close. We stood there silently while we waited for the ambulance. I texted Nana to let her know what had happened. As soon as Jimmy was in the ambulance, I would pick her up.

By the time the ambulance showed up, the fire was out, and more police had showed up. Something felt *wrong*. I couldn't quite put my finger on it, but I glanced around nervously, anyway.

Two paramedics gingerly helped Jimmy onto the stretcher.

"I'll meet you at the hospital," I told him and kissed him again as they rolled him into the back of the ambulance.

I wanted to watch them drive away, but the nagging feeling wouldn't let up. I closed my eyes and sent out a few tendrils of thought as my feet followed the feeling.

"Dot?"

I opened my eyes. Chief was staring at me with a bewildered expression on his face. "Something's wrong," I managed to say and kept walking toward the building in front of us.

The back door was slightly open. With everything going on, neither of us had noticed. Gingerly, I reached out and pulled it open all the way. The scent of blood wafted over me and I let out a little gasp of surprise.

"What is this place?" I asked Chief over my shoulder. He had followed me out of curiosity.

"Lou's Sandwich Shop. The propane delivery was probably for him. You smell that?"

I nodded. "Blood."

He drew his gun and slipped in front of me, pointing it into the kitchen, the lights overhead flickering.

He walked forward, pointing his weapon wherever he looked. The smell was coming from someone I assumed was Lou. He was lying on his back across a stainless-steel prep table, his chest shredded and glistening with every flicker of the overhead fluorescent lights.

"What the hell?" Chief holstered his weapon and closed the distance, grabbing Lou's wrist and vainly feeling for a pulse. There was no way in hell he survived having the front of his chest turned into coleslaw. It wasn't as bad as Frank Dunbar's body had been, but it was still pretty gross.

"What could have done that? Don't tell me the bears and wolves moved downtown?"

"Those aren't wolf *or* bear tracks." He pointed at a set of bloody foot and hand prints on the white tile, leading away from the body and into the restaurant.

I moved closer to get a better look. Whatever it was, had three toes on its feet and hands. They were bigger than a human child's but smaller than an adult's. The feet, closer together, had wider toes than the longer hand prints. It almost looked reptilian in appearance.

"Either we have a velociraptor on the loose or the nuke plant is leaking," I said half-jokingly.

Chief nodded, grabbed his phone and took a few pictures. I turned to look around when I heard the crash. Spinning, I saw the thing land on Chief's back, acoustic ceiling tile falling around them. It had been hiding in the ceiling above us. Four-inch fangs glistened as it opened its mouth to bite the back of Chief's exposed neck.

"*Tintreach*!" Without thinking, I had cast my spell...

Every outlet in the kitchen sparked and shot electricity at me. My shield coalesced visibly as all the power I could call arced around me and filtered into my outstretched hand, shooting the creature about to bite through his neck. It struck its side and blasted it into the wall across from me. The problem with using a magical taser is the properties of electricity. The thing had been touching Chief when I hit it and he caught a jolt of power, too. It knocked him forward onto the blood covered floor. He skidded to a stop and looked up at me over his shoulder, shaking.

"D-d-dot!"

"Sorry. You okay?"

He shot me a death glare, but spun over as soon as he was able, staring at the smoking, hairless creature groaning pitifully on the floor in front of us.

It shook its head, looked up, and snarled.

Chief shakily reached down for his holstered gun, trying to calm his fried nerves enough to actually draw it. I raised my hands again, ready to unleash fire when the door behind us blew open. A black and brown streak leaped through the room and landed on the mutated gremlin, jaws clamping securely around the creature's throat as it began shaking its head violently, snapping the creature's neck.

"Dar?"

My familiar let go, dropping the thing from his jaws with a sickening thud, black blood dripping from his muzzle.

"Good boy!"

Good boy? You get attacked by an imp, don't kill it, I save you, and get a good boy? You owe me a steak.

Chapter 9

I dropped a very quiet Nana, and a disgruntled Dar, back at the house, hopped in the shower, and headed over to the hospital. I'd been texting Jimmy the entire time, with no response. My nerves were frayed. I'd even resorted to texting Dennis, but he was just getting off work himself. He told me he'd meet me there.

I found a relatively close parking spot and practically ran into the ER. The receptionist was less than helpful, and I was about to magick her underwear into a knot when I spotted Doctor Shapiro walking behind her.

"Doctor!"

He looked up and saw me, recognizing me instantly.

"Miss Blackwell. What are you doing here?"

"My boyfriend, the fireman, was brought here after an accident. I'm trying to see him."

"I explained to this woman that he was being prepped for surgery and that she couldn't see him," the nurse interrupted, testily.

"Yes, well… Let her in, please. I'll take her back."

I tried not to give her a snide, shitty look. It was really hard not to, though. At least I didn't say, "Ha! In your face, bitch."

The doctor opened the side door and ushered me into the ER. "It's dangerous being your boyfriend, isn't it?"

"What?"

"Well, he was shot a couple of weeks ago. Now his back is broken in three places…"

I gasped in shock. I knew he was hurt, but I wasn't expecting a broken back. His leg had been the least of his problems. "I didn't know."

"You healed his leg?" He whispered his question.

I nodded.

"He mentioned the shard. I couldn't even see a scar and the x-rays are clean. Nice work. I'm assuming you want to heal his back?"

"If I can."

"I'll see if I can get you in the room. He's not in the OR yet."

"Thanks, Doc."

He nodded and lead me to the ICU. A nurse was taking Jimmy's blood pressure when we walked in. She looked up and narrowed her eyes at the doctor.

"Give us a minute, would you, Karen?"

"He's about to go in–"

The doctor sighed. "I know. Just give us a minute."

She shrugged, wrote something on his chart and removed the cuff from his arm before leaving us alone with Jimmy, who was out of it completely.

They had him lying flat on his stomach, ready to go. Thankfully, we wouldn't have to flip him over. I sincerely doubted my healing ability would be able to repair a severed spinal cord. I couldn't even fix a dishwasher.

"Go. I'll cover the door."

He stood in front of the glass square in the door, blocking most of it with his head and shoulders. I took what little time I had and put my hand over Jimmy's spine, just below his neck. I'd work my way down since I had no idea where the breaks were.

I started slowly, sending tendrils of power and whispering the canting for healing. I found the first one between his shoulders. It took a *lot* of power to heal it. It wasn't just a break, it was almost a shatter. I had a feeling he hit the side of the firetruck there first. Hopefully, the other two spots wouldn't be as bad.

Luckily, I was right. For once.

The other two vertebrae had a slight fracture going through them. Thank the goddess, none of them seemed to do any damage to the spongy cord running through them. Jimmy had been *very* lucky. Insanely.

I was working on the third break when the door handle behind Doctor Shapiro started rattling.

"Dot?"

Jimmy woke up.

I started to panic and forced the last bit of healing energy into him. "Shh, sweetie. You're okay now."

"Again?"

"Yes," I managed to say before passing out in a heap on the ICU floor.

∞ ∞ ∞

I woke up getting lightly slapped on my face.

"You awake?"

I blinked and Jason was standing over me. "Jason?"

"In the flesh," he said with a little smile. "Jimmy had the doc call me when he couldn't get a hold of Chief."

"Where is Jimmy?"

"Getting x-rayed for the thirtieth time since you healed him. They don't quite believe the story that his back was never broken…"

"Where's Doctor Shapiro?"

"At the center of an investigation."

"What investigation?"

"How a civil servant who showed up with multiple fractures in his spine was miraculously healed without surgery."

"What do they think happened?"

"You. The nurse who got kicked out of the room is mouthing off how Doctor Shapiro brought you into the room. She thinks you're some kind of nanite-wielding mad scientist or something."

"I'm something, all right. I was monumentally stupid and deserve to get caught. I just couldn't let them cut him open."

"The doc feels the same way," Jason said reassuringly, putting his hand on my leg. "He feels the healing is worth the investigation. Good guy, that doctor."

"Yes, he is."

"So, what is he saying?"

"That Jimmy woke up feeling a hundred percent better and that you fainted when he got up and started walking."

"Good story."

Jason nodded and handed me a glass of Pedialyte. "He said to give you this when you woke up. Something about electrode lights or something."

"Electrolytes."

"Yeah. Those."

I downed the glass and handed it back to him. The room actually started spinning when I sat up. "Whoa."

"How many times did you use your magic today?"

I briefly did a tally in my head and winced. "Quite a bit."

"Well, if anything else needs to be magicked today, I'm doing it. You're cut off, boss."

I nodded, not even wanting to argue. My channels were a little raw and I had about enough power left to flip on a light switch. "How long was I out?"

"Three hours. That's how I knew how drained you were."

"Shit."

"Yeah."

The door burst open. I was expecting a team of medical doctors, security, maybe even the police. I wasn't expecting a pissed off Asian vampire to come storming into my room.

"Hey, Yuki."

She just glared at me and sat down on the green cushioned chair by my bed.

Jason shot her a questioning glance. He didn't know she was my familiar. I think he had only met her once, at thanksgiving dinner. Not the best impression, either.

"You two haven't been introduced, have you?"

"No," Jason said curiously.

Yuki remained silent. She was pouting. She usually did when I was in danger and she couldn't be around. I don't know why, but daytime was usually a lot more dangerous for me than nighttime.

"Jason, this is Yuki, my vampire friend."

"I met her at Thanksgiving, but nobody introduced us." He reached across the way and held out his hand. She stared at it.

"Yuki, introduce yourself to Jason, my personal assistant…"

She stood up, taking his hand in hers and pumping it. "I am Yuki, vampire and familiar to Lady Dorothea," she replied almost forcibly. She had let it slip she was my familiar, but I don't think she had a choice. I told her to introduce herself. As soon as she was done, she shot me another dirty look. I just smiled apologetically.

"Familiar?"

I nodded, not explaining. I'm sure he knew what a familiar was. Every witch did. If the ritual wasn't so goddess damn complicated, we would all be walking around with kitty cats following us around. When I was younger, I wanted a black cat, but kept screwing up the ritual enough to warrant police intervention. Mother had been less than impressed. So had the mountain lion…

"Well, it's a pleasure to meet you," he repeated and flashed his dazzling smile at her.

"What are you doing here?" I hadn't been hurt, so I wasn't really quite sure why she'd shown up. I assumed it was because I passed out.

"You fought a demon. Your boyfriend was blown up. You had to heal him twice and then passed out. Why do you *think* I'm here?"

"Demon?" Jason took a step back.

"Yeah. It killed the guy who owns the sandwich shop across from the diner and probably ignited the propane tanks on the delivery truck."

"Lou? Why?"

"That's what imps do," Yuki answered. How she knew it was an imp was beyond me. I didn't even know it was an imp.

"How did you know?"

She looked up at me and furrowed her eyebrows. "Dar told me."

"He knew what kind of demon it was?"

"Yes," she answered.

"That's one smart dog."

"Dog?" Jason looked totally confused. "Who is Dar?"

"My other familiar. He's a German Shepherd."

"You have two?" He sighed and sat down next to Yuki. She patted his thigh.

"Her ladyship is hard to keep up with. It's kind of frustrating. Especially when you can't go out in the sun, you know, when shit tends to blow up."

I sighed, my head hurting way too much to deal with her angst.

"Well, I'm fine now, guys. You can take off if you want."

They both shook their heads violently.

"What?"

"Dar and I talked it over. We are your familiars and neither of us has been acting like it. We are going to be by your side at all times. Him during the day and me at night.

110

I already let George know, not that it matters to them. They're busy with the blood bank takeover and my father has pretty much disowned me."

"He did what?"

"Yeah. My bank card was declined. He cut me off. I thought our discussion went pretty well, but since I am now the property of a witch…"

"You became the witch's problem."

She nodded and I saw the tear roll down her cheek.

Fuck me. I need a bigger house.

"Move in with me."

"What?"

"You heard me. If you're mine, you *are* mine. I take care of mine. We'll set up the spare room for now and I'll find a bigger house, or buy the one next door. We'll figure something out."

She nodded and sniffled a little bit. Jason was staring at me with a peculiar smile.

"What?"

He coughed when he realized I'd caught him. "Nothing."

"No. You were smiling about something. What?"

"Just how you take care of everyone around you. You're like supermom."

"Shut up."

Yuki started chuckling.

"Well, it's probably a good idea to get the hell out of here before they start coming to ask me questions I don't have the answers to. Jason, follow me home, make sure I don't crash. Yuki, ride with me."

"I'll do one better and drive you home," he said, leaving little room for argument.

"Okay, but we're taking my car. I'm not riding in yours. My tetanus shots aren't up to date."

"Funny."

"I know."

I opened the door and faceplanted into Doctor Shapiro's chest. We should have left sooner. "Play dumb," he mouthed the words and motioned me back into the little room.

"Dorothea Blackwell," he said out loud, "this is Doctor Materos. He's on the board of directors and wants to ask you a few questions…"

Fuck.

"Is this about Jimmy? Did you figure out what happened to him?" He wanted me to play dumb. I could do that. Until I got pissed off. I might not have enough juice to mindwipe the guy in the suit, but Jason did.

"You have no idea how his fractures miraculously vanished?" Snide didn't even begin to describe his tone. He sounded like a pompous prick as soon as he opened his mouth. This wasn't going to end well. For him.

"I can only assume that your technician screwed up and my boyfriend wasn't really injured."

He blinked. Twice. And opened his mouth. "You're joking," he practically snarled at me, immediately calling my bluff.

"I never joke about gross malpractice. It's a very serious matter."

"I reviewed both the x-rays and the MRIs myself, Miss Blackwell. His back was broken in multiple places."

"Maybe he's a quick healer."

"Or maybe he had a little help."

I had exactly one option left before Dr. Materos ended up forgetting everything and maybe drooling on himself. Mindwipes were tricky…

"If you have questions, you may direct them to my lawyer. I will be contacting him in the morning regarding your incompetence." I walked past him, half-expecting him to grab me by the arm. Make them question what they think they know and be an asshole about it. It worked for my mother the better part of her life. It could work for me, too.

I strode down the corridor, praying I didn't hear their footsteps behind us. We didn't. If there was one thing a board member feared, it was litigation.

"That was fucking hilarious," Jason said when we were out of earshot.

"I saw his face after you were out the door. He looked like he was going to piss himself. I smelled fear. If you want me to go back and eat him, I will…"

"We'll see how it plays out. I'm too tired to care right now. I just want to go home."

"That's the safest idea you've had in a while," Yuki said with a giggle.

Jason put his arm around my shoulders, noticing my unsteady trek toward the elevators. "Thanks," I said and gave him a tired smile. His arm felt good draped around me, comforting and familiar somehow. Almost like it *belonged* there.

"Just glad you're not driving."

We made it out of the hospital, unhindered by hospital security. It was a small miracle. I just hoped Jimmy made it out of there sometime in the near future. If they decided to make him a lab rat, I'd have to orchestrate a rescue mission. I texted him to keep me posted.

I will. Be safe. Thank you, was his response. I smiled at my phone when we got to the car.

I handed Jason the keys, letting him unlock my door and shove me in the front seat. I put my elbow on the door, holding my head up and staring out at the eerily quiet parking lot. When I looked up, I could see the fine snowflakes falling in front of the yellow-tinted sodium lights illuminating everything in a soft warm glow. None of the snow was sticking, yet, but we were supposed to get a few inches over the next few days.

Jason and Yuki got in, and he started the car, blasting the heat for me. I sighed, trying to tell myself everything would be all right. The off feeling I'd been experiencing over the past few days just wouldn't go away. Hopefully a night in my nice warm bed would chase it away.

Chapter 10

"Dot…"

It wasn't his voice that woke me up, although I did hear it and incorporated it into my dream, a dream that faded away to nothing as he gently shook my shoulder.

I pulled the comforter down, exposing my face and blinking in the bright morning sun pouring through my window. I had forgotten to pull the blackout curtains before collapsing into bed.

"Somebody better be on fire, Jason."

"Jimmy called. He's on his way home. The hospital released him."

"Why didn't he call me?"

"He did, three times. You left your phone in the kitchen."

"Oh. What are you doing here so early?"

"It's almost noon…"

I sat up, the comforter falling away. Jason glanced down at my bare breasts and I saw a bit of color rush to his cheeks. I smiled briefly before the panic really set in. "Shit."

"What?"

"I didn't want to sleep that long. I have five million things to get done."

He cocked an eyebrow at me. "What can I do?"

"First of all, get ahold of Herb while I hop in the shower and get dressed. Actually, make that second. Coffee first. Would you mind grabbing me a cup?"

He nodded and left the room, leaving me a little more comfortable getting out of bed naked. I slipped out from under the blanket and grabbed a T-shirt, throwing it over myself as I walked into the bathroom. I closed the door and relieved my overburdened bladder and brushed my teeth before heading out into the kitchen. I shivered and turned around, deciding pants might not be such a bad idea, either.

I finally made it back into the kitchen. He was holding out my coffee and my phone. Josie got up from the couch, too. "Morning, sunshine."

"Morning yourself," I shot back at her. "Why didn't you wake me up?"

"Jason told me not to. Should I not have listened to your assistant?"

I shifted my gaze to his guilty looking face. "Should I not have?"

"No. You're fired." I'd meant it as a joke, but his panicked face sucked all the fun out of it. "I'm kidding!"

He cocked an eyebrow at me and gave me a stern look. With his angular face it was quite effective. I blushed and took a sip of my coffee in contrition.

"Herb says he has three houses that might be suitable, depending on her tastes."

"Speaking of the devil, where is she?"

"She said she was going to pack up a few things at home and come back when, and this is a quote, my lackadaisical granddaughter gets her sorry bones out of bed," Josie said and pointed at the portal to Ashville behind her.

I sighed and stared at it, wishing she had at least made it a little more modern looking. It completely clashed with the rest of my living room. I'd hoped it was only temporary, but she assured me it would probably be standing long after my dump of a dwelling collapsed around it. My grandmother was quite the ray of sunshine. At least I wouldn't have to fly in a damn airplane next time I wanted to visit home.

The fear that my house would become a transportation station settled somewhere between my fears that my mother would pop through at any time, or that it would collapse into a black hole, swallowing a greater portion of New York. Since the other end of the portal ended in my grandmother's house, I suppose I didn't have to worry about the station or my mother, but a black hole was a legitimate possibility. I did have to admit, it would be handy when *I* wanted to visit Virginia…

Moving to the dining room, I sat at the table and opened my phone, checking what I'd missed when I was dead to the world. Jimmy had texted he was going home and taking a shower. He'd see me later. Chief texted wanting to know what the hell had happened. The only other thing of interest was a couple of missed calls from the Johnson Brothers. They probably needed a check.

"Anything I can do?" Jason settled in the chair next to me.

I slid him my phone. "Call the Johnson Brothers. See what they need, call my grandmother and tell her we're going to look at houses, and then grab your notebook. We need to go to the bank. I'll add you to some of my accounts. That and I need food. I'm going to go take a shower."

I left him there with his list of things to do while I got clean.

By the time I finished, so had he. My grandmother was even at the table next to him, patiently sipping a cup of tea and staring at him as he shifted uncomfortably.

"Hi, Nana."

"Granddaughter."

"You ready to pick a house?"

She nodded, finishing her cup.

117

"Freddy says they need a payment on the construction. I have the total. Says they need to purchase materials and they should be done in two weeks."

"Holy shit!" I tried not to squeal in excitement, especially with my grandmother sitting there. Decorum and all that. She made a face at my expletive. If I had squealed, it would surely have earned me an eyeroll.

I went to grab my phone and he showed me the underlined number written on the notebook page with the total. I nodded and dialed Jimmy.

"Hey," he answered on the second ring.

"I'm heading downtown in case you were planning on heading over here."

"I was going to after my shower. I need my Dot."

I chuckled softly, turning my back on Jason and Nana, walking away for a bit of privacy. "Well, we're stopping by the bank and then heading to the diner. Meeting Herb and grabbing some food if you want to meet us."

"No. I'm going to take a shower and lie down. Hospital beds suck. I'll have a nap while you're running around."

"Okay," I tried to keep the disappointment out of my voice. "I'll call you when I'm done. Let's grab some dinner."

"Okay."

"Hey."

"What?"

"I'm glad you're okay."

"Me, too. Thank you, Lady."

I let it go. "You're welcome."

"Dinner?"

"Sure. Where?"

"Feel like Italian?" He chuckled sexily.

Heat creeped up my face and I was *very* grateful I had turned around. "Um. How about something a little less exciting."

"Steak?"

"Yes."

"Let me know when you're on your way. I'll meet you there."

"I'll just pick you up."

"Even better. See you tonight."

"See you tonight. Lo–" I stopped myself. I just couldn't quite say it...yet.

"I know," he said, and I heard the feeling in his voice. And his smile. I hadn't even known you *could* hear a smile, but you could.

I got a warm and fuzzy feeling when I shut off the phone.

"Let's go," I called over my shoulder. "You want anything to eat, Josie?"

"Go ahead. Candace and I are going to lunch."

"Have fun!"

∞ ∞ ∞

The bank had been almost exhausting. Instead of adding Jason to a bunch of my accounts, I opened a new business account and put him on it, and then gave him a mile-long list of things to get done for the bookstore, paperwork wise. Incorporating was the first thing. I told him to take the new bank card and get a laptop. How he lived his whole life without one was beyond me. For what he probably spent on porn magazines, he could have bought five computers and then streamed all the porn he wanted.

I doubted I would have time to teach him how to use it, and some night classes might be a good idea. He was hesitant at first, until I told him it wasn't an option and that I'd be paying for them. It was time to see exactly how smart he was.

"Brought the whole gang," Marge said jovially as we slid into my booth.

"Yeah. Herb's showing us some houses."

"He told me. How's Jimmy?"

"He's fine."

"That was pretty scary yesterday. Tommy's Glass Repair has been up and down the street all morning. Poor Lou," she said sadly.

I nodded, briefly wondering how they had explained his death. "Yeah."

"Can't believe a bear snuck in the back door. And Ralph, crashing his propane truck when he saw it… I mean what are the odds?" She shot me an accusatory glance.

Apparently, she wasn't buying the cover story.

"Yeah… Weird."

"Be right back with your drinks." She turned around and walked away without taking our drink order.

"A bear?" Jason asked with a smirk.

"Don't ask me, it's probably Chief's explanation."

"He needs to take a creative writing class." Jason toyed with a sugar packet from the holder next to him.

Nana chuckled.

"How would you have explained it?" I smiled at him.

"Freaking ninjas."

"Ninjas?"

"Ninjas. From the Owatatori Village, hidden deep in mountains."

"You're pretty good at this."

"I read a lot of manga."

I blinked in surprise. He didn't strike me as the type. "Really?"

"Really."

"Guess there's a lot more about you I need to learn."

"I look forward to it," he said with a little blush.

"Are you two almost done flirting? I would like to retain what is left of my appetite."

"We're not flirting, Nana."

"He wasn't. You were."

I blinked in surprise, blushing uncontrollably. Jason moved his hand in front of his mouth, stifling his laughter. Thank the goddess, Marge brought our drinks. She set my usual Coke and coffee in front of me, tea for Nana, and a Coke for Jason.

"Know what you want to eat?"

"Burger, well."

She turned to Jason. "The Dot."

Nana just shook her head, not wanting any food. I hardly ever saw her eat other than dinner. She probably drank the blood of her enemies from a skull. Or drank Ensure...

Herb walked out from the kitchen with a file folder and his fingers jangling with keys. "Hey, everybody."

"Hi, Herb," I said and gave him a smile. "Sorry we missed you yesterday."

"That was quite the commotion. Glad it's over. I had a bear-proof lock put on the back door, just in case," he said with a wink. Chief must have filled him in.

"Well, you two enjoy your lunch and flirting. I'll go with the nice man to look at the houses."

"Nana..."

"Hush, Child. I'm perfectly capable of picking out my own damn house. You told me I should trust this man."

"Most definitely. Take care of my Nana, Herb."

"Yeah. I don't think she needs my help, either," he said with a chuckle, clearly afraid of her.

"You were right, Granddaughter. He is a wise man." She strode toward the door, Herb scrambling to catch up.

"I hope we see him again..." I chuckled.

"Is your mother as bad as her?" Jason hadn't met my mother and was trying to get a perspective.

"Sometimes worse, sometimes better. Depends on Nana's mood, I guess."

"You're not going to turn evil and enslave us all one day, are you?"

121

"Would that be so bad?" I asked, jokingly.

"Not at all," he answered with a little grin.

Marge brought our food and we ate quietly. Since we didn't have to go house shopping with my grandmother, that freed up my day a little. We still needed to run next door and drop off a check for the book store construction, but that was the last thing on the agenda until dinner with Jimmy. I smiled at the thought of that, looking forward to it immensely.

"How's your sandwich?"

He blinked and gave me a little smile. "It's delicious."

"Well, no more jokes about the name."

He chuckled. "Well, I do enjoy eating it."

"Do you?" I smiled slyly as I reached for my Coke, taking a sip, letting the straw drag over my bottom lip as I pulled it away. A move that wasn't lost on him, either. He was blatantly staring. Then I realized what I was doing, gave a little cough, and attacked my burger.

Bad Dot. Jimmy Chief. Jimmy Chief.

The chime sounded over the door. I half-expected to see Chief walking into the diner. I sighed when I saw it was Derek. I'd told him I would let him know when I got back into town. Knowing full well that I should have, just to let him know how things stood between us, I just couldn't bring myself to do it.

"Dorothea," he said as he passed by, not stopping at our table.

I blinked in shock.

Jason noticed.

"You okay?"

"Just surprised. He must be pissed at me."

"You do seem to have that effect on people…"

"True story. Oh, well." I took another bite of burger, wanting to finish as quickly as possible and leave.

"Want to go?"

I nodded, finishing off my burger and leaving most of the fries. "Just need the check."

"Should have asked for it sooner. He's coming back."

I was facing the door, but I could feel the slow burn of Derek's gaze as his footfalls sounded as he crossed the diner. "Shit."

"Want me to stay?"

"No. Give us a minute."

He nodded, not questioning my decision. That might have been one of Jason's most endearing qualities. I smiled at him as he stood up and headed for the restroom in the back. I'm sure he would be keeping an eye on things from the dark hallway.

Without so much as an invitation, Derek slid into Jason's recently vacated seat, snagging one of the French fries off my abandoned plate and taking a bite from it.

"Was waiting fer you to let me know ye got back yesterday."

"Yeah. There was an explosion and my boyfriend got hurt."

"Which one?"

"Jimmy. The fireman."

"He okay?" He might have been pissed, but it faded away in genuine concern.

"Now. Shrapnel and broke his back in a few places."

"He's okay? With a broken back?'

"I healed him."

"Oh. If I recall correctly, healin' wasn't one of yer many talents."

"I got better."

"Apparently."

"So… What's new with you?"

"I don't know. I had grand plans of settlin' back in Ashville, maybe rekindlin' something between us, if ye wanted. Then yer ma' told me you were here, and I should run after ye. Now, I'm doubtin' her sanity. Ye seem happy."

"I am."

"No surprise with two of 'em."

I blushed, not even remotely wanting to talk about it with him.

"We'll you're still welcome to stay, but we have an apothecary already in the works. You might be hard pressed to find something to do."

"Or someone?"

"Oh, I doubt you'll have any trouble finding anything in that department… Unless you meant me. Then, yes. You would be hard pressed," I answered levelly.

He nodded, half-expecting that answer, but not looking disappointed in the least. "Not much fer sharin'."

"Well, then. What are your plans *now,* then?"

"The apothecary was me mother's life, not mine. I'm more into *entertainment.* Owned a few pubs in Cork. Sold them to move back. Might open a tavern here to keep me occupied. Think I'll stick around, if ye don't mind."

That kind of shocked me. I'd been sure he would have packed up and moved back when I turned him down. Hell, I was surprised he hadn't already, if I was being honest with myself. When he found out about Chief and Jimmy, he was less than impressed.

"I don't mind, at all. Town needs all the help it can get."

He nodded while I debated internally how in the hell I was going to break the news to Chief. Jimmy might not be happy about his decision, but he was a lot easier to deal with.

"So, the guy standing in the hallway keepin' an eye on me, another boyfriend?"

I chuckled. "Jason is my assistant."

"Not from the way he looks at ye."

"Pardon?"

"He likes ye."

"Well, he is a sweet guy."

Derek let it go with a little sigh. "Mind if I join yer coven?"

"I'll need to put it to a vote... But I don't see a problem."

"Not what I asked, but I wasn't expectin' ye to lie..."

"Excuse me?" I cocked an eyebrow at him.

"I asked if *you* minded." He annunciated very carefully, dropping the accent to let me know exactly who he was talking about. "*And* I'm sure ye meant run it past yer boyfriends when ye said ye'd put it to a vote."

I leaned across the table and looked him straight in the eye. "Aye," I said, mockingly, to let him know he'd hit the nail on the head.

He nodded. "At least yer bein' honest."

"One of us has to be. If I recall correctly, it was you who lied when you told me you loved me, and we would be together forever. Did you even blink when your mother asked you to move back to Ireland with her?"

"Aye."

I sighed, not wanting a couple's therapy session in the middle of the diner. I picked up my drink and took a sip, looking up and seeing Chief standing in the window, staring at me sitting with Derek.

Before I could motion him in, he shot me a look and headed back toward the police station.

Shit. Now I have two things on my agenda.

I kept my face straight, not wanting Derek to know what had just happened. He'd probably find it amusing. If he was going to stay in Cedar Falls, it wasn't going to be easy on my relationships.

"Well, I'll be going," he said and slid out of the booth.

"Talk to Herb when he gets back. He can show you some properties for your bar."

"Looking forward to it," he said and gave me a little wink before heading back up to the counter to pick up his order. Jason came back and sat down as he was walking out the door.

"You okay?"

"No. Let's pay and get out of here. Need to drop off a check and go assuage the Chief."

"You're going to do what?"

"Assuage. Reassure him. He saw me and Derek sitting together."

"Oh. Fun."

"Sure. Let's go with that."

∞ ∞ ∞

The bookstore was starting to look like a bookstore. It had walls, paint, floor, and even a new entrance. The broken rolling doors were gone, and they filled in the gaping holes with windows. It was beautiful. I swallowed the lump that seemed to have lodged itself in my throat and gladly handed Freddy Johnson his check.

"Should have your shelves and all the finishing touches done in a couple of weeks. It's going faster than I thought. You might wanna order some stock for your store," he said with a chuckle.

In all seriousness, he was right. I did need to and set up everything else, especially the business licenses. "If I do, is there a place to store it here, out of the way?"

"Sure, in the storage room. It's finished, unless you want some shelves in there?"

"I do."

"Tell you what, go to the Depot and order ten or twelve of the metal racks. Have them delivered here, and I'll have some of the boys put them together for you."

I stared at him, incredulously. Stepping forward, I threw my arms around him, unfortunately it was like hugging a mountain. I think my head came up to his shoulders and I ended up wrapping my arms around his belly. My fingers barely touched. "Thanks, Freddy!"

He patted me on the head and gave me another chuckle. "Well, I need to deposit this and find a buttload of suitable wood for your shelves. Wish me luck," he said and stepped around me as I let go.

"Good luck," I said loudly, and whispered, "*Ádh mór,*" to up the odds, pouring a little power at his back.

"What's next, boss?"

"Well, I need to talk to Chief. Feel free to look around some more."

"I will. Unless you want me to go with you..."

"No. I'll handle this one," I said with a sigh and headed out the open front door, crossing the parking lot between my bookstore and the police station.

An officer I hadn't seen before was sitting at one of the desks. I knew Chief had hired someone to replace Dane. He must be him. "Hello?"

He looked up from whatever he was doing on the computer. "Hello, ma'am. I'll be right with you."

"No worries. Just looking for Chief."

He stopped what he was doing and cocked an eyebrow at me. "You must be Dot."

"Guilty as charged."

"Chief said if you stopped by to tell you he had some things to take care of and he would see you tomorrow."

"Oh. Okay. Thanks," I said in kind of a daze and turned around, walking out.

That chicken shit son of a bitch.

I pulled my phone out of my pocket and texted him.

Where are you?

I blindly walked back to the bookstore, staring at my phone waiting for a response that never came.

"Bill not there?"

127

I squawked as I almost ran into Jason while distracted. I tucked my phone back in my jeans and frowned. "No. He's not answering, either."

"That's not like him."

"He must be more pissed off than I thought."

"Well, you just got your chance to find out." He pointed across the street. Chief was walking toward the station, looking at his phone. Without texting, he shoved it in the holster on his side.

He hadn't seen us yet. I pulled mine back out and texted him a quick, *Hello*? It was childish, I know. I stared as I saw him reach down and pull it back out, ignoring me once again. My heart cracked a little. It was official, he was ignoring me…

Crossing my arms, I stood there tapping my foot until he looked up. He literally skidded to a stop. I could see the internal conflict within. He was debating crossing the street to talk to me and running. Running, probably would have been the safer choice at that point. Then the realization that I was acting like my mother set in.

Sighing, I turned around and walked away, Jason quietly following me.

"You're not going to talk to him?" He finally broke down and asked as we got into the car.

"No. If he doesn't want to talk to me, just because he saw my former boyfriend talking to me, then fine. I'll let it go."

"You sure that's the reason?"

"If you had seen his face in the window when he saw us, you wouldn't be asking." I reached down and started the car, putting it in reverse while Jason slipped his seatbelt on.

My phone buzzed in the center console. I didn't even want to see if it was him.

"Want me to look?"

I shrugged.

Jason picked up my phone and said, "Yep. It's him."

"What did he say?"

"Hi."

"Jason?"

"Yes?"

"Shut my phone off."

∞ ∞ ∞

"Mom, Dad, I'm home," I hollered as I opened the front door, determined not to let Bill's behavior affect me in any way shape or form.

Unfortunately, nobody was home, and the tears started falling as I pressed my back against the front door and slid down it until I was a sobbing mess on the floor. I'd forgotten that Candace and Josie were going out. I shouldn't have dropped Jason off at his car, still in the hospital parking lot. Being alone wasn't going to help distract me.

My eyes were closed, trying to stop my tears from falling, so I nearly had a heart attack when the tongue slid across my cheek, wiping the wet saltiness from them.

"Hey, Dar," I managed to say when I finally realized who was licking me.

Are you all right?

"No. Not really. Stupid relationship issues."

Want me to bite someone?

The mental image of a hundred-pound-plus German Shepherd latched onto Chief's posterior made me smile.

"Next time you see Chief, bite him on the ass for me."

My dog nodded at me.

"I'm going to bed, you need anything?"

No. Wait, can you crack the door to the back for me? Your pet roommate locked it and I might need to go out later.

"Okay. Thanks, Dar." I stood up and walked over, clicking the lock open and pulling it open just a hair, enough for him to get a paw in and pull it open if he needed. I needed to have a doggy door installed. I'd look up a handy man later.

I pulled my jacket and hoodie off on the way to the bedroom, tossing them on my dresser as I passed by and fell into my bed, but I couldn't seem to fall asleep. The look on Chief's face kept playing back across my vision, every time I closed my eyes.

The doorbell going off didn't help either. I sighed as I slid over the edge of the bed and stood up, praying silently it wasn't Chief. It became a chant of, *Don't be Chief, don't be Chief,* with every footfall.

Leaning forward slowly, I pressed my eye to the peephole, sighing in relief when Jason's face stared back at me from the other side. Turning the deadbolt, I opened the door.

"I thought I gave you the rest of the day off?"

"I figured you could use some company."

"You mean you came to make sure I didn't do anything stupid, like getting falling-down drunk."

"Shit, no. If you're going to do that, I came over to join you."

Chuckling, I let him in, heading to the kitchen to grab a couple of beers. Dar peeked at us from over the back of the couch.

"Aren't you supposed to bark or something?"

"Woof."

"Good boy."

He lay back down on the couch.

I handed Jason his beer and clinked the neck of my bottle against his. "You're pretty sweet, checking up on me."

"Well, I worry about you."

"As I said, you're pretty sweet."

He blushed as I wandered over to the couch, plopping down in the middle next to Dar and absently scratching his head. He shifted around and put his head on my leg. I could feel the flow of energy between us, like a pleasant humming in my fingers.

You have two-hours to knock that off.

Only two, huh? I chuckled softly.

"What he say?" Jason plopped down on the loveseat across from us.

"That I may continue scratching his head."

"He's a beautiful shepherd."

Dar lifted his head off my lap and pulled back his muzzle over his teeth. I expected him to growl, from the snarl he was giving him, but I think it was a doggy attempt at a smile. Especially since he put his head back down on my lap.

"Your dog just smiled at me."

Dar *harrumphed.*

"Sorry. Your *familiar* just smiled at me."

"He's a good boy," I said jokingly and scratched him a little harder. His leg started kicking against the arm of the couch.

That's the spot.

I took another swig of my beer, debating turning the TV on, but settling on the silence and company. Jason was looking at Dar and smiling softly. The guy was just too damn cute. I loved the tiny smile that he had when he thought nobody was looking at him. But I doubted he could go anywhere without someone looking at him. He just had one of those faces, a face you could never get tired of looking at.

He tilted his head back, and I swear the beer poured out of the bottle and just went straight down into his stomach. He polished it off in seconds. It was pretty amazing, in a frat-boy sort of way. I blinked in surprise.

"Uh, want another?"

"I'll get it. You want one?" He stood up and headed for the kitchen. Mine was only half-empty but I nodded anyway, determined to have it finished by the time he got back. We were on a mission it seemed.

I managed to get mine down to the foam by the time the second appeared over my head. Grabbing it with the hand I'd been scratching Dar with, I leaned forward and set the empty on the table in front of me. Jason walked around the side of the couch and headed for the loveseat. My eyes played over his ass as he walked away.

"Why you sitting way over there? Not like we're having a meaningful conversation anyway." I probably shouldn't have invited him to sit next to me.

Bad Dot, I said to myself. Maybe Dar, too. He made a doggy noise that sounded like a laugh.

Jason turned around and blinked but came over and dropped down on the cushion next to me. I leaned against his shoulder and resumed my ear scratching. On Dar, not Jason.

"So, how come you don't have a girlfriend?"

He tensed a little and gave me a little shrug. "I live in the middle of nowhere, in a rusted-out shithole trailer with a big gaping hole in the middle of it. Up until recently, I worked all night, slept all day, and it's not like my vehicle is going to be scoring me any points with the ladies..."

"Shit! I forgot to fix your trailer."

"No worries, I put some plastic over it. I tried fixing it myself, but my magic might have made it a little worse..."

"Well, stay at Farrell's until it's fixed. I'll come do it right away. I should swat you for not reminding me."

"As I said, it was totally worth it to see you drop Chief into it. He's been a lot more...nicer since then."

"Until today."

"Yeah. Well, there is that. But, look at the bright side, he's internalizing his anger instead of being an asshole."

I nodded my head, not thinking about it that way. Again, Jason shocked me with his observations and perspective. "Sweet, hot, and wise," I said without thinking. "Tell me again why you don't have a girlfriend?"

"I'd never really wanted one. Until... Never mind."

I looked up at him. "Until?"

"Nothing," he said shyly and took another sip of beer.

I wanted to push him, needing to know what he was going to say, but I let it go. My beer seemed way more interesting than it had, moments ago.

Want me to give you two some more room? Dar was looking up at me from my lap.

I should have said no. Hell, I should have left Dar on the couch and gotten up myself, but I didn't. *Please.*

Without another word, he slid off the couch and stretched before meandering over to the love seat and making a nest there. I took the opportunity to turn sideways, stretching my feet out and putting my back against Jason's side. He was far too muscled to make a good pillow.

He must have sensed it. He reached over and grabbed the cushion beside me. "Sit up for a second."

I leaned forward and he put the cushion between me and him, inviting me to lean against his leg. "Thanks," I said and leaned back again.

"I should be the one saying thank you. Not every day a guy like me has a beautiful lady in his lap..."

I could see him from my new angle, catching the blush as it slowly colored his cheeks. He stared at the off television and drank more of his beer. Nervously polishing off my second one, I set it on the table, rolling over and lying on my side, cheek pressed against the cushion over his leg and sighing very happily.

His hand slowly slid down the back of the couch and found my shoulder, resting there gently. It seemed so natural, but I could feel his nervousness. I smiled, loving every moment of it.

"Thanks for being here, for me." I put my hand on his leg, just above his knee. "I *really* didn't want to be alone."

"My pleasure," he chuckled nervously.

"This cushion smells like Dar," I said and slid it out from under me, putting my head directly on his leg. It wasn't as comfortable, but I enjoyed it more.

And what, pray tell, do I smell like?

Shush. I'm using you as an excuse.

I can see that. He chuckled.

I could feel a tiny bit of movement coming from somewhere by my ear. If it hadn't been pressed so close, I might not have felt it...

"You want another beer?" Jason's voice cracked as he lifted my head and slid out from beneath me, gently shoving another cushion under me before he practically *ran* into the kitchen.

I put my hand over my mouth so he wouldn't hear me laughing.

Chapter 11

I didn't try to put my head back down on his lap. Maybe it was for the best. When he brought the next round of beers, I sat up next to him and tucked my feet underneath me. At least I would be able to see his eyes when I teased him.

"Been a while, huh?"

"For what?"

"Since you were close to a woman."

"Yeah. Long while."

"How long?"

He grinned awkwardly and swallowed some beer. "Too long."

"Well, at least I know you think I'm pretty. Or has it been so long you would have had the same reaction if Dar was sitting next to you?"

Dar lifted his head and whined pitifully.

I nearly spilled my beer, I was laughing so hard. Jason just hid his eyes behind his hand, shaking his head in embarrassment and more than a little bit of laughter. At least he could laugh at himself. I doubted there was a better quality to be had in a person. Chief and I, both, could learn a thing or two from Jason.

"You're wrong about one thing," he managed to say after the blushes passed.

"What is that?" I pulled his hand away from his face and caught his eye in mine.

"I...um. I don't think you're pretty. I think you're beautiful."

It was cheesy, and it was corny, but I knew he meant it. My heart melted a little as I leaned closer with the intent of kissing his cheek for being sweeter than pure cane sugar. He turned and was leaning back, maybe out of fear, maybe out of shock. I closed the distance between us, and my lips found his, instead of his cheek.

He stopped moving away and leaned into the kiss, his lips hungrily meeting mine.

Without looking, I set my beer down and wrapped my arms around him, pulling him into me as I leaned back across the couch. He scrambled to kneel over me as he slid his bottle onto the table next to mine before using his hands to hold himself above me.

My tongue danced against his as he slowly lowered himself against me, my breasts pushing against his oh-so chiseled chest. My hands slid over his back and down his ass, grabbing and pulling with the heat blazing between us.

Ding Dong.

I stopped kissing Jason and turned my head toward my front door.

Want me to get it? Dar asked jokingly.

If you had hands, I might take you up on that. Not sure I want whoever it is to see me like this, though.

It is the one you call Chief.

How do you know?

Gunpowder. I can smell it. And his aftershave.

Yep. That would be Chief.

"It's Chief," I told Jason, letting him pull himself off me.

"Dot, I'm sorry!"

He looked close to panicking. I put my hand on his shoulder. "Why? I kissed *you*."

He breathed in, and nodded, trying to calm himself.

I got up after he gave me enough room and walked over to the front door, opening it without looking through the peephole.

"Is your phone broken?" He had his hands on his hips when he asked. I reached down to my jeans pocket but remembered I had put it on the kitchen counter. I made a face at him and went and got it. As soon as I picked it up, I knew I had never turned it back on.

"It's just off. Why?"

"Hey, Jason," Chief said with a nod before answering me. "There was another attack."

"What? Where?"

"Antonio's Pizza."

"But we killed the damn thing."

"Apparently not all of them."

"Jason, lock up when you leave," I shouted over my shoulder as I ran to my bedroom to get my hoodie and jacket. The sun would be down soon, and I didn't want to freeze my ass off.

"You got it, boss."

"Give us a minute, would you, Chief?"

He gave me a strange look, shrugged, and left through the front door. I waited until I heard the click before calmly walking over to Jason. "Thank you, for a wonderful day," I said *shyly* and meant it. Having him with me had not only made my life a little easier, but exciting, too.

"You're welcome. I'm glad I could be of assistance." He smiled and I did my best to wipe that smile off his face with my lips.

When I pulled away, he stared at me and gently reached up and touched his lips with two fingers.

"Was that okay?" I wanted to make sure he didn't mind. Judging from the smile on his face, he hadn't.

"Um… Yeah! Feel free, any time."

"Well, we'll just have to see," I said and touched his nose with my finger, laughing as his eyes crossed before

137

turning around and leaving him standing there, bewildered. Before I could shut the door behind me, Dar shot out of the house and mentally yelled at me for trying to leave him behind.

∞ ∞ ∞

Sure enough, the moment I got away from him and into my car, guilt settled in like ton of lead bricks. The ten minutes it took to get to Antonio's was spent chastising, berating, and belittling myself.

In my own defense, I had little protection from the sweet, intelligent, and incredibly sexy package that was Jason Bradley.

I pulled my SUV behind Chief's Jeep and shut off the engine before opening the door. Dar stepped over the center console and jumped down onto the cold wet pavement.

"Smell anything?"

Pizza, marinara, and... Another imp. He's gone, though. Took off across the street and through the park.

"That's quite the nose."

Thank you.

"Now if you could just smell where all these hellions are coming from…"

Probably from the rift.

"Um… What particular rift are you talking about?"

Chief walked up. "You coming in? Antonio is pretty scratched up, but alive. Paramedics patched him up, but he didn't want to go to the hospital. What?"

"Dar says the imps are coming through a rift. I was asking him where."

"Ouch! What the fuck. Your dog just bit me on my ass!" Chief narrowed his eyes at my familiar.

"Dar!" I wrapped my arms around him and pulled him away from Chief's posterior. "What are you doing?"

You told me to.

"I wasn't serious!"

Well, next time you tell me to bite your boyfriend on the ass, you might want to clue me in if that is not your actual intention. I can hear your thoughts, but I'm not a mind reader...

"Sorry," I said trying very hard not to laugh my ass off. I wouldn't want people confusing me for Chief. He was rubbing the part Dar had gnawed on and was sticking his finger through the holes in his jeans. "Sorry, Chief. That was my fault. I told him to do it earlier."

He shot me a look of pure something. I wasn't sure what the something was, but it made me laugh harder.

The rift was here, but it keeps moving, Dar continued, ignoring the mumbles about his pedigree from a very angry Chief.

"So, it's a magical moving rift that leads to...?"

Are you dumb? Where do demons live?

"Magical, moving rift to hell."

Gehenna. Hell is a mortal fabrication.

"Whatever. How did it get here?"

How in the hell would I know that? It just appeared. Poof. Disappeared the same way.

"Did it appear at the trailer the other night, when we found you?"

Yes.

"So, it wasn't a bear or a wolf that killed Frank Dunbar? It was an imp?

No. An imp couldn't do that. It was a pit fiend.

"A fiend? There's a pit fiend, somewhere in Cedar Falls? Running around and munching on people?"

Unless it went back through the rift.

"Why didn't you say anything sooner?"

Why didn't you ask? I told you about the imp, where the hell did you think it came from?

"I don't know. Detroit?"

Funny.

I looked up at Chief. "There's a portal to hell floating around town. A pit fiend ate Frank Dunbar, and you know about the two imps. The one that attacked Antonio ran that way through the park but is long gone."

He stared at me incredulously. "Your dog. Told you all of this?" He scratched the back of his neck, trying to process the information.

"You know he's not a normal dog."

"Yeah. No, I know, just trying to figure out how I'm going to write that in my police report."

"Just say it was a rabid trash panda attacking people," I said and turned to walk away. "Come on, Dar."

"Dot… Wait."

"Yes?"

"Can we talk?"

"I tried. You ignored me. That window has now been closed."

"I'll buy you a cup of coffee and a slice of pie."

"You slick bastard."

"No. I'm incredibly stubborn and–"

"Stupid?"

He sighed and nodded. "Yes. That, too."

"A la mode?"

"Excuse me?"

"You said pie. Are we talking a la mode, or just whip cream?"

"I'll even tell Marge to warm it up."

"Yeah. That's kind of what a la mode means. Hot with ice cream. Pie noob."

"I'm more of a cake, guy. Or a nice brownie." He gestured toward the cars.

"Uncultured swine," I said and got in my Sportage, letting him close the door with a sigh.

We could have walked to the diner, but whatever. It took forty-eight seconds to get there and then I didn't have to worry about walking back to my vehicle.

"Do you want to wait outside, in the car, or run home?"

I'll wait in the car. Crack the window or I'll call the ASPCA. Sarah McLachlan hates people like you.

"You watch too much damn television," I said with a chuckle.

Chief pulled in behind me. I waited at the door for him and pulled it open, letting him go first. "Do you want to eat dinner instead?"

"Shit! No. I'm having dinner with Jimmy. Pie and talk." I grabbed my phone out of my pocket, fingers flying over the keys, frantically.

There was another demon attack. Got into a fight with Boyscout. He's apologizing and then I'll come pick you up.

He replied almost instantly. *No worries. Chinese? We can have dinner here if it's easier.*

Most of the men in my life had flashes of brilliance. And then there was the one standing in front of me. *You're brilliant. See you shortly.*

K.

I fought the urge to snarl at my phone. I hated the K.

Seriously. How fucking hard is it to type an O in front of it?

"Everything okay?"

"With Jimmy. Yes."

"Ouch."

"You know, we wouldn't have to keep having these charming conversations if you would stop being a douche."

He sighed and we entered the restaurant. I waved at Marge and plopped down unceremoniously in my spot. He skulked into the booth across from me.

"Let me start off by saying, I'm sorry."

"Wise choice."

"I have my moments," he said proudly.

141

"Few and far between, but yes."

"You're still pissed."

"What can I get for you two?" Marge asked as she idled up to the table.

"Cherry pie, a la mode, and a coffee. Unless you're hiding a bottle of bourbon behind the counter."

"I'll see what I can do, sweetie. What do you want?" She turned to Chief. "Or should I ask, what do you deserve?"

"Do you call her when I screw up, just to torture me?"

"No, but I should. It's probably just instinct," I said with a laugh.

"I'll have the brownie sundae."

"Does he deserve it?" She asked me.

"No, but he'll cry if he doesn't get it. Not worth the hassle."

She scoffed and walked away.

"I swear, that woman…"

"Is gold."

"That, and so much more."

"So. Where were we? Oh, yes. I'm still pissed. My old boyfriend shows up, I tell him that I'm happy with who I'm with, and then I see you spying on me? What was all that about? But then I text you after you run off, you hide, and ignore me? Damn skippy, I'm pissed."

"Dot…"

"Spill it. Let me hear what the hell was rattling around that spacious warehouse on top of your shoulders."

"I went to talk to him."

"Who?"

"Derek."

"You did *what*?"

Marge was standing just outside of earshot, holding a tray with coffee and desserts, but not wanting to interrupt. I turned and smiled at her, letting her know it was okay.

142

She set the stuff down quickly, and practically ran for the hills, not that I could blame her. I was surprised I hadn't shattered any glassware when I hit the high C note on the what part of my question. Even Chief looked a little scrambled.

Instead of apologizing, I scooped a schlarf of pie and ice cream into my mouth and let everything go for a moment, breathing with the taste of heaven in my mouth. "Could you repeat that?"

"Huh? I'm sorry, I'm having a little trouble hearing at the moment."

"Not a good time for jokes, Chief."

"Sorry. I said I went to talk to Derek."

"Why? Did you not trust me?" I reached down and picked up my cup of coffee, taking a swig and nearly choking as it burned all the way down. It wasn't even that hot. The whiskey Marge poured in it cooled it down quite a bit. I turned and looked at her standing behind the counter. She winked at me and gave me a thumbs-up. I gave her a crooked grin in thanks.

"Quite the opposite."

I took another bite of pie. "Do you want me to guess or are you going to tell me what the hell is going on?"

"As soon as I turned around and walked away, I realized that my jealousy of a man you dated forty years ago was probably the most childish and idiotic thing I'd ever done. Okay, maybe not the *most,* but it was definitely in the top ten. I turned around to come back when he came out of the diner. I was going to let him go, but I figured it was a good place to start. I stopped him and took him to O'Malleys for a drink."

"You did what?"

"I took him for a drink and did like I promised you. I reserved judgement until I got to know him. He's actually a pretty nice guy. So, we bonded, and he asked me about joining the coven. I told him he had my vote and that I would talk to you."

"So why did you tell your deputy to tell me you would talk to me tomorrow?"

"Well, he's not a deputy. He's an officer, and I texted him from the bar because I figured you would run to the office to chew me a new one."

"Weren't wrong."

"I figured."

"So why did you blatantly ignore my texts, right in front of me."

"I was texting Jimmy about my meeting with Derek and was trying to plan a dinner tonight with the four of us to show there was no hard feelings. I was ignoring you until I heard back from him, and then I ran into you on the street and panicked. I'm sorry. I tried calling you, but you had shut your phone off, apparently."

I had finished all of my pie and my coffee flavored whiskey by the time he finished explaining. "I'm sorry."

"What?"

"I said I'm sorry, Bill."

"Uh oh. She said my name."

"Do you really want to continue making me squirm?" I already felt like shit and was kind of proud of the big lug.

He leaned back in the booth and flashed me his boyish smile. "I'm sorry, too. I was trying to be the bigger man, but I shouldn't have kept you out of the loop. You were angry and I should have realized, no matter what my intentions, you would only get angrier. I just didn't plan on you shutting off your phone."

"Technically, I didn't. Jason did. I told him to, though."

"Semantics."

"Well… I have a confession, too."

"You kissed Jason," He replied. Not angrily, either. It was almost as if he was proud, which was kind of creepy.

"What? How the fuck did you know?"

"Dot. I'm a cop."

"He called you?"

"No. I called him. I went to your house and your clothes were all rumpled. You were acting like nothing happened, but you didn't see Jason standing behind you. He was flushed and looking like he had a cactus stuck in his colon. It didn't take a rocket scientist to figure it out. Especially since I know you have a soft spot for him. So, I called him to ask him on the way to Antonio's. He was crying, so I'm glad I called him. He thought I was going to shoot him."

"Are you?"

"Me? No? Why?"

"You're not jealous?"

"Did you want me to be?"

"It would be the normal reaction. For you."

"Dot, I don't know if you realized this. But there isn't a fucking thing normal about us..." He chuckled. He wasn't lying either. He wasn't jealous that I had kissed Jason, I could hear it in his voice and see it on his face. I was just glad I *hadn't* kissed him to make him jealous. That would have been the backfire of the century.

I was glad I did it, though. Guilt be damned.

"He's a sweet guy."

"That he is. This is Jason we're talking about. That's probably why I'm not even the slightest bit jealous. You want to take care of him...and so do I. He might be your assistant, but you'll be good for him, too."

"So, no jealousy."

"Nope. Derek on the other hand..."

"Yeah, yeah. I get it."

"Maybe after I get to know him longer."

"What?"

He realized what he said and frowned, knitting his eyebrows. "Did I just say that out loud?"

"Yes. You did."

Chapter 12

"Hey, beautiful."

"Hey, handsome. Smells like eggrolls."

"Thanks?"

Jimmy almost shut the door on Dar. My hand shot out and stopped him until the shepherd walked past him, shooting him a murderous glare.

"Oops. Sorry, Dar."

Tell him I forgive him. This time. But now I have acquired a taste for human flesh.

"He says it's okay."

I most certainly did not!

Shush. And no tushy nibbles. That's my job!

He sat and his tongue lolled out of the side of his mouth, his expression of humor. There was a knock on the door behind us. I turned to Jimmy. "You invite your other girlfriend?"

"No. I told her I'd call her tomorrow. You expecting your other boyfriend?"

"*Touché*," I said with a fake smile, swallowing the rage in my chest. I knew he was joking, and it was my fault for setting it up, but still.

Mine.

He opened the door and Yuki stood there. "Sorry."

"Hey, Yukester," Jimmy said with a smile. He stood there for a moment while she waited patiently outside his door.

"You have to invite her into your home, Jimmy," I said and rolled my eyes. "Don't you watch vampire movies?"

"That's real?"

"Yep," Yuki said, embarrassedly.

"Dear Yuki, would you please enter my domicile?" He bowed and swept his arm under him, gallantly.

"Why, thank you, good sir." She chuckled and crossed the threshold nervously.

"Dinner's on the table," Jimmy said and shut the door, staring at it a moment to make sure nobody else pushed through or knocked. "Gangs all here, huh?"

"Yeah. They're being over protective."

"With a bunch of demons running around," Yuki added sarcastically.

"You figure out where they're coming from?" Jimmy sat down at the table.

I took the seat next to him. "You two can go watch TV or hang out. Up to you," I said to my familiars.

"I'll stay, I want to taste Chinese food." Yuki looked at Dar and I saw something pass between them, hearing a faint echo in my head.

"You two can talk to each other?"

Yukie stared at me wide-eyed. "You can hear us?"

"A faint echo. Why?"

We say bad things about you behind your back, Dar said dryly.

"I'm sure you do."

"What do you two talk about?" I asked Yuki.

"Mostly your safety. Sometimes your boyfriends."

Jimmy chuckled nervously.

I let it go. We could discuss things later. I turned to Jimmy. "Where's Dennis?"

"Right here," Dennis said softly as he came out of his bedroom. "Holy shit, that's a big dog." He stopped walking forward and backed up a few steps.

"It's okay, Dennis! He's my familiar."

"Cool," he said, not taking his eyes from Dar, skirting around the far side of the table, keeping as much distance and as many obstacles between them as he could.

"Not a dog guy?"

"Not a big dog guy. Got bit as a kid."

"You and Chief should start a club."

"He got bit when he was younger?" Dennis sounded surprised.

"No. Tonight."

"What?" Jimmy and Dennis asked at the same time. Dar just gave a throaty doggy chuckle and lay down on the floor.

"I was pissed at Chief earlier," I narrowed my eyes at Jimmy, who looked around innocently, "and told Dar to bite him on the ass next time he saw him. I forgot about it until Dar saw Chief. Chomp."

Jimmy chuckled, Dennis looked afraid but noticed Yuki as he was sitting down. "Hi, Yuki."

"Hi, big guy."

Jimmy slid my *moo goo gai pan* in front of me, which worked out perfectly since I wanted something light. I hadn't even told him what I wanted and smiled at his selection. "Thanks, handsome."

"You're welcome. What do you want to drink?"

"No alcohol. I have to drive home."

"Or you could stay the night..."

"I have to take Yuki and Dar home."

"It took me less than a minute to run here. I can get back just fine if you want to stay..."

Dar even *woofed*.

The thought did sound appealing, in so many ways...

"Okay, but let Josie know when you get home," I told her. "I'll have a beer," I answered Jimmy and nearly snorted at the look of excitement on his face as he opened the fridge. He danced all the way back to the table.

We ate. Jimmy and Dennis devoured theirs, I picked and forced myself to make Yuki happy. She was controlling her reactions since Dennis didn't know she was my familiar, but she kept glancing down longingly at my plastic takeout container. It was *very* easy to tell she wasn't a fan of baby corn. I'd never seen a vampire turn green before.

"You okay?" Dennis seemed genuinely concerned when he saw her face.

"Somebody has garlic in their food," she lied, smoothly.

"Sorry. I ordered garlic chicken," Jimmy said and blushed.

"It's true about garlic and vampires?"

Yuki shifted her attention back to Dennis, shaking her head. "No, but our noses are about a thousand times better than a human's. Not the most pleasant of amplified smells."

"Ahh. Makes sense."

Nice cover, I thought at her.

Yeah. I should probably just tell him. Half the damn coven knows, anyway.

Well, you can trust Dennis. He wouldn't hurt a fly. Plus, it's not like you have to hide it from the vampires anymore.

True.

She stood up at the table and looked down at us. "My name is Yuki Abernathy and I'm a witch's familiar. It's been seven minutes since my last embarrassment."

She sat back down, and Jimmy started laughing. Dennis was staring at her and processing the information. He turned to me and I smiled. "Yuki is your familiar?"

"Yeah."

"That's friggin' cool! I wanted a familiar when I was a kid. Probably would have ended up with a toad or something."

Rat, Dar's voice popped into my head.

150

I didn't share the revelation.

You can tell what familiar's witches would have?

Yes.

What would Jimmy's be?

He looked over at my boyfriend and narrowed his eyes. *Cat.*

Chief?

He made a clucking noise with his tongue, as if tasting something…or remembering the flavor of Chief's ass. *Chihuahua.*

Seriously?

No. He'd definitely have a wolf.

That's no fair. I have a German Shepherd.

My dog turned to me and cocked an eyebrow over his golden iris. *You, my dear pain in the ass, could have an unlimited amount of familiars. You have so far acquired a vampire and me. Be thankful.*

I am. I was just teasing you. Sheesh.

∞ ∞ ∞

Have fun! >:)

I laughed at Josie's text. Yuki must have gotten home and told her I was spending the night at Jimmy's. Dar, on the other hand, seemed quite comfortable curled up on Jimmy's floor in front of the television. That probably had more to do with the belly full of Chinese leftovers. He'd refused to leave me alone, and I was touched.

Don't be. You die, I die. I like living.

Way to ruin the moment, Dar.

I snuggled against Jimmy on the couch and smiled at Dennis. He seemed a little off. "Where's Alista?"

His face darkened a little. "She flew back to Virginia to start moving and getting everything ready."

"When she coming back?"

Dennis just shrugged.

"Everything okay between you two?"

Jimmy elbowed me in the ribs, shaking his head slightly but not looking at me.

"Don't know."

"Oh, sweetie. I'm sorry. Do you want to talk about it?"

"Thanks, Dot. No. It will work out or it won't."

"What happened?" I whispered as softly as I could to Jimmy.

"She accused him of being in love with you."

It took me a moment to decipher his words, he whispered them so softly. "Nuh uh."

"Yep."

"What did he say?"

"That she cared more about her brother than him."

I could almost hear the trombones playing, *Waah wah waaaah,* in the background. "Dennis, you moron."

I gave him a stern look and instantly regretted it when he blushed and then looked at me with those sad, sweet eyes. "I know."

"Oh, honey," I said and got up, walking over to him and hugging him gently.

"She was pissed when she said it, and instead of denying it, I just told her she was too close to her brother. I'm a fucking idiot."

"Yes. You are. But, look at the bright side. You have all the time in the world to tell her that you're stupid." I squatted down beside him, looking him in the eye. "Just take things slow. I'm sure they'll work out the way they were meant to."

"I know. Thanks, Dot."

"And for future reference, if anybody else accuses you of being in love with a crazy bitch like me, just tell them you're not into insane." I stood up and kissed him on the forehead before going back to Jimmy.

"Awww," Jimmy said and winked at Dennis who launched a pillow at his head, completely missing and blasting me.

You could have heard a pin drop until Jimmy started chuckling evilly. "Somebody's in trouble!"

"They are," I said coolly, picking up the pillow and swatting my boyfriend in his smug, laughing face. "He wouldn't have thrown it if you weren't such a shit."

He just laughed harder.

I jabbed my finger in his thigh and whispered, "*Pléisiúr.*"

His ass lifted off the couch and his eyes rolled up into his head as pleasure spread out from my finger. He may even have convulsed once or twice. "Holy shit."

"Did you learn your lesson?"

"No. Do it again."

I should have known better. The spell was for pleasure, but an overwhelming amount, almost to the level of pain. Leave it to Jimmy to actually like it. "There's something wrong with you."

"Yeah, but you love me."

That stopped me in my tracks. I probably should have denied it to teach him a valuable lesson, but it would have been a little hard with a grin plastered on my face…

"Yeah. I do."

"Awww," Dennis said from the recliner.

Jimmy launched the pillow back at him, catching him squarely in the face, *then* he leaned down and smiled at me lovingly, capturing my lips with his. I held up my hand while we kissed, not wanting to get in the middle of a pillow fight with my teeth almost touching Jimmy's.

"Did you like that?" I asked after he pulled away.

"Bet your ass, I did." His grin was bigger than mine. "Say it again?"

"I do."

"No, say it, say it."

"What?"

"Please?"

Well, it's not like I had a choice after he said please and gave me a gentle smile. "Fine. I love you. Happy *now*?"

"You have no idea."

"Yeah. I think I do." I waited for him to say it back. He just smiled. Until I pointed a finger at him, letting sparks arc across the tip. "This one is set to stun..."

"Well, if I say it under duress, it doesn't really mean anything, now does it?"

"Jimmy..."

"I love you, Dorothea Blackwell. I love you with all of my heart," he said and leaned forward, kissing me again a hundred times harder.

He leaned back against the arm of the couch, pulling me with him. I could feel his need through his lips. He wanted to devour me, and I wanted to let him. His hands slid up my back, under my hoodie, igniting wherever he touched. When he realized I wasn't wearing a bra under it, he groaned and reached up to my shoulders, pulling me against him harder.

Involuntarily, my back arched as I felt his hardness press against me, breaking our kiss. He let go of my shoulders, letting his hands leave tingling trails as they glided over my back, down my sides, and then back up over my ribs, stopping only to cup my breasts as I leaned over into another kiss.

He caught my nipples between two fingers of each hand, and I shuddered in ecstasy. "Take this into the bedroom?" I managed to ask after shaking my head.

"Why?"

"Dennis?"

"You don't want him to watch?"

I felt myself twitch as the thought raced through what few working braincells I had left. A twitch that didn't go unnoticed by Jimmy.

"Somebody likes that idea."

"I think two somebodies do. Maybe three," I said and looked over at Dennis, who was pretending to flip through channels. I caught his eyes as they shifted away from us, focusing on the infomercial he had stopped on.

Jimmy squeezed my breasts again, my hips bucking involuntarily. "Take off your sweatshirt."

I reached down and grabbed the bottom, pulling it over my head and tossing it on the ground. Jimmy's eyes feasted upon my exposed flesh. From the feeling I was getting from Dennis' direction, he was, too. I grew even wetter, making my jeans mighty uncomfortable.

"Take off your shirt," I said imperiously above him. I wanted to see his chest, almost as much as he had wanted to see mine.

He leaned forward and I lifted myself off him, letting him pull his shirt over his head. Before I straddled him, I pushed my jeans down and off, sitting on him in my panties.

"Holy fuck," was all he managed to say.

"I don't know if I'll go that far," I replied with a grin.

Dennis' gaze became a steady heat at my back, warming my chilled, exposed skin. I wasn't sure if he was watching, but just the thought of it had me on edge.

I reached down and undid Jimmy's belt, struggling to get the prong out of the hole, a thought that wasn't wasted on me. I chuckled throatily as I watched him watching me, unsure if he was watching my hands or the front of my panties. He answered my question with the tips of his fingers as he lightly brushed them across the lace front.

I had undone his belt, but the button on the jeans was giving me trouble. Jimmy laughed at my struggling and reached down with both hands, popping it open.

"Thanks."

"My pleasure."

"I'm sure it will be."

He wasn't wearing boxers, and I don't know why but it excited me more. Carefully unzipping him, I reached in and pulled him out with my fingers. His soft hardness blazed in my fingers, I could only imagine how warm it would feel inside me. Pulling him against me, I rubbed him against the silkiness of my panties as I stroked him slowly.

He half-closed his eyes, enjoying the sensation. I could see his gaze flicker from me to Dennis behind me as the corners of his mouth lifted ever so slightly in a pleased smile.

I'd never been more turned on in my life.

"Put it in you," he whispered softly.

I gasped, not sure if I could go that far. I shook my head.

Jimmy cocked an eyebrow at my reluctance and smiled even more. "You want to."

It wasn't a question, and he wasn't lying... I wanted to. I wanted to feel him inside me while his friend watched. I wanted to, so bad.

"Are you sure?" I whispered my question, almost begging for his approval.

It came as a small nod.

Not wanting to stand, I pulled my panties to the side, exposing myself completely to the man I loved in front of me. His eyes locked on to me and didn't shift in the slightest. He watched hungrily as I lifted myself up, parted myself, and used my other hand to place the tip of him at the very opening he craved.

Instead of dropping on him, I lowered myself and slid forward, pushing him into me. I gasped with every inch and every ridge. When he could go no further, I stopped moving and lowered my face to his, trailing my tongue over his bottom lip as pleasure flowed through me.

"You feel so fucking incredible."

"So...do you," I stammered through the pleasure.

I pulled back a little before pushing myself forward, his cock driving the last of my thoughts from my mind. I managed to make only a few strokes like that before my body took over, demanding more. Almost crazed, my rhythm intensified as my hips began bucking on their own. My face in his neck, I curled into him over and over until I felt his hands on my shoulders.

He gently lifted me up and looked at me like no man had ever looked at me before. There was heat, and passion in his eyes, and something else. Love.

"You should turn around," he said and gave me a gentle smile.

He wanted me to finish while Dennis watched. He wanted Dennis to see my pleasure. A shiver started in the back of my neck and bounced down the length of my spine. I clenched and felt myself squeezing Jimmy as the thought raced through my brain, lighting the rest of my pleasure centers.

There was no way to say no. I wanted it too much. I'd become a slave to the show, and I hated how Jimmy knew me better than I did. He wasn't telling me what to do, he was telling me it was okay to do what I wanted.

Lifting myself off him, I closed my eyes and turned around, using my hands to guide me back down. I repositioned him and let him slide inside me, the curve of him sending waves of pleasure in different places than moments before. I was on fire and I put my hands on his thighs to steady myself.

I couldn't lift my head, unable to look Dennis in the eye as ecstasy swirled inside me like a small storm. Concentrating on my breathing, I began lifting myself up and dropping back down with every breath until Jimmy slid his hands up my back and around my sides, straightening me and stopping me from hiding.

Sitting up, I took one last breath and opened my eyes, letting my exhale bring Dennis into focus. He was still in the recliner, the long forgotten remote on the floor beside him. He had put one leg over the arm of the chair and unbuttoned his jeans, his fist slowly stroking himself as he watched us.

Feelings I couldn't even begin to describe, drowned out the pleasure emanating from inside me. He was gorgeous. His light brown hair bobbing with each stroke as his hips curled up to meet his fist while he watched *me*. His gaze drank it all in from my head to my toes, sipping on the agony of my ecstasy.

I stared hungrily at his cock. It was almost as handsome as he was, straight and cut. He was little smaller than Jimmy but thicker. I could almost feel it in my hand, wanting to draw it in my mouth. But Dennis wasn't mine. I hadn't laid claim to him or even discussed it with him. His eyes alone told me he wanted me, but that was a decision best made between just the two of us and not engulfed in the throes of passion.

Jimmy began to tense beneath me. He was nearing his limit and I picked up my pace, not once tearing my eyes from his best friend. It pushed me over the ledge I'd been holding onto with everything I had. It started deep within me and the rhythmic motions of my hips took on a jerky, needy motion. "Oh, goddess," I managed to draw out over the space of twenty syllables as my body betrayed me, turning me into a quivering wreck as I gasped for air.

Jimmy's orgasm ignited my secondary fuse and the world around me exploded in patterns of light and sound. The only clear point in my vision was the tip of Dennis' cock as he cried out as he came all over the gray T-shirt he wore, staining it dark.

Falling backward, Jimmy lowered me slowly to his chest, my angle forcing him out of me. Even after unloading, he was still hard as it flopped back against me.

I lay there, panting, trying to think straight.

Dennis looked at me guiltily, blushing a furious shade of crimson. Still holding himself, he slipped out of the recliner and padded quietly to his room.

That was going to be an awkward conversation, later.

And you people call us animals, Dar said in my head with a little chuckle.

Chapter 13

Waking up with my head on Jimmy's chest, naked in his bed, was something I could definitely get used to. His arm was around me, his fingers tracing gentle circles over my shoulder. I grinned and rubbed my face against his chest, stretching languidly.

"Morning, beautiful lady."

"Morning, handsome man."

"Did you sleep well?"

"Uh huh," I said sing song, relishing in the moment.

"Beautiful and cuter than a fucking button, all rolled into one."

"Somebody's in a good mood. Or did something wrong. Two compliments in the same sentence? What did you do?" I popped my head up concernedly and stared into his eyes, ignoring his soft laugh.

"Nothing yet," his hand slid down and aimed for my ass, which was just out of reach.

"Haha. No tushy for you."

He extended his arm and brought his palm playfully down on it, swatting me. I laughed and put my face back in his chest, snuggling closer.

"So. Anything interesting happen beside the pesky demon attack?"

"No. Oh, wait. I kissed Jason," I added almost as an afterthought. I thought I saw a brief movement down under the sheets, but maybe I was just imagining it.

"Say that again?"

"I...kissed...Jason."

"Why didn't you tell me this last night?"

"We were uh...kinda busy."

"What kind of kiss?"

"The kind that could have melted stone. It was sweet, hot, and very wet." I traced a circle around his nipple, teasingly. "One of those kisses where you thank the goddess that Chief rang the doorbell and interrupted you, kind of kisses."

He groaned and there definitely was movement under the sheet. "Damnit, Bill."

I let out a little bark of laughter and kissed the nipple I'd been teasing.

"You gonna kiss him again?"

"Probably. You okay with that?"

"Absolutely."

"You working today?"

"No. I've been placed on leave because of the accident."

"You're not in any trouble, are you?" I lifted my head.

He shook his. "No. Just investigating the accident. The other three all have the same story. The Fire District was made aware of the extent of my injuries as well as the subsequent lack thereof. I have to go for physicals and testimonials. They want to make sure I can still fireman."

"Can I ask you something?"

"What?"

"Is that what you want?"

"To be investigated?"

"No. To be a fireman. You did your time. Isn't there anything else you would like to do?" I propped myself up on my elbows, eager to hear his answer. We were witches, and we were immortal, but not if a flaming building came down on us. If I were being honest with myself, I didn't want him to put himself in danger every time he went to work. It wasn't up to me, but I would help him if he wanted it. Dennis, too.

"I don't know. When I was younger, it was all I ever wanted to be. Now, I'm not so sure. The only time the job ever feels worth it is when I save somebody's life."

"I can see that. I was curious, but I'll be serious. I worry about you. I don't like you putting yourself in danger every day, but that's not my call. You're a big witch. But... If you ever decide it's not what you want to do anymore, let me know."

"What? Why?"

"Because, I love you. If there's something else you want to do and you need to go to school for it, or train for it, or whatever. Let me know. I'll help if you let me."

"You mean pay, don't you? Damn it, Dot, when are you going to realize you can't fix *everything* with money?"

"I already do realize it," I said solemnly and rubbed my hand over his chest. "That's why I fix what I can, when I can."

He pulled me against him a little tighter, kissing my forehead. "I *will* think about it. How's that?"

"More than I was expecting honestly."

"I love you, too."

"Dennis, too."

"Huh? Why?"

"Because you love him," I answered. "If something ever happened to him, and you weren't there... It would destroy you."

"More than you know. Losing Richie was bad enough. Dennis is more like a brother than a friend."

"Ew. We had sex in front of your brother."

My head bobbed up and down as he laughed. "Now it's my turn to ask you some things."

"What?"

"Did you enjoy last night as much as I think you did?"

"Maybe a little more," I admitted, honestly.

"So, let's say, in the future, if that were to happen again…"

"Don't push it."

"I'm just asking, hypothetically. Let's say we did have another audience… Would you want them to join in? You seemed like you wanted to last night."

I blushed and hid my face a little. "I almost did. If I were dating Dennis, I probably would have."

"Well that settles it."

"Settles what?"

"You're just going to have to start dating Dennis."

I pinched his nipple and he yelped.

"Going to let the dust settle from last night, first. Let him decide on his own what he wants to do about Alista. How many men do you think I can handle in my life? I have my hands *full* with you and Chief."

"And Jason."

I sighed. "We kissed. Can't say we're officially dating."

"You tell Chief?"

"Didn't need to. He took one look at Jason and knew."

"Was he pissed?"

"He didn't even bat an eyelash, because it was *Jason*."

"That guy's strange," he said sarcastically.

"And you're Captain Normal."

"With Abs."

"You are quite cut." I rubbed my hand over his six-pack.

"I meant Captain *Ab*normal."

I chuckled, seeing what he did there. "Yep."

"It ever bother you that I'm a little strange?"

"What fun would it be if you weren't?"

"Now we just need to figure out what to do with that sexy hunk of an Irish ex you keep dodging…"

I groaned. "Chief told me he was trying to play nice and getting you to go along with it. Seriously, I appreciate the sentiment, but if it's too much…"

"Let him hang around and join the coven. Maybe we'll like him after we get to know him."

"Uh huh. Sure."

"Never know. His accent gave me a partial stiffy at Thanksgiving."

∞ ∞ ∞

"Take my laptop, I'll use Josie's and order a new one."

"You're sure?" Jason pulled it against his chest, afraid he might drop it.

"Yes. I'm calling in sick today. I won't need it and you have a ton of shit to do. You have your list?"

When I finally strolled through my front door, Jason was there with a cup of coffee in hand and a notebook in another. While I drank my coffee, we made a list of things to accomplish before the book store opened. First and foremost was incorporating and business licenses. The rest of the list ranged from book distributors to coffee cup suppliers. He was going to be very busy over the next few weeks. I trusted him completely, though. I'd seen firsthand how keen his mind was.

"Yes. Uh… Dot?"

"Yes?"

"I don't have internet at my house…"

I stared at him incredulously. How the hell did he even live? "Then park your ass at Mickey D's. They have free WiFi. Or better yet, call the cable company and set up service at the book store. Stay out of Freddy Johnson's way, but I'm sure you can set up shop in the kitchen. They're not doing much in there."

He nodded. "Okay. Call me if you need anything," he said proudly and turned to walk away.

"No kiss?" I asked him, half-jokingly.

"Not supposed to kiss your boss," he said and gave me a little wink before taking off and hopping in Bessie.

I almost made it to my bedroom when Josie came out of hers.

"Um, excuse me. Who are you?"

"Yeah, yeah. I missed you, too," I said with a chuckle. Josie walked right past the kitchen where the coffee was, just to give me a hug. I'd never felt more loved in my life.

"Did you have fun last night?" She pulled back and wiggled her eyebrows. She gasped when I blushed. "Oh, my goddess. Spill it!"

I just shook my head. "Maybe later," I managed to spit out. "I'm going to take a shower. Dar, don't let her in my room!" I ran in and shut the door, putting my back against it and letting out a sigh.

Suddenly, Josie was pounding on the door, followed by some growling and snarls. I heard her squeak and run away.

Good boy.

Talk is cheap, show love with meat.

I couldn't resist. *That's what she said.*

There is something wrong with you.

I chuckled as I stripped and got into the shower, gladly letting the hot water massage the last of the tension out of my shoulders. Without opening my eyes, I reached over and grabbed the shampoo off the shelf, pouring a good dollop in the palm of my hand. I flipped it closed and started scrubbing.

There was a sudden drop in pressure and my ears popped as a blast of hot wind blew the stream of water away from me and nearly dried half my body. I couldn't open my eyes and had no way to get the shampoo off my face. I reached for the towel I kept draped over the glass door and found nothing. No towel, no shower door, nothing.

I pawed at my eyes and opened them, screaming in fear.

I was still in my shower, but between me and the door was a ribbon of darkness, undulating in two dimensions. I blinked, seeing shapes moving inside coming toward me and clawing their way over red sands under a blood red sky. The figures were horned and bipedal, standing taller than me with fanged muzzles and dagger-like claws. They groaned hungrily.

The door to the bathroom kicked open and Dar shot through it like a black and brown streak. He barked at the rift and looked around frantically, trying to figure out a way to get me out of the shower.

I kicked the glass wall beside it, wincing as it shattered and tore my foot to shreds. My blood splattered the tub and floor, but I had an exit. Sparing one last look at the two creatures nearly through the rip in reality, I dove through the broken glass, landing in a heap on the shard-covered, cold tile floor.

Josie grabbed me, pulling me across the floor and into the bedroom. Dar put himself between me and the bathroom as Yuki's rage flowed through me from the other room. She was awake but helpless in her sun-proof prison.

The two hungry demons shattered the rest of the glass as they exited the shower around the rift, their gazes staring hungrily at me and warily at Dar. He snarled and grew, fur and muscles rippling as he tripled in size and two-foot-long horns grew from his head as his flesh began to sizzle and smoke.

I watched through half-lidded eyes as he leapt and rendered the demons limb from limb, their dying screams sounding oddly metallic in the small bathroom as Josie's offered an almost semi-melodic counter harmony. I blacked out for a moment and heard nothing but silence as I swam in my own head, enjoying the peace.

Getting slapped awake was becoming an occurrence I could live without.

I opened my eyes and blinked at Candace, who looked oddly angelic in the sunlight filtering through the curtains in my bedroom. "Am I dead?"

She smiled and shook her head.

I lifted my head from the pillow to see I was lying on my comforter naked. Glass was protruding from most of me and I felt the wetness beneath me that I hoped wasn't blood. I'd just bought the damn comforter. At least I wasn't still on the floor.

"Stay still. Josie is getting my med kit from my apartment. I'll remove the glass and get you healed up. Jimmy, Chief, Dennis, and Jason are all on the way to help."

"Dar?"

She nodded at the ground next to me. "Yuki has also calmed. As soon as you collapsed the rift disappeared. All is well."

"What happened to those things?" I raised my voice so Dar would know I was talking to him. I didn't have the concentration to try and mind-speak.

Dead, he answered almost nervously.

"Thank you," I let my hand drop off the side of the bed, wincing in pain as my fingers stroked the fur on his head. "Hellhound?"

Yes.

I nodded, understanding completely. He wasn't Frank Dunbar's pet German Shepherd. He was a hellhound who had snuck through the rift after the pit fiend. He hadn't been completely truthful with me, but I couldn't blame him. I probably would have freaked out if I found out I had accidentally bound a hellhound to me.

Sorry, he said, oddly meek as he nosed the palm of my hand.

Just glad you are what you are. Otherwise, I'd be demon chow right about now. The pain in my everything was ebbing. It had faded from a searing pain to a light burn, like I had spent a few too many hours in the sun. Hopefully I wasn't losing too much blood and dying.

Candace gasped and backed up a step, covering her mouth with her hands and staring at me incredulously.

"What?" I asked, frantically. Lifting my head, I stared down at my stomach which had several large shards sticking out, not to mention my arms and legs. Diving through a glass door hadn't been my crowning achievement.

I screeched and then stared in fascination…

The largest shards were the most noticeable. They were waving in the air violently, working their way out of my flesh. The burning sensation turned into an almost unbearable itch. Even the smaller ones were wiggling as they backed themselves out, like they were being pushed away from the inside. Pieces of glass that I couldn't even see were popping out of cuts that looked clean.

The biggest one slid from a gaping wound just above my navel and slapped against my skin wetly. I reached down and picked it up, staring at it. It was nearly opaque with blood. Candace ran into the kitchen and grabbed a large plastic mixing bowl, returning to hold it out in front of me. I dropped the six-inch piece of glass into it with a thud. Carefully, she started picking the rest off me.

"What's going on?"

She shook her head again. "I do not know. It's almost like your body is rejecting the glass. I've never seen anything like it, unless magic was involved."

Dar, who had extricated himself from the floor beside me, stared. He leaned forward and sniffed the air around me. *You smell like the vampire…*

Like blood?

No. Yes, that as well, but you smell like a child of the night.

I smell like a corpse?

169

Vampires are not dead, just different. Do they teach witches nothing?

I skipped witch class a lot.

I can see that.

I was joking. Vampires are rare these days and very secretive. Blame them. So, what, am I turning into a vampire?

As you are a witch, that is not possible. You do seem to have their regenerative power, though. He leaned closer and nosed one of the wounds. *You are healing yourself.*

No, I'm not.

Your body is healing itself, dolt.

Oh. Wait. Could it be because I have a vampire as a familiar? Could I be gaining the power from her?

Interesting. Perhaps.

I sighed. Mystery solved. Hopefully. "Candace, grab a wet towel from the kitchen, please?"

She ran off and was back in a moment. She used the rag to wipe the blood away from my stomach. There wasn't a single mark left, not even a white-lined scar. I sighed in relief and let my head drop back to the pillow, breathing in and out gratefully. She stared at my stomach in awe. "Would you help me to the shower? Your shower. I don't want to step in demon guts."

"Yes, Lady." She reached out a hand to help me up.

I was halfway to my feet when Chief kicked the door open and ran into the house. He took one look at me and dropped to his knees outside my bedroom door.

"I was hurt, but my doorknobs work just fine."

"Don't joke, Dot. Please. Not now. Not ever when it comes to you."

I received the biggest shock of the day when I saw the tears sliding rapidly down his cheeks.

"Oh, Chief," I said with a breaking heart, wanting to go to him to comfort him, but not wanting to cover him in blood. "I'm okay. I'll explain everything once I've gotten all this blood off me."

"You. You're okay?" he asked disbelievingly, taking in the amount of blood I was covered in.

"I nicked myself shaving."

"Dot, I swear to the goddess. If you don't stop..." He wanted to be angry, but he gave a short bark of laughter.

I chuckled. My mission successful. "Shower." I said the word and got to my feet, unaided. I even gave a little jump to check for any remaining pain. I'd forgotten I was covered in wet, sticky glass. The majority of it fell from me and made tinkling noises as it hit my hardwood floor. "Oops."

"I'll clean it up," Candace said softly.

"Thank you, sweetie."

She nodded and gave me a brief smile over her shoulder, relief clearly etched on her elfin features.

"How did you kill it?" Chief asked as I walked to the bathroom on the opposite side of the house.

"I didn't. Dar killed them. You're lucky he was only playing when he bit your ass. He's a hellhound, not a shepherd."

Chief blinked and turned his head to stare at the dog who was obediently following me. He gave a short proud bark. I was ordering takeout steaks with his name on them. He was the bestest boy.

I paused by Yuki's door and gingerly reached out, putting my hand against the white wood. *Thank you,* I sent softly.

You're welcome, came her sleepy reply. *For what?*

Tell you later. Sleep tight.

Quit making so much fucking noise.

I chuckled as I entered the rift-free guest bathroom.

Chapter 14

I exited the bath with an oversized towel wrapped around me, nearly tripping over Dar who stood guard across the bathroom door. He got up and moved out of the way as I walked out into the hallway in a cloud of steam.

My living room was empty, as was the kitchen. I started to panic until I got to my bedroom where everyone had gathered to magick the damage caused by me, the rift, and the two demons. I gasped as Candace stroked away the last bloodstain off my comforter.

I walked through the room and peeked in my bathroom. You couldn't tell an unholy war had been waged in there barely an hour before. Even the dismembered demons had vanished.

"Oh, guys. Thank you," I said. Josie shot me a dirty look. "And gal," I added with a smile.

"Well, we wanted to do *something*." Jimmy said. "But you're not allowed to call my job dangerous, anymore."

"I didn't get blown up."

"*This* time," he said with a chuckle.

"I'm ordering steaks. You're all staying for dinner."

"Would you like me to call Bunyan's? I can pick them up," Jason said.

"Sure, but take my car."

He nodded, knowing better than to argue. "I'll get everybody's order. You relax," he said and squeezed out of the overpopulated bathroom, kissing my forehead as he walked by.

"Thought you weren't supposed to kiss the boss."

"I'm off the clock."

Chief laughed and was the next to get out of the tiny room, kissing me firmly on the lips. Then Jimmy pulled me into a hug and breathed in the scent of my wet hair, kissing my neck. Dennis walked out, blushed, and kissed my cheek.

Josie leaned in for a kiss and I covered her mouth with my hand, shooting her a dirty look. I felt her tongue wiggle against my palm, and I pulled it away screaming and wiping it on the towel I was wearing. She wisely ran out of my bedroom.

Candace walked around the other side of the bedroom after propping the broom and dustpan against the wall. She reached up and put her hands on my shoulders, pulling me a little lower. She leaned over when my head was at her level and gently kissed me on the forehead, *exactly* on the mark that couldn't be seen, the one the goddess herself had anointed me with, and breathed against my skin.

"I am glad you are safe, Child," she whispered in a voice that wasn't her own. I blinked in surprise as a faint golden glow faded from her eyes. She shook her head and smiled, pressing her face against my shoulder. "I'm so glad you are safe, Lady. You scared me. I don't think I've ever been that afraid, even when the creature had me in his grasp."

"Oh, sweetie," I said and hugged her to me. "I'm a tough, old broad," I said and my voice broke. I hugged her and cried while she began rocking me gently.

A cold, wet nose slipped under my towel and poked me in the rear. I let go of Candace with a yelp of surprise.

Could you tell your new boyfriend I want a porterhouse, rare. No potato. No veggies. Double meat?

"Sure thing, Darling."

Darling?

"Yeah. Your name is Dar... So Darling."

I'll allow it.

I rubbed his head. "If you ever stick your nose in my ass again, you'll be eating kibble for the next six months, though,"

He let out a high-pitched whine and ran out of the room. Candace was holding her belly as she laughed musically.

Candace left behind him, still chuckling. I tried very hard not to think about how she had been possessed by the goddess only moments before. I was going to keep that one to myself. The witches in my life already thought I was weird enough.

Without closing the door, I dropped the towel. I kicked it in the general vicinity of the laundry basket in the corner and slipped into some jammies. I absolutely, resolutely refused to go anywhere for the remainder of the day. Hopefully, by the time the orders were placed, and Jason got the takeout, the sun would be down, and Yuki could enjoy the steak with us. Dar's double order of meat didn't sound like a half-bad idea. I was ravenous.

I slipped out of my bedroom and sat down in the only open space on the couch, right between Chief and Jimmy. Right where I wanted to be. I leaned against Chief and put my legs over Jimmy, who looked at me with his hands over my legs to make sure it was okay to touch them. I nodded and gave him a smile for his thoughtfulness.

"Dot, what kind of steak do you want?"

"King cut, prime rib. Extra rare. No veggies or potatoes. Make it two of them."

He blinked in surprise.

"Dar wants the same thing but make his porterhouses."

Everybody else blinked in surprise.

"What? I lost a lot of blood."

"Dot, that's almost three pounds of meat."

175

I looked up at Chief and smiled. "Insert dick joke here."

He sputtered and turned red.

Totally worth it.

"You shouldn't use the words insert and dick in the same sentence, sweetness," Jimmy added.

He and I started laughing harder. I was crying by the time we stopped. Everyone else was just kind of staring at us. I was a little loopy from almost dying. Jimmy was just weird. We made quite the team.

Candace extricated herself from Josie's side, and slipped into the kitchen, returning with a glass of wine for me. I was almost afraid to drink it until I got some food in me.

"Gonna go call in the order and pick up the food. I'll be back shortly," Jason said and grabbed his coat, heading out the door.

"Seriously, though," I stopped and looked around the room at each and every one of the witches that I loved, in one way or another. "I can't thank you for enough for taking care of me and everything. I am blessed with you."

"Not that you needed us. What the hell was that? You were covered in blood and don't have a single scratch on you," Chief turned a little, and my head slid off his shoulder, landing on his chest.

"I can only assume it's from having a vampire familiar. While I was healing, Dar said I smelled like a vampire."

"And Dar killed the demons?"

I nodded, not looking at him. "Yeah. He's not a German Shepherd at all. Hellhound."

"I've heard of them, aren't they demons, too?"

I nodded. "Obviously."

"Are you sure he didn't eat Frank?"

"Dar… Did you eat the nice fellow by the grill?" I asked a little sarcastically.

No.

"He says no."

"Oh, well in that case… Dot! He's a demon. How do you know he's not lying?"

"You're not very trusting. Anybody ever tell you that?"

"Comes with being a cop. We suspect everybody." He didn't sound angry, just stating a fact.

Tell him we are not demons. We are the guardians of hellmouths, portals, and rifts. We're the ones who keep the humans safe from the denizens of Gehenna.

I repeated it word for word to Chief and everyone else in the room.

"Bang up job," Chief snarked.

This rift is different. It appears and disappears in a random pattern I cannot predict. If I were to hazard a guess, I would presume it is not a natural phenomenon.

"You mean someone *made* it?"

Or caused it.

"Who would do such a thing?"

Again, I do not know.

"What did he say?" Jimmy asked while rubbing my leg gently.

"He can't tell where the rift is going to show up because its random and therefore man-made, either intentionally or unintentionally. He doesn't know who did it, either. I asked."

"So, someone opened a portal to hell and just left the door open?" Chief said testily.

"Yep. And the door likes to move around a lot."

"Well, none of us could have done it. We don't even know how to make potions."

Every eye in the room turned and stared at me, accusingly.

"Don't fucking look at me… I didn't do it."

"Are you sure, sweetie?" Jimmy winced when he asked.

"What do you mean?"

177

"Shit has a tendency to go a little *fucking abnormal* when you're around. Don't get me wrong, I love you, but you're an 'oh shit' magnet."

I couldn't even deny it.

"Yeah, but it wasn't me. This time."

"Well, if nobody here knows how to do it. And you didn't do it… What about one of our visitors?"

I opened my mouth to give him a scathing retort, when reality set in. That was Chief, throwing around his fucking logic like confetti. I hated it when there was a minute chance his assumptions were correct. "Maybe? But doubtful? I mean, creating rifts and portals is extraordinarily complex… I don't think any of them could have done it," I said dismissively. "I know I couldn't do it… Maybe with a spell book I'd get luck–"

"Like with one of the *stolen* Blackwell spell books?"

"Yeah. One of those."

"Hey, Dot?"

"Yes, Chief?"

"Is that a new door?" He pointed at the ancient oak door my grandmother had created as a portal to her house in Ashville…

"Fuck me six ways to Sunday…"

"Let me guess, your grandmother?"

"Chief. Shut up. Goddess damn it, Nana… What were you thinking," I shouted and stood up, walking over to the door and flinging it open, staring at a blank wall. I shut it slowly and opened it again to the same effect. It was literally just a door opening to my wall.

"It wasn't like this before. It led to her workshop in her house in Ashville. Now it's just a door."

"Maybe a spell to activate it?" Jimmy had gotten off the couch to check it out.

"I don't know, but it's safer not to muck with it until Nana comes back. Let me call her."

I swiped my phone off the counter in the kitchen angrily, dialing Nana and slapping the phone to my ear. Of course, it went straight to voicemail. I dialed my mother.

"Greetings, Daughter."

"Hello, Mother."

"What can I do for you today?"

Instead of acting indignant that she assumed I wanted something, I got straight to the point. "Have you seen Nana?"

"You lost your grandmother, dear?"

"Mother... Not a good time. Have you seen her?"

"What did she do?"

"Opened a portal into my house and accidentally opened a wandering rift into Gehenna that seems to be floating around town releasing demons... You know. Usual Nana stuff."

She sighed heavily on the other end of the line. "Damn that woman."

"She's your mother, Mother."

"She is a consistent pain in my arse, *Daughter.*"

"Starting to think it runs in the family."

"As I am sure it does. Obviously, it was her who removed the grimoires from the museum... How she got in, I can't even begin to fathom, but even she could not have opened these portals without a ritual. I'm quite positive she did not memorize it, either. When did it start?"

"A few days ago."

"You do not have much time, then."

"Uh... Until what?"

"I swear you slept through the majority of your lessons, Child."

"Mother, what is going to happen?"

"The longer a portal is open, the more stable it becomes and without framework to contain it...the more it wanders. You should start noticing an increase in the frequency in attacks until it settles in a final location and grows."

"How big?"

"How big is Cedar Falls?"

"You're kidding me."

"I do not jest, Daughter. Only rarely, and usually at your expense."

"Gee, thanks."

"How long ago was the last attack?"

"Maybe two hours? In my bathroom."

"Are you all right?"

"Yeah. My hellhound familiar tore them to shreds."

"Hellhound? Familiar?"

"Long story."

"One I would love to hear. Later. We need to work on our communication skills."

"We tried therapy. You slept with the counselor."

"Mmmm. Mr. Mackey. He was quite excellent at pillow talk."

"Ew! Mother!"

She chuckled through the phone. "If half a day passes until the next occurrence, you will have more than a day before it finalizes. If it happens sooner, you will have less time. Contain the demons, Daughter. I shall find your grandmother and ship her to you as soon as possible. Carry a knife with you to cut the bindings I'm going to wrap her in," she finished icily and hung up the phone.

"We're in so much shit."

Chief's phone rang.

"Yeah, Marcus? On my way. Keep everybody out of there."

"Please don't say it's a demon," I said, giving a silent prayer to the lady.

"Okay. I won't say it. But you might want to put on some pants and shoes."

I thought longingly of the prime ribs I was going to have to ruin in the microwave later. Sighing, I ran into my room and changed into something a little more combat friendly.

Chief, Dar, and I were on the road in less than two minutes. I'd made everybody else stay at my house, much to their dismay. Especially Jimmy. He wasn't happy about being left behind, but I didn't want to see him hurt again.

"Where is it?"

"The hospital…"

"You're kidding me," I said in disbelief. "What about all the people?"

"*Luckily,* it's a smaller demon and the security guard has it pinned down in the boiler room."

"Nobody got hurt?"

"Janitor and one of the doctors got scratched up pretty bad, but they're alive."

"Hopefully it wasn't Shapiro."

"Don't know. Marcus was pretty scared. He saw it."

"How you gonna explain it?"

"I'll send him for a random drug test…"

"That's horrible."

"I'm kidding. He's a good guy. I'll think of something."

We pulled into the hospital parking lot with the lights on, but the sirens quiet. I'd only ever seen them flash behind me. It was weird being in the car and seeing the strobing effect all around you.

"Hey, Chief?"

"Yeah?"

"How are we supposed to get Dar into the hospital?"

"You mean Officer Dar? Our new K-9?"

"Oh. That was easy."

"Helps to be a cop."

I turned to the back seat. "Listen to Chief while we're in the hospital."

If he tells me to roll over or play dead, I'm biting his junk.

I snorted and got out of the car.

Chief wasn't running but I practically had to in order to keep up with his much longer stride. He yanked open the door and ushered the two of us in before him. As soon as the security guard at the desk saw Chief, he snapped to attention and dropped his sandwich.

"Downstairs," he said to Chief and motioned for the stairs on the opposite wall from the elevator.

"She's with us," Chief called over his shoulder and barged through the heavy stairwell door.

I let Dar go ahead of me and brought up the rear. Watching him sniffing the air around him as he padded down the stairs set my nerves on edge.

Smell it? I struggled not to lose sight of him.

Yes.

Imp?

Yes. And something else.

"Of course, there is," I said with a little sigh. Nothing was ever easy. I wanted to punch something. If another rift had opened already, we were literally going to be in hell very soon. "There's more than one, Chief," I called down the stairs. He was just reaching the bottom.

He pulled his gun and the light flickered above his head. He ducked instinctively. The entire floor went dark with an audible *clack*. It didn't sound like a breaker popping, it sounded like a microwave blew up. Surprisingly enough, I knew what that sounded like.

"Got a flashlight?" I said drolly, knowing full well he didn't. Most cops had a superhero utility belt full of useful shit. Chief had a gun and a holster for his cell phone. I didn't have the heart to tell him he looked like a dork and that nobody used them anymore. It was amazing I found him as attractive as I did, sometimes.

"No," he said exasperatedly.

Pulling out my cell, I whispered, "*Solas*," and forced a bit of power into the case. It lit up like a beacon and I held it above my head, just in time to see the shadow scream and pull back away from Chief. It had snuck up on him without a sound. Even Dar hadn't heard it.

Shadow demon. Not good.

Not good?

Ever try to bite a shadow?

Not good.

That's what I said, he said with a shake of his head.

Ten billion hellhounds in hell and I had to get the smart ass.

How do you kill a shadow?

He lowered his head, not wanting to answer. *You let it attack you. It has to become real to hurt you.*

He just volunteered to get hurt to kill the damn thing. There had to be another way. *Don't you get hurt on me, Dar. That's an order.*

I shall try.

I sighed, assuming that was the best I was going to get. I nodded at Chief and moved a little closer with the light.

"Stay behind me with that so I can see what I'm shooting at."

"Don't think a gun is going to hurt it. Might have to use magic for this one."

"Shit."

"Yeah."

"What about the imp?"

"Fire away."

"After you fry it."

"I'll try not to hit you this time."

"Please. Most of my eyelashes fell out the last time."

"It could have been worse," I said and lowered my eyes below his belt, holding the light in front of my face.

"Yeah. Let's be careful out there."

I chuckled evilly.

Done flirting?

Never.

Chief kept walking down the corridor. I sent a bit more power into my phone case and it got even brighter, keeping the monster at bay. The only problem was, we couldn't leave it running rampant in the hospital.

"Marcus," Chief called out.

"Down here," the reply echoed from the right.

Chief turned down the adjoining hallway, pausing until I caught up with the light. Marcus and a very frightened security guard were leaning against a set of metal double doors.

"I'm assuming it's in there," Chief said and pointed.

"No. Just tired and leaning on the door," Marcus answered with an eyeroll. Chief seemed to have that effect on people.

Can you handle it, Dar?

Easily. And I'm hungry.

"You should let the dog in, Chief," I said, hoping he caught my meaning.

"That's a darn good idea. Marcus, let the dog in."

"Chief, I saw that thing. It's some sort of mutated ape. It will tear that dog apart."

"He's a…uh…special military K-9 as it…uh…turns out. Dot was lucky to find him at Frank Dunbar's."

Either Marcus knew Chief was full of shit and didn't care, or he was just used to weird shit happening and bullshit explanations. "Military K-9. Sure. Go ahead, doggy." He pulled away from the door and opened it enough for Dar to slip between it.

"What now?" The security guard asked, nervously.

"We wait," Chief said with a smile and rocked on his heels while I kept an eye out for the other thing.

"That's a hell of a flashlight you got on that phone," Marcus said. He almost sounded suspicious.

"Yeah. Got it off the internet. It's the case so it doesn't drain your phone's battery. Have to keep them both charged, though." I chuckled nervously. Chief wasn't the only one who sucked at subterfuge. At least my stories weren't as hokey as his, though. My delivery just needed a bit of work.

Marcus just shook his head.

Snarls of rage and growls erupted in the room behind the door. Something was thrown against it hard enough to dent the thick metal right by the guard's head. He squawked and fell to the ground, Chief immediately leaned over him and held the door tight.

"Hopefully that wasn't your Military K-9," Marcus said in a voice that screamed, 'I told you so.'

You okay?

Yes. No talk. Feisty bastard.

I shut up and let him do his job.

I'm coming, Yuki's voice sounded in my head. Apparently, the sun was down.

Hospital, basement. Don't be seen.

I know. And I always know where you are, I can feel you.

I remembered when we were in Ashville and I felt her barreling at me like a rocket. Closing my eyes, I could feel her again, crossing town like a flash of lightning. Vampiric speed was a scary thing.

A clawed hand swiped the wrist holding the cell phone above my head. I screamed out and dropped it, plunging us into darkness as it shattered against the floor.

There was no emergency lighting in the basement. We were in complete darkness. My eyes adjusted and shapes began to come into focus, but everything had a silvery sheen to it.

"At least they got the lights back on," I said and picked up my phone, wincing at the shattered screen. I tucked it in my back pocket.

"What happened?" Chief said, turning his head back to look at me, but he wasn't. He was looking to my right, his eyes reflecting strangely.

"Something hit my wrist and I dropped my phone. My...uh...flashlight broke, right before the lights came on."

"What is she talking about, Chief?" Marcus was looking up at the ceiling. The security guard was huddled on the ground, still beneath Chief.

"Dot? The lights aren't on..."

"Oh. Then how am I seeing you?"

A high-pitched squeal caused us to wince before it echoed off into nothing but a wet sounding gurgle.

"I hope that wasn't your dog."

Got him.

I heard.

"It wasn't. You can open the door. That thing is dead," I said as a black, wet looking, scaled hand reached out from the shadows. It grabbed the security guard and dragged him away, screaming.

"Chief!"

There was a wet squelch and the sound of cracking bone and the screaming stopped.

"Dar!"

The door burst open, flinging Marcus back against the wall. He slid down to the floor, quite unconscious. The mass of a six-hundred-pound hellhound turned out to be an effective anesthetic.

Instead of running down the hall after the thing, Dar skidded to a stop, sniffing the air around him. He turned his eyes to me, and I saw them glowing red.

Do you trust me?

Yes, but why?

It's about twenty feet behind you. It circled around. I can smell the guard's blood covering it, even incorporeal.

It's going to go for you next. Duck when I say duck and don't hesitate.

Dar...

Duck!

I dropped to the floor with a little squeak, watching in fascination as Dar launched himself without even a ripple of preparation. He almost turned to liquid in my vison as he became a blur of speed. I saw the hand swipe above me in my peripheral vision, exactly where I'd been standing less than a moment before. If I had hesitated, my head would have landed by Chief.

The sound of a shadow screaming would haunt my dreams for months. I made the mistake of looking over my shoulder. Not giving it a chance to vanish, Dar had aimed for the kill, shredding its neck and chest with his massive maw and talons. No blood flew from the massive wounds, thankfully. It vanished in a wisp of ash and sulfur smelling smoke when it died.

I lay back against the cold concrete floor. "That was fun."

Dar turned around and walked over to me, lowering his head to my face and giving it a lick. *You okay?*

Yes. Your timing was very impressive.

So was your reaction time. Good puppy, he said and licked me again. His wet hellhound tongue felt like a giant slug. I was just grateful to be alive to find out that disgusting bit of otherworldly trivia.

"Damn it!"

We all spun on Yuki, who had finally shown up.

"What?"

"I miss all the fucking fun."

Chapter 15

Yuki set me down on the ground in my front yard and I stumbled and staggered for a few steps before dumping the contents of my stomach in the snow. I dropped to my knees and rolled to the side, not wanting to fall in my own puke.

"Never ever again," I managed to say and groan simultaneously. I sounded like a Tibetan throat singer.

"You okay?"

"No, I'm fucking not. Humans weren't meant to go that fast unless it's on four wheels. My face feels like I spent an hour in a wind tunnel!"

"I kept it under eighty and it was for like two minutes."

"Never again, Yuki. Don't ask me."

Chief had to stay at the hospital to do his chiefly duties and tell Marcus what had happened when he woke up. I didn't envy him the amount of paperwork he was going to have to fill out about the dead security guard. At least the poor bastard died almost instantly. Lady rest his soul.

Chief had been adamant that Yuki, Dar, and I get out of there. It would make it easier to explain things. At least Dar hadn't left a piece of imp big enough to examine. Chief planned on burning everything, including the guard's body, and chalking it up to a missing person and an escaped animal. He was also going to wipe Marcus' memory, if Dar didn't do a good enough job with the door.

Instead of a nice, leisurely walk home, Yuki had picked me up in her tiny little arms like I was a pillow and *ran* all the way home. I was nauseous, wind-burned, and frozen down to my underpants.

"I need coffee."

"Not what people usually say right after they puke," she said with a stifled little giggle.

"Laugh it up, fang face." I lifted myself off the cold ground.

Yuki opened the door, the smell of steak wafting warmly over us. I groaned and nearly crawled up the front steps, my stomach driving me forward.

"You're hungry?"

"Ravenous."

I got to my feet and ran the rest of the way, ditching my jacket and hoodie on the floor on the way to the dining room. I smiled when my family came into view. Josie and Candace were practically sitting on top of each other, munching on salads. I noticed Josie's had chicken covering it. Jimmy and Dennis sat on opposite sides of the table, Styrofoam containers in front of them and knives and forks poised to cut into their steaks. Jason was waiting, his container still closed as he nervously looked up at me and smiled. My family.

"Welcome back," Jimmy said with a smile. "Get em?"

"Yeah. Dar munched 'em to bits. I love you all, but where's my food?"

Jason got up and walked into the kitchen, returning with two containers of food. It didn't smell like beef, it smelled like it had been carved from a god. I practically snarled as I swiped them from him and plopped down in the closest chair. I may have torn the lid off the first one, but I can neither confirm, nor deny, that fact. Jason set a knife and fork in front of me.

All I saw was red. Red meat. Beautiful, glistening red meat. Ignoring the heat, I picked up the slab of prime rib in both hands and shoved it at my face like a fucking sandwich. The blood and flesh hit my tongue and melted as

I ripped it away, almost swallowing it whole. I instantly felt a hundred times better.

Staring in front of me at the wood grain of the table I ate, listening for danger and trying to sense if anybody got too close, trying to steal even a morsel of *my* meal.

"Dot?" I heard Jimmy's wavering voice as his chair slid backward. Somebody must have stopped him from approaching me, because I continued my meal uninterrupted. When I stuffed the last piece of meat into my mouth, I looked up.

Five utterly *horrified* faces stared at me in confusion and fear. Even Candace, sweet Candace, who would love me if I grew horns and wings, was looking at me like I had kicked a puppy.

"What?"

"You just ate a cow with your bare hands and teeth, were practically snarling and drooling through the whole ordeal, while making what could easily have been mistaken for sex sounds. You're going to sit there and ask what?"

I focused my attention on Jimmy, since he had been the only one coherent or brave enough to answer. "I don't know what you're talking about."

"Dot. Look at the floor beside you."

I looked over the side of my chair. Yuki was lying on the ground, still writing in ecstasy and almost touching herself inappropriately.

"I'll admit, the steak was good," Jimmy continued, "but it wasn't *that* good. Your familiar had three orgasms while you gorged yourself. I'll ask again, what the hell is going on?"

"I… I don't know."

You're taking our powers, Dar said from outside the front door. *And our appetites…*

Yuki came to, got up in a fluid motion, and walked to the door, letting my hellhound inside.

"I'm taking what?"

191

He sat down on the floor and Yuki set his containers of food on the ground in front of him. He picked one steak up and swallowed it down like a snake gobbling down a mouse, just much faster. I could see it as it slid down his throat. Suddenly, I felt very nauseous as I pictured my neck swelling as I ate. No wonder everyone looked horrified.

Our bonding is nearing completion. You have garnered not only vampiric healing, but vision as well. You have gained my appetite to start. I am interested in seeing what else you inherit from me. Hopefully my intelligence and wisdom, but that might be a bit much to hope for.

"Why would I gain your appetite? Doggy eating abilities isn't a super-power. There's no Kibble Man comic books."

He ignored me and gobbled down his other hunk of meat. When he finished, he shook his whole body like he was shaking off the rain. He resumed his hellhound appearance. Then the air rippled around him, as did the flesh down his back. He lifted himself onto his hind legs as his flesh became hazy and almost impossible to focus on, like my brain was denying what it was seeing as he shifted into a man. Not a human, but he was male...and quite naked.

His flesh was blue, dark blue, almost royal. His eyes were completely red, the color of blood that matched the two three-inch horns protruding from his forehead with a slight upward curve. I found myself wanting to run my fingers through his mane of black hair that swept behind him to below his shoulders and run my fingertips along the ridge of his tapered, elf-like ears. He was beautiful in a devilish sort of way. I found it very hard to keep my eyes focused on him from the waist up. I didn't want to look lower...

"Wait a minute!" A flash of realization hit me. "All those times I...in front of you! You even stuck your nose in my ass!"

I figured I might as well since you thought I was a dog anyway.

You bastard! You could have told me. I mentally pouted at him. At least I think I did. I tried, anyway.

I apologize. It was not my intention to bind myself to you. When I realized what had happened, it was already too late. I figured I would just remain as you found me until I could find an open rift to slip back through. My hope was that it would break the bond forged between us. Then the demons attacked, and I took the form of a hellhound to better defend you. Now that the bond is nearing completion, my only option was to tell you the truth. We need to find an open rift and I need to leave. I fear what you might become should I stay.

He pulled out the last open chair and sat down on it. I ignored the fact that his demon ass was naked on the upholstery.

"What could I become?"

"Dot? What's going on?" Jimmy asked, nervously.

I held up a finger to silence him for a moment. "Can you speak, speak?"

"Yes," he answered, his voice flittering over my skin like a warm breeze.

"What could I become? What is happening to me? No secrets from my family."

"When a denizen of Gehenna mates with a human... A cambion is born. A nephilim. Some have great powers, some are horrid wretches. It mostly depends on the type of demon. I fear the bonds forged between us might have the same effect, but on you. You are a powerful witch, even though you are young. I am a... You have no word for me as my kind have never before left the planes of Gehenna. We are the guardians, the peacekeepers, and the rulers. The nobles. We are dominus."

"That's Latin..." Josie translated in her head. "Lord."

He nodded. "*Verum.*"

"Lady, I do not need this right now." I dropped my head into my hands, elbows on the table. If my grandmother were there, she would have slapped me on the back of the head, right after I beat her senseless for causing this whole mess. Okay, maybe not beat, she would wipe the floor with me, but she'd get a stern verbal warning. "We need to find my grandmother. She needs to fix this complete fuck up…"

"Okay, how do we do that?" Jimmy leaned forward and put his elbows on the table.

"I don't even know if she's here in Cedar Falls, or back in Ashville, terrorizing the residents there."

"You need a way to check both places. Like a shadow walker?" Josie asked with a smile.

"Josie, you're brilliant. Contact Shea, ask him to come here. I may need his services." I ignored Jimmy as he wiggled his eyebrows lecherously at me. Josie, on the other hand, was actually being helpful and got up to get her cell phone.

"Was she not looking at homes with Herb? Shall I see if she settled on one? Maybe she is there?"

"Thanks, Candace. That would be awesome."

She beamed as she took off after Josie.

I texted Nana one more time. Hoping she had finally turned her phone back on. Staring at the text, I prayed the notification would turn from sent to delivered with no such luck.

"No luck with Shea. I left him a message begging for him to get here as soon as he gets it. I gave him a head's up as to what was going on, too."

"Thanks, Josie."

Candace walked out of the bedroom still on the phone. "Thank you, Herb." She walked back over to the table and set her phone down, shaking her head. "She did purchase a home but went back to Ashville to secure the funds. Your grandmother is meeting him at the diner tomorrow morning."

"That's better than we've done so far. Thanks again." I gave her an appreciative smile. "I guess we wait," I said to the rest of the people seated around me.

"Well, I need to get home," Dennis said and stood, looking at Jimmy.

"I'll stay with Dot. I don't have to be at work tomorrow, like some people."

"Dennis? Can I talk to you for a minute?" I got up and headed to my bedroom, wanting to make sure he was okay in the head. I would absolutely *hate* it if things got uncomfortable between us. He was my little rock of calm in my crazy world.

"Sure, Dot."

I grabbed the door as soon as I made it into the room, closing it softly with a soft *click* after he passed through. He had his hands in his front jean pockets and was shifting uncomfortably under my questioning gaze. "Everything okay?"

I could almost taste his fear.

Resisting the urge to throw my arms around him and comfort him, I answered. "You tell me. I'm not getting a weird vibe or anything, I just wanted to make *sure* everything was copasetic between us? I know things got a little hot and that you ran off before I could check on you. Are *you* okay?"

"I don't know."

"Are you mad at me?"

"No! Goddess, no. Not even remotely."

"Jimmy?"

"No. I'm used to his antics."

Rage and jealousy swirled inside me in a tempest of hypocrisy. "He have a lot of sex with women in front of you?"

"What? No!" He saw I was pissed and rushed to explain. "I'm just used to him having no filter around me. I swear the guy has no shame. He hasn't even had *that* many girlfriends. He has a tendency to get under people's skin and not in a good way. And I can swear to you one thing, he hasn't so much as *looked* at another woman since you rolled into town."

"Okay. I'll let him live, then," I said with a wink to let him know I was joking as my anger quickly faded. "For now."

"Sorry. Didn't mean it that way."

"No worries. Little green monster and all that."

"I see that," he said with a chuckle.

"So, what's bugging you? Are you embarrassed that you were jerking off in front of me? Cuz I'm not going to lie, that was kind of hot."

"Really?"

"Really, really."

He beamed a little at the compliment. "Thanks."

"No. Thank you."

"I just feel horribly guilty. I mean, I didn't touch you, but I watched. Now, every time I think of Alista, a horrible knot forms in my stomach. But, what was *really* bothering me was you, to be honest. I was afraid you were going to get weirded out by the whole thing and not want to be around me anymore."

"Oh, sweetie." This time I did wrap my arms around him and hug him, putting my head against his chest.

"I just didn't want things to get weird between us. I know I'm not boyfriend material for someone as beautiful, gorgeous, and amazing as you, but I do want to be your friend. Forever."

I didn't have a clue who broke my sweet Dennis in the past, but I knew one thing… If I ever met the bitch, I was going to shove a few thousand volts up her ass. "What the hell are you talking about, you stupid, sweet dolt? I would be lucky to have *you* as a boyfriend. You're sweet, caring, sweet, loving, sweet, and gorgeous. Did I mention how sweet you are?"

He chuckled. "Once or twice, yeah."

"Well you are." I pulled back and looked up at his face. Tears were rolling down his cheeks, steadily. I reached up and wiped them away. "None of that. Thank you. Thank you for being you and being my friend. Things will never be weird between us, okay?"

He nodded.

"Good." I lifted myself up on my toes and gently kissed him on his cheek.

He didn't wrap his arms around me and try to make it into something more, but I had a feeling he wanted to. I could almost feel him shaking in anticipation.

He's not ready yet.

I know.

See how things play out with Alista first. Give them a chance to be happy.

I know.

You have enough boys to play with for now.

I said I fucking know! Sometimes, I really hated talking to myself. I was such a bitch.

"Wow. You even smell sweet and you feel like the sun," he said shyly after I let go of him.

You sure, self? Cuz this guy is like... Yeah. Wow.

Maybe...

I sighed and decided to go with my initial reaction. "You. You little sexy sweet talker, you. You're going to make me melt in your arms."

"Well, then I'd just have to lick you up," he said and blushed.

"Okay, one more word and I might seriously have to strip you and have my way with you... But... Dennis. I am going to say this and only once, I'm not going anywhere. I think you should, and this might be the hardest thing I've

197

ever had to say, try and make things work between you and Alista. I would hate to come between the two of you when I think you have a real chance at being happy. Talk to her like you just talked to me," I said with a soft smile. "I would never do anything to come between you two, either."

He sighed, almost expecting my answer. "Thanks, Dot. That, and you, mean a lot to me."

"And you to me. Good luck with Alista."

"It's kind of funny... I *almost* hope it doesn't work out," he said with a small, sad smile and kissed me on my cheek before he pulled the door open and left me standing there, struggling not to call him back and change his mind...

I counted to ten before I walked out of the room. As soon as I joined the others, who were busy talking animatedly to Dar, Jimmy looked over at me and raised his eyebrow questioningly. I gave him a small shake of my head and a smile. He nodded in understanding. *That*, to me, was a marker of an outstanding relationship, when words didn't even have to be spoken to have a conversation. My heart felt a little lighter.

"Night everybody," Dennis said and headed for the front door.

"Night!"

He spared one last look and a wave for me before slipping out the door. I sighed and wished him the best of luck.

Pouring myself a glass of wine first, I sat back down at the table, tucking a foot underneath me. Dar gave me a smile and resumed talking to Candace, about what, I had no idea. I was only half-listening, just enjoying the company. I spent most of my first ninety-nine years alone, sometimes with Josie, sometimes with Derek, but I'd *never* been surrounded by a group of people, simply because they wanted to be there. Now it was more common than not. It was a striking difference between my mother an me. The only groups of people around her were men pawing at her, or if I was going to be honest, her pawing at them. They weren't lovers. They weren't boyfriends. They were just walking sex toys that talked, sometimes. When she removed the ball gags.

Jimmy, Jason, Dennis, and even sometimes Chief, I *wanted* to hear. Wanted to know what they were thinking and feeling. Sometimes I just wanted them to tell me everything was going to be okay. I couldn't imagine being with someone just for sex.

You okay? Yuki's voice intruded on my thoughts.

Other than the rampant demon problem? Actually, yes. Just enjoying the crowd.

You looked lost in thought.

Just thinking about how special each and every one of you are to me.

Even Dar and me?

Especially the two of you. It might have been a couple of happy accidents, but I'm glad you're mine.

Me, too. She gave me a shy smile from across the table.

I do not understand, you do not wish me to leave? Dar's voice held a confused tone. I'd been unaware he was listening, or that he could.

If it weren't for the whole turning into a witch-demon thing, I'd let you stay in a heartbeat.

He'd been speaking out loud, holding two conversations at once, which was impressive to me since I couldn't rub my head and pat my belly at the same time, but he gave a short bark of laughter, mid-sentence. Candace looked from him to me, almost like she knew.

The game was on. I wanted to see how many times I could make him laugh while he was talking to other people.

This might be more fun than Sudoku, I thought to myself.

"In the planes of Gehenna, both food and drink are hard to come by. Most of the denizens, the ones capable of social interaction, have banded together in cities," he told Candace who seemed to be enthralled by his words.

You know. I think I might actually like the blue skin and red eyes thing...

His eyes darted to me and then settled back on Candace, as he continued his tale.

Wish all guys had horns like yours. Those would make good handle bars.

He stumbled over his next words and continued on, valiantly, until Yuki started snickering next to him.

"Lady, you are being impolite," Candace chastised me. I gave her a wink.

"What's she doing?" Jason asked, slurring his words a little. He had a half a dozen empty beer bottles in front of him and was working on another.

"Trying to disrupt my conversation with mind speech."

"I'm jealous. I always wanted telepathy," Jason said as he took another sip of his beer. He seemed to have slowed down, but there was no way in Gehenna I was letting him drive home.

"You wouldn't want to have telepathy around Dot. You'd blush to death," Jimmy said with a chuckle.

"Probably. But what a way to go."

"You ready for bed, sweetie? I'm exhausted," Josie said to Candace.

She nodded and gave Dar a smile as thanks for his stories. "Good night," she said softly and walked around the table to give me a hug before following Josie.

"I'm tired, too. Jason, you're staying here."

"I am?" He looked up at me in shock.

"Yeah. I'm not letting you drive like that."

"Oh. Okay." He sounded disappointed.

I noticed Jimmy staring at him, a small smile playing across his face. He was up to no good, I recognized the look and could almost smell the smoke from his plotting little brain. I rolled my eyes and got up from the table.

"Night, kids," I said to Yuki and Dar.

"Night, Lady," they both said harmoniously. It was beyond creepy.

I downed my wine and headed for my bed. Jimmy could plot all he wanted, but I was tired as fuck. If he woke me up, he was going to find out just how part demon I could be.

Chapter 16

Waking up with a heavy arm draped over my stomach was *really* nice, except I'd been woken up by my bladder. Not so nice. I reached down to slide Jimmy's arm off me to sneak out the other side of the bed when I noticed the bare back sandwiching me in the middle of the bed...

I looked up at the hair and new it was Jason in an instant. The name of Herb's special, the Dotwich, took on a *whole* new meaning.

Holy shit.

You okay? Yuki's sleepy voice penetrated my panic.

There are two guys in my bed. What do I do?

Google it. I'm going back to sleep.

Sorry.

Ironically, I *had* googled two guys in bed before... I don't think it would help my situation any.

I started slowly inching my way to the end of the bed, trying desperately not to wake them. Maybe if I peed and went and had some coffee, they would snuggle up to each other and forget I was there.

Holy shit that thought is hot.

I almost gasped at how much I really *did* like that idea.

What the hell is wrong with me?

I shouldn't have paused to daydream. I should have got while the getting was good. Jimmy's hand slid back over my waist, pulling himself closer to me and resting his head above mine.

"Love you," he mumbled in his sleep.

My bladder took second place to the goofy grin that spread across my face. But then bladder came around the outside and passed goofy grin to take the lead when he started kneading my stomach with his open palm.

"Ji-ii-im-my," I hissed at him in undulating tones.

His eyes blinked open and he drew in a breath as he stretched, pressing down on my tummy even harder.

"Stop!"

"What's wrong?"

"I have to pee, quit pushing."

"Oh, sorry." He lifted his hand, and decorum aside, I flew off the end of the bed and raced to the bathroom. I'd worn an oversized T-shirt and panties to bed. I didn't do well under pressure and the panties had to be abandoned into the hamper. At least the T-shirt was long enough to cover me completely. It hung down to my knees.

I washed my hands, ran my toothbrush over my teeth, and quietly opened the bathroom door. Both of them were lying on their backs, asleep. Jimmy had both of his hands on his stomach over the comforter and Jason had pulled an arm over his eyes when he rolled over. They were quite adorable, and I could have stood there watching them for a while… but coffee.

I tried sneaking past Jimmy to head into the kitchen, but he held his hand out for me. I couldn't resist. He was better than coffee, most of the time. I put my hand in his and he pulled me closer, wanting a kiss. A kiss was acceptable. Smiling at him as I tucked my stray hair behind my ear, I leaned over to give him a gentle one so I could caffeinate myself properly.

Trusting him had been a huge error on my part.

As I leaned over, he let go of my hand and snaked it around my back, pulling me over on top of him and trapping me in his embrace before rolling me back over into the middle of the bed.

"Where do you think you're going?"

"Jimmy," I whined. "I want coffee."

"Just think how much better that coffee is going to taste after I hold you in my arms for five more minutes and plant little kisses on your neck and face."

I shuddered. That did sound awfully tempting...

"Five minutes," I whispered.

"You fool, now that you are in my trap, I shall never let you go!"

I squealed as quietly as I could as he started gnawing on my neck while he rolled on his side to face me. I rolled away from him to save myself the indignity of exposing myself as being super ticklish. I counted slowly, backward, in Spanish as he made nom-nom noises on my neck and bit me playfully with his lips.

"Damn it. You're not ticklish," he whispered.

"Nope."

"That's just wrong. Beautiful women such as yourself, should always be ticklish. It gives us mortals even ground."

"You are such a sweet talker. But there is a flaw in your logic. You're not mortal," I said and turned my head, kissing the side of his mouth.

"But I feel mortal when I'm around you. Like I was born yesterday, grew up loving you, begged to grow old with you just to die in your arms, and start the whole cycle over again each day."

"What the fuck, Jimmy?" I managed to stammer as the tears burst from my eyes like an un-dammed river.

He turned me into a blubbering, gibberish monster with one sentence. I flipped around and buried my face in his chest as he kissed my head and stroked my back. I fell back asleep, my last thoughts of gratefulness I had skipped the coffee.

I must have just dozed off for only a few minutes because I woke back up in the same position with a still-damp face, Jimmy still holding me, but Jason spooning me from behind. His arm was tucked between my stomach and Jimmy's.

Jimmy had a strange look in his eye...

"What?"

"Nothing," he said with a smile.

"Don't be getting any ideas."

"It's not me you have to worry about," he whispered back, kissing me on the nose.

Jason softly called my name in his sleep as he pulled himself against me with the arm wedged between Jimmy and I, grinding himself against me and whimpering softly. His hardness was pressing my T-shirt where it didn't belong, too.

"Somebody's having a good dream," Jimmy whispered with a little chuckle.

"I'm going to wake him up before he embarrasses the hell out of himself."

"You just don't want him to finish on your shirt."

I glared at him and he chuckled harder.

"You should roll over. The movement will probably wake him."

"What are you plotting, Jimmy Duncan?"

"I know not of which you speak."

"Uh huh."

He kissed my nose again. "Please?" He gave me a crooked grin.

I sighed and rolled over. Jason's arm didn't move, he didn't roll over, nor did he wake up... "Now what?" I whispered over my shoulder.

"Nothing. My arm was asleep, and I wanted you to roll over."

My head snapped to the side. "You're a shit."

"Yep." He leaned in and caught my lips with his.

I melted into the kiss, leaning back for more as his hand settled on my hip, gently sliding up and down. Even in the throes of a passionate kiss, I couldn't help but notice he was inching up my shirt. It barely covered my ass when I pulled free and narrowed my eyes at him. "Really?"

"Really," he said and kissed me again. Harder.

I started to moan into his mouth when his hand reached down and slid back up under my shirt, gently caressing the skin over my hip. Little ripples of pleasure sent goosebumps down my leg as I tried to roll over more. His hand stopped me.

"What are you doing?"

"You'll see."

His hand glided forward, tracing little circles over my lower tummy, unable to go higher with Jason's arm over me. He let his fingers brush through my tuft of hair and gently touch my lips below. The breath I'd been holding without realizing escaped in a soft moan.

His lips grazed my shoulder as his teeth playfully nipped, never biting, but sending chills down my spine. He brought his hand back over my hip, sliding over my ass and down to the juncture of my thighs. He pushed them forward until my knees were tucked against Jason.

Moving from my shoulder, he kissed the base of my neck. I pushed my head against the pillow, exposing more of the side, wanting him to kiss me more. He was eager to please and suckled on the skin below my ear. My moan became a groan as he slipped a finger over my lips between my thighs. I spread my legs a little more for him.

Two more fingers joined the first as he found my opening and spread my wetness around. Gently, his middle finger slipped inside me as the other two continued their caressing motion. My hips angled backward, exposing myself more to him. Deeper he went and faster he rubbed. My breathing became panting and my eyes opened in shock as Jason's hand began caressing my back.

He was awake, for how long I don't know, but he was watching my face with a curious little smile. I gasped as Jimmy's suckling became a more than playful bite. As I groaned at the sensation it caused, Jason leaned in and kissed me, stifling the sound. My hands slid over his chest and clenched his shoulders as I rode the pleasure.

Jimmy shifted behind me and his fingers left me for a moment, only to be replaced by something much longer and thicker. I felt the tip of him as he aligned himself and then drove it inside me. Involuntarily pulling away from the kiss with Jason, I threw back my head in ecstasy as he filled me in one fluid motion.

"Fuck me," I whimpered.

"I am," Jimmy replied.

Trying to ignore the pleasure from behind, I studied Jason's eyes. They had met mine and refused to look away. His lips were slightly parted, and his breathing was far from normal. He was enjoying watching me.

"You can touch me. I won't bite," I said between ragged gasps.

He looked down at my exposed chest, and I could feel his hunger. I could also see his hesitation as he blushed furiously. It made me want him even more and for the life of me, I couldn't understand what was going on with me. We hadn't done anything more than kiss, but all of my inhibitions had flown out of the window as my guard around him fell.

"Are you sure?" His voice quivered as his eyes began repeatedly darting from my eyes to my chest.

"If...I weren't...I wouldn't have, oh my goddess, yes." I paused to take a breath, Jimmy nearly pushing me over the edge as he picked up his pace. "I wouldn't have offered, Jason."

He reached out tentatively, letting the tip of his finger glide over my nipple, testing the water. I shuddered from the sensation, reached down and grabbed his wrist, bringing the finger to my lips. I stared into his icy blue eyes and licked the tip before taking his finger into my mouth and wrapping my tongue around it as I sucked.

He groaned and pulled the finger away, before diving to my chest, finding my right nipple with his lips as he awkwardly sucked me in. He grazed my flesh with his teeth and a gasp escaped my lips. Unfortunately, he mistook it for a sigh of pleasure. He had nowhere near the amount of experience as Jimmy or Chief, but I had all the time in the world to teach him.

"Easy," I whispered, running my fingers through his baby soft hair.

"Sorry," he said.

I shook my head and pulled him tighter against my breast.

He switched from lips and teeth to suction and tongue and he knew he had the right combination when I groaned his name.

Jimmy pulled my hips against him, driving himself in as far as he could before beginning a slower rhythm that felt incredible. My senses were quickly becoming overwhelmed from everything they were doing to me, yet I still wanted more.

"Touch him," Jimmy whispered in my ear.

I reached down and found Jason straining against his boxers. "Take them off."

Without stopping, he reached down and slid them over his hip, using his legs to shimmy them down far enough to lift his leg and push them down and off him. As soon as he settled, I reached for him. He was hard and hot, silky and smooth in my hand as I began pumping him. He pulled away from my breast and slid up, kissing me as he gently cupped my breast.

I had to break the kiss when he delicately pinched my nipple between his thumb and finger.

"Oh, Jason."

"You are the most beautiful woman I have ever seen."

A ripple of pleasure ripped through me that had nothing to do with the fingers on my nipple or the cock pounding inside me. It was enough to tip the scales as my orgasm took over. I started shaking and bucking against Jimmy as he increased his pace. As it passed, I opened my eyes, reaching behind me and stopping Jimmy's thrusts for a moment while I breathed in some much-needed air.

"Don't move for a minute."

Jimmy chuckled behind me and leaned in to kiss my shoulder.

"I said don't move!" I laughed as his shifting sent another few waves of pleasure through me, almost triggering another orgasm. "Just lay still. Just for a minute."

"Wow," was all Jason could manage to say.

"Save the wows for when our work is done," Jimmy said over my shoulder.

Jason's eyes got a little wider and I stifled a giggle. He really was too cute for his own good. I reached back down and took him in my hand again, just holding him. He propped his head up on his hand and drank in my body. I swear I could feel his gaze as it traveled over every inch of me.

With a smile, he leaned over and kissed my chest, just above my breasts. I gave him a little squeeze and started stroking him again.

"Do you want him in you?" Jimmy's voice whispered in my ear, giving me a chill.

I turned my head until I could see his eye. A thousand arguments flittered through my head on why I should say no, but I didn't. I nodded.

"Roll over."

Jimmy pulled himself free and ran his hand over my hip. I straightened my legs, and rolled over to face him, offering myself to Jason. Jimmy watched his face as he looked me over like a kid on Christmas. He didn't know what to do or where to touch first.

"Jason," I said over my shoulder. "I want you." I gave him an encouraging smile. He scooted down and his legs curled up against mine. I knew he wasn't a virgin, but it took him a few tries to get the correct position before he slipped inside of me.

I smiled at Jimmy who was watching me with rapt fascination. Watching for the pleasure that was to follow. He set his head on his hand, trailing fingers all over my chest, stomach, and thighs.

I reached down, grabbed his very wet cock in my hand and stroked him, smiling as his hips thrust to meet my hand.

Jason was pumping into me and trying to find a good pace. I began to buck my hips to subtly help him find it. He did and the pleasure quivered through me with every thrust. "Jason," I breathed heavily arching my back.

Jimmy's fingers slid between my thighs as he lifted my leg. I put my foot flat against the bed, propping myself open for him. He smiled at me lovingly as his fingers danced against my clit, barely an inch from Jason as he continued to pound into me.

I cocked my eyebrow at him but let the pleasure flow through me. Between Jason's cock and Jimmy's fingers, I wasn't going to last much longer.

"Yes," I panted over and over again. Jimmy got to his knees and lowered himself to me. I gladly took him in my mouth as he reached back down and continued his caresses. Jason was starting to pump a little harder and faster, nearing his end. I moaned in anticipation of him coming inside me. Jimmy shuddered as I moaned with him in my mouth, and I loved it. I began being more vocal as I sucked on him. His caresses stopped as he used one finger to put pressure on my clit, forcing it against me as he made tiny circles, over and around it.

I closed my eyes as another orgasm washed over me. My clenching and bucking triggered Jason's as he grunted and forced himself against me, pumping with short rapid strokes as he filled me with wet heat.

I gasped and began pumping Jimmy with my hand as I held him in my mouth.

"Dot," he warned me with a grunt.

I pulled him out of my mouth and aimed him at my chest as I leaned back against Jason. He began bucking in my hand as it burst forth, landing in hot rivers across my skin. I groaned as I kept moving my hand over him, smiling. He reached down and grabbed my hand when the sensations became too much, lowering himself to the bed in front of me.

"That was amazing," I said loud enough for them both to hear me clearly. I figured I'd better say it before they both asked.

"Yeah it was," Jason said contentedly behind me. I leaned back a little further and gave him a quick kiss on his lips.

"I'll go get a towel," Jimmy said and slid off the bed, slipping into the bathroom and returning with one.

"You're the bestest," I said and smiled at him as he leaned over and gently wiped his painting off my chest. I lifted my chin for him.

"That was hot," he said and grinned at me.

"You didn't get any on Jason, did you?"

He looked over me and shook his head.

"Ew," Jason said with a chuckle.

"Would you really have complained?" I looked over at him.

"Probably not at the time. But after, maybe."

I started laughing and Jason slipped out of me. Jimmy reached down with the towel and patted me down. Then he did the absolutely hottest thing I could have ever imagined, he leaned down and kissed me on my clit. I stared at him wide eyed as he looked up at me, gently ran his tongue over my opening and winked at me.

I came again with a little shudder, gripping the sheet in my hand as I breathed through it.

"Did he just lick you?" Jason asked incredulously.

I nodded, still unable to speak.

"Jeez, remind me never to bitch if he gets any on me."

∞ ∞ ∞

I got my wish and the three of us took a shower together, but we were so spent there was no fun and games. We'd have to try that later. I just stood between them as we all gently washed each other. Jimmy washed Jason's back, but that was as close as they got to each other.

I was the first one dressed and at the coffee maker.

Finally. I greedily sipped from my *Shud duh fuh cup* mug.

Did you have fun?

I looked down at Dar, lying by my feet. He had snuck up on me and I hadn't even heard him. At least he didn't shove his nose where it didn't belong, and I didn't mean that figuratively.

Yes. She did. Yuki answered for me. She'd been my familiar much longer than Dar, could taste food through me, *and* enjoy my little love making sessions.

Why aren't you asleep? I was starting to worry about how much she was awake during the day.

I don't know. I've been lying here since you woke up the first time. Do you think sleeping pills would work on a vampire?

Probably not. Want me to buy you a television?

There was a moment of silence.

Yuki?

You'd do that?

I walked over to her door. *Yuki, if you don't stop doing shit like that, I'm going to throw holy water on you. Get it through your thick little skull. You are mine, I will always*

213

take care of you. If you have wants or needs, you fucking tell me. Got it?

Got it.

Good.

I could hear her sniffling through the door. It was probably locked, but I tried it anyway. I blinked in surprise as the handle turned.

I dove into the room quickly and shut the door behind me, letting in as little sunlight as I could. My eyes instantly adjusted and I could see everything in the room. Including her, sitting in middle of the bed, with her knees up to her chest and arms wrapped around them.

I sat down behind her and pulled her to me into a backward hug.

"You okay?"

"Yes. Just scared and sad."

"Why?"

"I hate being trapped in here during the day. You're usually always gone, and I have nobody to talk to. Josie and the pussycat are always running around giggling, thinking I'm asleep. I haven't slept the day through in weeks. I'm going a little batty."

A little chirp of laughter escaped my lips. "Batty. Vampire. That's funny."

I felt her chuckle against me.

"Well. You inherited my tasting food and my pleasure powers. I'm sorry you also got my diurnal tendencies."

She rubbed her face with one hand as she leaned against me.

"Thanks, Dot."

"For what?"

"Caring."

I kissed the top of her head. "If you ever need to talk, I'm just a mind shout away."

She laughed at that.

Dot. You may want to come out here.

What is it?

The door.

Who's here?

Not that *door. The* other *door…*

"Nana!"

I slipped out from behind Yuki and patted her on the head. Without thinking, I flung her door open and ran out. Her hiss stopped me in my tracks. I spun around and reached in her room to grab the handle. "Sorry!"

"Dot!"

"What?" I pulled it almost all the way closed.

"Open the door all the way. Please."

"What?"

"Do it."

I did. The sunlight wasn't flowing into her room directly, but there was enough ambient light filtering in that she should have been in horrid discomfort. She wasn't. She was staring at her hands, watching them as they were bathed in non-artificial light.

There was a boom and a crack of thunder from the living room.

"I'll be right back!"

She nodded without looking at me. There were too many things happening at once. I turned around and Josie flung open her door, wrapped in a blanket. Candace stood behind her blinking rapidly and slowly pointing at a visible Yuki in her room. I ignored them both and ran into the living room. The door in my wall was rattling and bellowing white smoke and flashing purple through the cracks. I wanted to find a big stick and whack my grandmother with it as she came through. It might be the only way I could get a shot in.

The doorknob turned just before the door swung wide. The smell of sage filled the air as my grandmother imperiously stepped through the portal to the other side, waving away the smoke.

"Nana!"

"Hello, Granddaughter," she said with a smile.

"Don't you hello granddaughter me! We've been looking all over for you!"

"Yes. Your mother finally got a hold of me. I rushed right over. What's this about floating rifts?"

"Nana. What. Did. You. Do?"

She sighed and shrugged. "Do you have any tea?"

Candace walked past me. I motioned to the dining table and Nana took a seat. Jimmy and Jason came into the room and Josie went to put some clothes on. Dar moved next to me, stared at the woman seated at my table, and growled.

Nana narrowed her eyes at him and barked something in Latin. Dar dropped to the ground and rolled on his back, tongue hanging from his mouth.

"Hellhound?" she asked but narrowed her eyes further. "No. Something else. *Cad a bhfuil tú,*" she canted in Irish, her native language.

Dar yipped and curled next to me, coughing and shifting. His bipedal humanoid form gasping in pain on the floor.

"You okay?"

He nodded, catching his breath. *Just caught me off guard. She's strong.*

And scary, I added.

And can hear you both, she added in both our heads.

We both looked at each other and back up to her.

"He's new. I don't think I've ever seen one quite like him."

"Nana, this is Dar."

"Greetings, Dar of Gehenna," she said as he stood. She raised her eyebrows as it became quite apparent, he was naked.

"Greetings…Nana."

"Cathleen, please."

He nodded.

"You've been busy, Dorothea."

She used my full name. She never did that. I was either in a shit ton of trouble, or she was impressed with me. Either way I was screwed.

I ignored her name calling and sat down at the table beside her. Dar shifted back and sat by me, more comfortable in his dog form. I didn't blame him. If I were a guy, I wouldn't want to be naked in front of my grandmother, either.

"So, what happened?" I finally mustered the courage to ask her.

Again, she sighed. "I screwed up. I'm sorry, Granddaughter."

I blinked at her. Repeatedly. She admitted making a mistake. It was probably the first time in recorded history such an admission had occurred, and I was certain the world would end before it happened again.

"Don't give me that look. Yes. I screwed the pooch."

Dar whined beside me.

She ignored him. "I wanted to cast the portal between us, but as you know, your mother locked away my spellbooks…"

"Yes. I know."

"Well, I thought I could do it from memory, but…" She paused a moment. "I may or may not have forgotten a particular glyph and well… It had nothing to anchor to. I could feel it popping in and out of existence here, so I released the spell. But it was already too late. The portal found an anchor the moment I let go. Unfortunately, that anchor was in the planes of Gehenna. So, with an anchor on one end, the other just seemed to flop around madly in your quaint little town. I thought nothing of it, not knowing it was still active."

"So, you stole your spell books back to try again."

She nodded.

"So, is what Mother says true? Will it find an anchor here and become massive?"

"Spilling an unimaginable number of denizens into this world. Yes. It will become a hellmouth."

"Fuuuuuuuck," Jimmy said wisely, behind me.

"Apt, but vulgar," Nanna said disdainfully.

"Sorry."

She nodded at my boyfriend. He took a step back, just to be safe.

"So, how do we stop it?" There had to be a way. There was always a way. At least in the movies.

"That's where I have been. Trying to find a way."

"Please tell me you did."

"Yes. Hopefully. But the price was very high."

"What was it?"

"The life of your mother."

"Nana!"

"I'm kidding, Child. It was a joke."

I sighed and shook my head, hiding my smile. "So, what was the price?"

"A night of passion with the elven king."

"You poor thing. How did you survive?" I asked sarcastically.

"How did I stay awake, you mean. Elves make love like they're painting a living room."

I stared at her aghast, sincerely doubting my ability to look at another elf again with a straight face, ever again.

"So, what was the solution?"

"We anchor it when it arrives again, *before* it can expand into a hellmouth."

"Sure. That's easy. Why didn't I think of that?"

She narrowed her eyes at me.

"Nana, I saw one of these things up close…in my bathroom. There's no way to anchor it. It's a two-dimensional ribbon. It's not like we can grab the edges and stretch it over a door frame like a balloon. That, and we have no idea *where* it will appear. We would have to start drawing the glyphs and casting the circle for *days* before it would appear. Even if we started now, *and* we knew where, it's probably going to go full nuclear sometime in the next few hours."

"All true. If we didn't have these," she said and reached into her pocket. Then her other pocket. Then her back pocket. Checked her bag, dumped the contents onto my table, shuffled through everything and muttered, "Oh!" She reached into her *jacket* pocket and pulled out a doe-skin bag, handing it to me.

I pulled the drawstring, snorting at the elvish runes embossed on the supple leather. "Painting a living room," I said and chuckled again.

I tipped the bag and three stones of blue, green, and crimson rolled into my hand. They were flat, but circular, with more elvish runes carefully carved in the stone and gilded in silver.

"Uh. What are these?"

"Charms."

"Lucky charms?"

"No, more of the fix a wayward portal type."

"How do they work?"

"One to anchor, one to bind, and one to… I forgot what the third one does. I'm sure it gets rid of it, somehow."

"Which one is which?"

"I don't know."

"How do they work?"

"You read the inscriptions on them and then hurl them at the rift. One at a time."

"Nana?"

"Yes, Child?"

"None of us can read elvish…"

"What?"

"I can," Candace said with a sigh.

"Can you read all three and throw them into the portal?"

"No," Nana said evenly. "It has to be three different people."

"I can translate them onto paper phonetically for you. Hopefully the stones will say which one is which," Candace said and walked over, nervously looking at my grandmother.

"This child is adorable!"

I kept Candace's age to myself, but from the way Nana was staring at her through half-lidded eyes, she might be figuring that out on her own.

I handed her the stones, and she rolled them over in her hands. She set the green one down first. "That is the anchor stone. Once it touches the rift, it will be stationary."

"Jason, toss me the pad of paper by the phone, and a pen, please."

He grabbed both and set them in front of me. "Here."

"Thanks." I wrote *anchor stone* on the top of the page and flipped it over to the next page. Candace could make notes under each one.

"Dot?"

Yuki's voice came from behind me. "Yeah, sweetie?" I turned around... She was standing. In the middle of my living room. Swathed in sunlight. She was staring down at her hands in front of the big window as the sunlight shined all over her. Dust motes were swirling around her, flashing in the beams of light.

"What's happening to me?"

I pushed my chair back, the stones temporarily forgotten. Crossing the distance between us, I smiled as I saw tears of joy streaming down her cheeks. They were tinted red, but still beautiful, just as she was with the sunlight playing with the purple in her hair. She sniffed as she turned to me.

"Do you like it?"

"It's so warm."

"Guess you inherited a little more from me than just food and fun, huh?"

She nodded at me, about three seconds away from a full-blown meltdown. I don't think I'd ever seen anyone as happy as she was, right then, at that moment.

"Hang on," I whispered, torn between wanting to watch her joy and having to deal with the rift. I did the best I could and walked back to the table, grabbing one of the high-backed wooden chairs. I brought it over to her, setting it down beside her in the sun and facing it out the window. "Enjoy yourself."

"Dot... *Thank you.* A million of them aren't enough, but you can have all of them."

"Happy for you, sweetie." I rubbed the top of her head and went back to the table, unable to stop smiling.

"She's going to make all the other vampires jealous," Jimmy said with a smile.

"I'm glad. They kind of kicked her to the curb, she should get a kick ass ability out of it."

Candace had the three stones in front of her and was hastily scribbling notes under each title, having ripped the pages off the pad. Standing over her, I watched her swirling script as she jotted it down. Her hand-writing was beautiful and made mine look like it had been done by an over-caffeinated six-year-old. I guess after seven hundred years you'd have plenty of time to practice.

The green stone was the Anchor Stone, the blue was the Binding Stone, and the reddish one was the... Sealing stone. I sighed in relief. There was a way to close it. The weight I hadn't felt in my chest became noticeable as it left. Now we just need to find it, bind it, bag it, and tag it. Then we could get on with our abnormal lives.

"Well, that's settled," Nana said and slapped her knees, standing. "I have a house to go buy. If you'll excuse me..."

"Nana?"

"Yes, Child?"

"Sit your ass down. You're not buying a tube of fucking toothpaste until this is over."

"Dorothea. While I might have been partially responsible for what is happening, don't ever presume to order me around. Ask your mother how well that worked for her..."

"Nana. Once this is over you can be as imperious and pompous as you would like. *Until* that time, you're staying right by my side. You broke it, you fix it. Do we have an accord?"

She took in a very large breath and let it out slowly through her nose. "Agreed."

"Good. Then we can go buy your house and I'll even help you move. And you're taking your door with you, I don't care how you do it."

She gave me a small smile, lowering her head briefly. She hadn't blasted me into bite-sized morsels. I might have impressed her with my refusal to back down. Then again, I might not have, and she'd make me pay for it later.

"Candace, put each stone with its translation into separate baggies, please. That way they won't get mixed up."

Dot...

Dar was looking up at me from the floor by my feet. *Yes?*

Let me go through the portal before you close it.

What? Why?

I've given you my reason. I'm afraid for you, but also, I do not belong in your world. Your vampire can protect you, even in the daylight now. You do not need me.

That may be true, but I like you. I don't want to lose you.

You are very kind. You have my thanks, but please... Let me go home.

If that's what you want.

I do.

Okay.

He nodded and settled his head on my foot. I was pretty confident that shutting the gate between two different worlds would sever the familiar bond.

My phone rang. I pulled it out of my pocket and a dreadful feeling washed over me as Chief's name popped up on the screen. I let out a little plea to the goddess as I answered it.

"Hey, Chief..."

"Yeah. You better get to the center of town. Now. I hope you got a hold of your grandmother."

"Be there in ten."

"Make it five, please. All hell is breaking loose down here. And that wasn't a figure of speech."

"Got it." I hung up the phone and looked at everyone around me. "Guess it's that time. Smoke 'em if you got 'em, I'm going to go put on some clothes. Jason, call every witch in the coven and have them meet us downtown. We're gonna need all the eldritch fire power we can muster."

"Yes, ma'am."

Chapter 17

We passed the diner and headed toward the big circle in front of Cedar Falls Town Hall. The closer we made it to the center of town, the darker the sky turned. Yuki frowned halfway. She'd been enjoying the sunlight. Hopefully we'd get through this quickly so she could enjoy it some more. Take out a couple of demons. Close the rift. That was the plan and it sounded like a damn good one to me.

As soon as we came around the bend before center square, I knew we were going to need a better one.

"What the fuck?"

I slammed on the brakes and we skidded to a stop. Jimmy, who had neglected to put on his seatbelt, tasted my dashboard.

"You okay?"

He nodded, rubbing his mouth a little. "Are those all demons?"

The center of town was literally *swarming* with imps, fiends, and various other species I hadn't seen yet. Chief and Marcus were firing their weapons, but being selective to conserve ammo, I assumed. They shot only at the ones chasing the few townsfolk trying to escape. Marcus got off a nice shot, blasting an imp's head just as it was about to pounce on a mother running away with her child.

I got out of the car with everyone else. Dar took off running and jumped at a fiend, transforming into a hellhound midair. Josie and Candace walked toward the fray wielding fire, not caring who saw. I nodded. Most of the town was holed up inside the buildings or had taken off running. The few remaining stragglers probably wouldn't be half as worried about a few people wielding magic more than getting eaten by slobbering demons. People did have *some* common sense.

Chief looked over his shoulder, saw me, and started backing toward us. "What's the plan?"

"Kill the demons, close the rift, grab some beers."

"Dot. There are probably over a thousand demons running around, and more are pouring from the rift."

"Where is it?" I couldn't see it, and we needed to get closer. A lot closer. "The park in the center?"

"Yes."

"It's in the park?"

"It *is* the park. The ground opened up and swallowed everything. It's not a rift, it's a pit."

"Hellmouth," I whispered to myself.

I hadn't noticed the pit fiend sneaking up on me. Luckily, Yuki did. In a blur of speed, she was in front of me and caught the things arms as it swung them. Yanking on it, she jumped and bashed her skull into the bottom of its chin, its razor-sharp fangs biting through its own tongue that fell to the ground beside them. It howled in pain and rage until she sliced through its throat with her claws. It was the first time I'd seen her fight, and I started to understand just how lethal vamps could be.

Chief did a double-take and looked at me for an explanation to her being out in the sunlight, even if it was filtered through billowing black clouds swirling over us.

"I'll explain later. We need to get to the rift."

"I'm with you," Jimmy said behind me.

"Jason, you help the girls and get people to safety. When the rest of the coven shows up, have them help. The townspeople are the priority, killing demons second. Got it?"

"Yes, Lady." He headed toward Josie and Candace, lightning crackling over his hands, flashing out if any imps got too close.

"Let's go," Chief said and stopped by the Jeep, pulling out his shotgun from the trunk. "Marcus, watch our rear."

"You got it."

I nervously palmed the bags of rocks nestled safely in my jeans pocket, making sure they were still there. We needed to hurry and get it anchored. I didn't even want to imagine a hellmouth shutting and reappearing elsewhere, even larger.

"Shall I help with the demons, Granddaughter?"

She had insisted on traveling by herself, not wanting to stuff herself inside my already over-packed Kia. Looking up, I smiled as she gently lowered herself from the sky on her broom. I'd never ridden one. It's not that I didn't know how, but seriously…it's a stick of wood. How comfortable could that be? Give me a sedan or SUV any day. Most witches only rode at Halloween in the safety of Ashville. The world was a much different place and the last thing we needed was to end up on Youtube.

"Yes, please, Nana."

She dropped off the side of the broom and landed on the ground. She shook the broom once and it became a wicked looking scythe. Now *that* was a trick I wanted to learn!

Nana held it in one hand, cleanly slicing through some of the closest demons and unleashing a torrent of fire from her other hand. I stared in awe before Chief coughed and pointed toward the park.

"Let's go," I said confidently, calling fire to both my hands. We needed to get to the rift, even if I had to burn us a new road to get there.

I took center, burning a swath through the demons while Jimmy and Chief walked side-by-side behind me, covering attacks from our sides while Marcus' gun could be heard going off every so often behind us.

Chief yelled behind me and I looked back. A winged monster had landed on his back, clawing frantically at his exposed neck and head. Rivulets of blood were already running down, staining his shirt.

Jimmy, quicker than I and closer, spun and grabbed the gargoylesque creature and turned it to stone, yanking it off Chief and shattering it on the street below.

I reached over and rested my hand on his neck. "*Leigheas,*" I canted, pouring a bit of power into the spell. The wounds closed beneath my hand. He could wash the blood off later.

"Thanks, Dot."

I nodded, turning at the horde before us. They were gathering, trying to keep us from reaching the portal.

Dar slipped up beside me, covered in black gore. *Your friend is hurt. Her lover is attending her. The humans have been driven from the square by the rest of your coven. Your grandmother scares me.*

Me, too. Any ideas how to get to the hellmouth?

Luck, Yuki chimed in as she appeared to my right, moving so fast I didn't see her until she was there.

"This isn't working, Dot. What else can we do?" Chief asked, echoing my familiars' thoughts.

"I don't know!"

"Pull back," Jimmy said. "We need to regroup and figure this out. It's just a handful of us against hundreds of these fuckers."

I hated to admit it, but he was right.

Turning to agree, a distant sound caught my ear. It was the blessed sound of sirens. Our cavalry had arrived. "Call Dennis!"

"Good plan," Jimmy said with a smile, knowing my intentions without my having to explain.

"What plan?" Chief asked confusedly.

228

"We got ourselves a battering ram," I told him with a sly wink.

"What? Where?"

Chief must have fired his weapon too many times without ear protection. It took him a moment to finally hear the sirens fast approaching. "Oh. *That* plan," he said and nodded.

"Get off the street!' I hollered as loud as I could, hoping *everybody* heard me. The five of us moved to the side, not attacking, just shoring up our defenses as they tried to surround us. Nana worked her scythe and flames, bearing down on us, albeit slowly. At least she wasn't in the middle of the road. Dennis would swerve. Hopefully.

Jimmy's defenses broke and he was covered in imps in a heartbeat. Yuki disappeared and came back into view beside him, tearing the offending creatures apart. I spared her a brief moment to nod my thanks.

"Hurry, Dennis," I hissed. They were close, the sirens echoing off the buildings around us.

Lightning flashed from the pit ahead of us. Fear that it was going to move and swallow up another part of Cedar Falls seized my chest. I couldn't breathe. We couldn't lose… There was way too much at stake.

Fly, Daughter…

A voice flittered through my mind, leaving a sense of well-being and an odd calm. A voice that wasn't either of my familiars or family members. I shook my head and smiled, blessed once again.

"Nana! Need your broom!"

She gave me a quizzical glance, not nearly close enough to throw it. She shook her scythe and it once again flashed into an archaic-looking broom. She tossed it above her and the demons surrounding her, shouting something that was drowned out by the screaming sound of the imp trapped in Dar's jaws.

The broom shot at me like an arrow, I grabbed it as it slowed, passing on my right.

My body became weightless as my hand gripped the broom. One handed, I forced it beneath me, settling it between my legs. It wasn't nearly as uncomfortable as I thought it would be. The weightlessness helped immensely. Otherwise I would have had the wedgie from Gehenna.

Taking to the air, the scene became surreal. A sea of demons stood between us and the pit, which wasn't fading or moving, it was getting bigger. The road that ran in a circle around it, had started crumbling and falling into it. At the edge, a massive demon was clawing its way out and into our world. Black horns sprouted from its head, curling upward wickedly. Flames danced all across its body as fear poured from it like a stench. I could smell it, even fifty feet above, and I was afraid.

I sent a mental image of it to Dar. *What the fuck is that?*

No...

Dar?

A balor! Stay away!

He was too late with his warning. The thing lifted its massive claws. Its piercing black eyes spotted me buzzing above its head and launched balls of fire ahead of me. It was smart enough to lead with its attacks instead of launching them directly at me.

Pulling back on the broom, I flew straight up, missing the first giant fireball. It sped past me and then reached the apex of its ascent before dropping back down and landing in a throng of demons, exploding and leaving nothing but ash.

The second one got close enough to singe both me and the broom. I began to question *why* the goddess had bid me to fly.

Think, Daughter... What is above you?

I looked up. There wasn't anything above me but a swirling mass of clouds, looking vaguely like a hurricane...

I couldn't make it rain unless there were clouds above me. It would negate our fire spells...but it might buy us some time against the flaming behemoth standing just outside the hellmouth.

I raised the hand not clutching the broom for dear life, aimed it at the sky and screamed, "*Fuascail!*"

It started as a drizzle, the droplets stinging my eyes as I made a wide pass back around toward my family. I could see Dennis bearing down the street, driving the rig expertly as it weaved through abandoned cars. When he hit the straightaway, he floored it, the diesel engine whining like the turbine of a jet as it lifted and rocketed down the road.

It hit the wall of demons and began splashing them away. I cheered as the truck made it over halfway before it started to slow.

"No. Keep going, Dennis. You can do it!"

The rain became a deluge and I spun the broom around, watching the flames of the balor flickering and sputtering. It looked down at its arms and roared out over the street in anger.

I urged the broom forward and swooped down. Just above the roof of the truck, I set my feet down on it as it sped forward, rain and demon guts obscuring my vision.

I held out my hand at the road in front of me and yelled, "*Reoite!*" I poured almost every ounce of power I had left into the spell. Blue light shot from my hand, striking the ground in front of us, turning the water that had so graciously fallen from the sky into a thick sheet of ice. The truck beneath my feet hit it and became an unstoppable freight train of destruction.

Exhausted, I toppled from the roof of the truck, but still managed to hang on to the broom and yell to Dennis to jump...

Hanging limply above the street, clutching the broom as much as I could, I watched as the truck kept barreling forward, whispering the word, "Jump," over and over again. I started breathing again when I saw three figures jump free, the demons scrambling to get away from their own death, ignoring them.

I had enough in me for one last spell, Jimmy's accident giving me the inspiration. I slowly lowered myself to the ground and whispered, *"Pléascadh,"* to the heroic firetruck's fuel tanks just as it struck the demon. It ignited, crashing into the balor and continuing on its unstoppable path. The demon and the firetruck slipped over the edge of the hellmouth.

Even with the broom steadying me, keeping me on my feet, the resulting fireball knocked me on my ass. Many of the demons were caught in the explosion, but not all of them. We were going to have a hell of a cleanup job to do. But, more importantly, the entire way to the hellmouth was completely clear.

Dar and Yuki slipped up beside me, acting like crutches. I let go of the magic flowing into the broom and felt my weight returning to me.

"That was fucking *awesome!*"

I chuckled down at Yuki smiling up at me. "Not from up there, sweetie."

She sobered and nodded. Dennis and the other two firemen reached us before Chief and the rest. The two firemen kept staring at Dar.

"Is that one of them?" The taller of the two finally built up the nerve to ask.

"No. He's with me."

"You're Dot, right?"

I nodded.

"*What* are *you*?"

"A witch…"

The both nodded, things they had seen clicking into place. "You saved Jimmy that day…"

"Yeah. Sorry."

"For what?"

"Can you keep all this between us?"

"Only if you tell me one thing…"

"What?"

"Jimmy's like you, isn't he? I mean seriously, beds don't walk by themselves, porn magazines don't just disappear in the middle of inspections, and a fucking Dalmatian can't talk. There's no way it was ventriloquism, either. Its lips were moving."

I couldn't help it, or deny it, if I wanted to. I was laughing too hard.

"Yep," the other fireman nodded, confirming their suspicions. Dennis remained wisely quiet.

"What do we do now?"

"We close the hellmouth."

"Where the hell did it come from?" The first fireman asked.

"Exactly," I answered.

"Oh. You didn't do this, did you?"

"No. That big ass demon did," I lied, not wanting to throw my grandmother under the bus. Firetruck. Whatever.

"Thank you, then. For saving all of us."

I nodded, just as Jimmy and Chief walked up.

"Everyone okay?"

I nodded at him. "Let's close the portal. I'm covered in demon guts and I want to take a shower." I turned to Dennis and the other guys dressed in yellow. "Stay here."

They nodded, backing up slowly and carefully on the ice.

"Let's do this."

It took a few minutes to finish crossing the small ice sheet in the middle of town. I could feel the heat radiating from the portal as it slowly melted the surrounding ice. I pulled the bag of stones out of my pocket and handed the green one to Jimmy and the blue one to Chief. "You're up first, Jimmy."

"Do I say it and then throw it or throw it and say it?"

I shrugged. "Go with say and throw. That way if it doesn't work, we don't have to jump in after it."

"This is why you're the boss."

He held the stone in one hand and the paper in the other, his mouth straining to make the phonetic sounds.

"*Il vath duodoth, mil tan thamar.*"

Immediately, the stone began humming and glowing. He gently tossed it over the edge of the pit. The ring of concrete around it flared brightly and made a loud *chink* noise, echoing off the buildings surrounding us. It had been anchored.

"*Il vath tuomoth, dan vil manar,*" The blue stone in Chief's hand did the same and he lobbed it a little more forcibly. The portal spun clockwise about three feet, twisting the road around it in a thunder of crunching gravel. It had been bound.

I held the crimson stone in my hand and closed it, turning to look at my familiar.

I'm going to miss you.

I know. He winked at me with his giant hellhound eye.

Fuck it. I'm getting mushy. I squatted down beside him and threw my arms around his neck. He smelled vaguely of sulfur, but it wasn't overwhelming or unpleasant. *Take care of yourself.*

You do the same. If you ever find yourself in the plains of Gehenna, call my name.

More like, scream it as I run for my life.

It's not all bad.

Sure.

I rubbed his head as I stood up, motioning for the portal. He nudged Yuki in her chest with his big head and she scratched his ears. Without another word, he turned around and leapt in.

I held up the stone again and read the words off the paper. "*Mil math domoth, mal brek veshnir.*"

The stone split in my hand and floated away on its own, I didn't have to chuck it. One half drifted over to my left, the other my right. They settled on both edges before drifting back together, dragging the wound in the earth closed, the concrete, grass, park, and fountain in the center all healing itself magically. It was pretty fucking cool to watch. An inch apart, the two stones slammed together in a clap of thunder and it dropped to the ground, the only one left in our world. The portal had been sealed.

I walked over and slowly picked the stone up off the ground, sticking it in my pocket as a memento of my friend.

Well done, Daughter.

Chapter 18

I winced as I looked at the jagged wounds across Josie's stomach. One of the demons had almost succeeded in gutting her completely. Candace had done as much as she could, but it was angry, wet, and still open in places. I wasn't sure if I had enough power to heal her, but I was going to fucking try.

Putting both my hands over the wounds, I tried to avoid putting any pressure on it. She was already in enough pain and her breathing was ragged and shallow. She was lying on the hood of an abandoned car and Candace was hovering above her, perched on the metal next to her. Candace had been crying, and her cheeks were puffed and swollen under her dark eyes.

I sent in a tendril of power, probing the wound. She had a tear in her intestines, a puncture in her stomach, and a scratch on her liver. Shuddering at the amount of damage she had taken, I knew I had to hurry. She'd lost a lot of blood. Too much.

"*Dún*," I said softly, pouring in a good amount of the tiny pool of power I'd amassed since dealing with the demon. I concentrated on the tear in her intestine first. I'd almost had it completely closed when I had to pour more power into her. Without a doubt, I knew I wouldn't have enough to save her.

"This isn't going to work. I'm depleted."

My heart broke when Candace began sobbing and Josie's eyes opened. She gave me a small, sad smile and nodded, knowing I'd done my best.

"Love you both," she whispered and closed her eyes.

"No! Goddess fucking damn it, Josephina! Don't you fucking die!"

I tried healing her again, I just didn't have anything left. But I didn't care. There was still magic in me. It was the magic that made me what I was and who I was. It was my core. Without a second thought I reached inside and felt my heart slow as I pulled the magic from its place inside my soul. The world around me started to fade until five sets of hands yanked me away from my best friend.

"No! What are you doing! I could save her!"

It was my grandmother who cracked me across the face. That sobered me the fuck up. "Nana?"

"You think she would want you to trade your life for hers, Child? Are you insane?"

"No," I said in surrender.

"Do not give up, but do not throw your life away. No matter how admirable your motives." She sighed. "Make that two lives."

I looked over at Yuki. She was deathly pale and leaning against the vehicle, panting. "Oh, my goddess. I didn't even think. Yuki! I'm sorry."

She nodded. "I could have stopped you. I was ready, too."

Candace jumped down from her perch and hugged my vampire.

Chief shot me the dirtiest, angriest, glare I think I'd ever seen. Worse than he usually looked at me when I did something stupid. "Maybe this will work." He rubbed his hands together and touched them to my chest, just below my neck. I felt the trickle of warmth as he poured power into me. I didn't even know it was possible, but he was doing it.

"How?"

"I don't know, either. I used to have to juice Rebecca up before major rituals. She didn't have enough power on her own. It's how I knew I could do it."

There was a minute flare of jealousy, but I wanted to kiss him more for handing me the solution to saving my friend. None of the other witches in our coven could share their power or were adept at healing. Candace had about as much healing power as Josie. My amped up abilities were leagues beyond that. If there was more time, they could have taken turns healing Josie, but she needed it all now. I was her only shot.

"Start healing, I'll keep feeding you. If you kill yourself, I'll never forgive you, though," he said sternly.

Nodding, I put my hands back on Josie and sent out my tendril of power, letting it finish closing the wound on her intestine. I moved on to the stomach, which was much easier. The liver healed even quicker. Her insides were fine, but there was still the wound to deal with and her blood loss.

Her flesh began to wiggle and become very warm under my hands. The demon's claws had been filthy, and I sent enough power into her to kill any foreign organisms, too. Healed and sterilized, I let go of her stomach through the gaping wound in her shirt. I used my hand to wipe away some of the blood and gore, sighing when I saw her whole again.

"Josie?" Candace asked softly, with no response.

"Any ideas on how to cure blood loss?" I asked the crowd.

"She needs a transfusion," Candace answered. "You could stimulate her blood production with magic, but it's still slow.

I could give her some of my blood.

That didn't work out so good the last time, I answered Yuki.

I think that was more you *than anything. You did the same damn thing to a demon. I don't think I have to worry about your witch friend stealing me from you.*

I'll leave it to you, then. It's your call. I'd never ask you to do anything like that, ever.

You just won't stop me, though, she said with a wink.

"Nope," I said aloud and gave her a smile.

She nodded once, and got a little closer, ripping her wrist open with her fangs and dribbling some of her blood into Josie's mouth before pressing it against her lips.

Immediately, Josie began suckling on Yuki's wrist, making little slurpy noises and moaning. I knew exactly what she was feeling. Vampire blood was like... Yeah. Wow.

Her eyes opened and she saw everyone watching the show. She let go with a little wet *pop*, glancing up at Yuki in embarrassment. "Woah."

"Welcome back," Yuki said and wiped her arm off on her T-shirt.

"Chief? What the hell is going on?" A silky-smooth voice asked softly behind us.

Everybody turned around to look at the forgotten Marcus.

"Where'd you go?"

"One of those things grabbed me and dragged me down an alley. Then there was explosions and rain and light. The thing screeched and disappeared above me."

I looked around and we were alone on the street. There wasn't an imp or anything even remotely demon-like left. They were all gone.

"What the fuck? Where'd they all go?"

"They disappeared when you activated the sealing stone, Child. They went back to where they belonged." Nana gave me a proud smile.

"So even if Dar had *wanted* to stay, he couldn't have?"

"Unless he belonged here."

240

"I kinda felt like he did."

"But he didn't."

"Thanks, Nana."

She nodded.

I let my eyes drift over all my friends, old and new, in thanks. We'd done it. "Can we go home now? I need a shower and a nap."

"The hellmouth is closed. The three of us shut that shit down!" Jimmy smiled at Chief and me, but then got a *very* serious look on his face.

"What?" I was almost afraid to ask.

"You, me, and Chief. I thought our first threesome was going to be *way* more fun.

"That's disgusting. There is something wrong with you," Chief said and shook his head.

"What?" Jimmy asked innocently. "Our other threesome was fun. You should have been there.

"Wait. What?"

"Jimmy!" I growled his name.

Chief turned to me and blinked once, and then stood there mouth agape.

Jimmy whistled and said, "Oops," before skipping happily back to the car.

"Fucker," I said at his retreating back.

Epilogue

I reached down and picked the cup of coffee off the teal tabletop, taking a welcoming sip. I let its warmth spread over my tongue and fill up my happiness tanks. Everybody worries about finding the perfect mate, having a successful career, and buying the perfect house, all without realizing that true happiness came in a mug and was black. Those cream and sugar people didn't want *true* happiness, just a watered-down sweetened version of it.

"Ahhh. That's the good shit."

"Language, Granddaughter," Nana said as she slid into the booth across from me.

"Sorry, Nana."

She sighed and took a sip of the cooling tea she had ordered before getting dragged into Herb's office to sign her life away. I smiled when she set the new key ring holding her shiny house key on the table in front of her. The mountain of paperwork, she shoved into a purse that shouldn't have been able to hold a decent sized wallet. Leave it to Nana to have a bag of holding.

"I almost forgot." She reached back in and pulled out three heavy, leather tomes and set them in front of me. "Those are for you."

"The grimoires?"

She nodded. "I suggest you start reading them thoroughly."

"What? Why?"

"Sweetie, that hellmouth? That was just the beginning. The Lady has many wonderful things in store for you. Unfortunately, you are going to have to work *very* hard for them. But have no fear, your Nana is here."

"Gosh. I don't know what to say."

"Your gratitude is very underwhelming. Come on! Get a little excited. The Blackwell witches are going to liven this little town up!"

Of course, she said it loudly enough for every person in the diner to hear her. The woman had no filter. I sighed in resignation. We were pretty much out of the closet, anyway. There was no hiding what the hell had happened in the center of town. People told tales of being rescued by magic wielding heroes, and there was no going back. Everybody knew, and they were remaining oddly quiet about it. It was almost…magic.

So, we were outed and well on the way to becoming a suburb of Ashville. The start of the dream I had for the little town I, and Nana, called home.

The door chimed behind me and I smiled as a familiar hand ran over my shoulder.

"Hey, Chief," I said without looking.

"How'd you know it was me?" He sat down next to me.

"Your touch. I'd know it anywhere." I leaned over and gave him a sweet kiss. "That and your aftershave. I could smell you coming up the street."

He narrowed his eyes and didn't reply. Reaching down to have another sip of coffee, I saw him pull his shirt to his nose and sniff. I smiled and sipped.

It was good to have things back to normal between him and me. He'd been kind of grouchy for like three hours after Jimmy mentioned the threesome. I just told him exactly what happened and that it was Jason. And then I made it up to Chief, all by my lonesome. It would be hard for anybody to be grouchy after what *I* did for him. I might even be back to walking normal, sometime tomorrow.

The door chimed again, and Jimmy plopped down next to Nana. Yuki slid an empty chair up to the end of the table. They'd walked down to the bookstore to check on how things were going.

"The place looks amazing," Jimmy said, surprised. "Freddie said they should be done by next weekend."

"Woah."

"Yeah. You should see Jason running around the place, trying to figure out where everything is going to go. I told him to make sure he plans on having a *huge* erotica section."

"Of course you did."

"Plenty of dirty magazines, too."

"Jimmy. You realize you're sitting next to my grandmother, right?"

"Sorry, Cathleen. Do you have any preference for dirty magazines? I can run back over and tell Jason to order them."

"No. I use the internet like a normal person."

Only Jimmy could have gotten away with saying something so outrageously outlandish to my nana and survived. And only my Nana could have come up with a retort to leave Jimmy stunned. But then he grinned and wiggled his eyebrows and I wanted to beat him with a shoe. I sighed and took another sip of coffee while Chief and Yuki started laughing.

"Where's Josie?" Yuki scooted a little closer to the table.

"She and Candace went across the street to Abe's. She wanted to find a bigger bed for the two of them. Candace kicked her in the eye last night."

"Honeymoon over?" Chief asked with a chuckle.

I shook my head. Those two were inseparable. It had even gotten worse since Josie got hurt. Candace loved her from day one, but almost losing her made her dote on her a little more. I even had to fetch my own wine in the evenings. I was happy.

"We have more people coming in tonight?"

I nodded at Chief. "Yep. Josie's mom should be in town any minute. She called Josie from the border a couple hours ago. It's Shea I feel sorry for. She practically forced him to ride with her. At least they're sharing the moving van expense."

"I saw Alista and her brother, earlier. That's about half the new members coming in. They're moving faster than I expected."

"Not Trevon. He's in Africa collecting herbs for the Apothecary. He won't be here for a few weeks. Once he's here, we'll hold the ritual. That's not something I want to do more than once."

"Gotcha. Still can't get used to the idea of an apothecary."

"Telling you. The town is going to love it. Just be careful what you drink around some of the single ladies stalking you."

"Yeah," he said with a shudder.

I raised my mug in a toast. "To brighter days and happiness."

"Aye," they gave a cheer.

"So, Derek will be a full-fledged member of the Coven of the First Moon soon," Jimmy said with a strange lilt in his voice.

"Oh, boy," I said and rolled my eyes, running my fingers over the third charm from our sealing ritual. I'd turned it into a necklace and wore it all the time now. Just as a reminder.

"Dar," I whispered his name with a smile.

A red light flared from the necklace and everyone at the table shielded their eyes. With a small crack of thunder, there was a six-hundred-pound hellhound lying broken and battered on the table, wounds smoking and giving off a sulfurous stench. The table flipped sideways under his weight, throwing Yuki to the floor as Dar slid on top of her.

"Dar!" I practically pushed Chief out of the way to get to him.

He wearily lifted his head off Yuki, shimmered, and turned into a German Shepherd.

Need power.

I put my hands on him and let it flow between us, watching in fascination as his wounds closed before my eyes.

"Are you okay?"

Now.

What happened?

The bond didn't sever, and I found myself being pummeled by the denizens of Gehenna. When you sealed the rift, they were practically dumped on me. Let's just say they weren't too happy. I'd been lying there for days when the ground opened up beneath me and dumped me in your lap.

Oh, sweetie. I'm sorry. I hugged his neck. *But I'm glad you're back.*

Me, too. I guess you're stuck with me.

Oh, no! I teased.

"Hey, Dot. I'm sorry, but only service animals are allowed in the diner."

"Sorry, Marge."

I led him out as soon as he could stand. We had just made it out the front door when he growled and spun, leaping up in the air in front of me and catching the arrow meant for my chest between his jaws, snapping it cleanly in half.

"Where the hell did that come from?"

The elf in the tree at the end of the street...

Bonus Scene

Read on for a bonus scene from Dennis's point of view in
Chapter 12.

In the Hot Seat

Oh, she's there?

I sighed and stared at Alista's text for a minute before
answering. Even *if* I lied to her, which I didn't want to do,
it would be the wrong answer. So, I typed, *Yes. She and
Jimmy are on the couch watching TV.*

Where R U?

I'm sure she was just making conversation, but it felt
like an inquisition. Probably because I felt guilty in my
heart. I was in my room, but that's not where I wanted to
be. I wanted to be out in the living room, just to be around
Dot. It made me feel like a pig. Don't get me wrong, Alista
was amazing, when she wasn't accusing me of being in
love with our high priestess, but Dot was...Dot. Alista
wasn't wrong. I'd fallen in love with her when she smiled at
me the first time all of us had gone for drinks. When I'd
delivered her furniture, I wanted to ask her out. Helping out
at the firehouse, I'd wanted to ask her to marry me.

The problem was my best friend.

He loved her more than I did. I'd backed away from
Dot to give him a chance and he hadn't been afraid to take
it. I hated him for that. Not that he took it, but that the man
lived without absolutely any fear. We'd been friends since
we were kids and he'd been like that since the day he was
born. Fearless, amazing, a burning light to match Dot's
inferno. They belonged together. I belonged...on the
sidelines. Watching. Like I always did.

In my bedroom, folding clothes. Where else would I be? I typed a little sadly. Setting down my phone, I picked up my stack of boxers and put it in the top drawer of my dresser.

My phone dinged. I walked back over and picked it up, afraid to look at it. *Sorry, that probably sounded bitchy. Still sad and sorry, and I just miss you.*

Miss you, too. That wasn't a lie, either. Having a best friend like Jimmy and a wallflower personality made it difficult for me to meet women. I'd heard the phrase, "Who's your friend," too many times to count. Alista was one of the few women who had been instantly attracted by both my body and my quiet, safe personality. Don't get me wrong, I'd had plenty of women *show* interest, but my shyness was almost like a disease. Some women found it cute, others found it weak. Alista had seemed like the perfect fit.

I should have stayed away from Dot completely. It's not like I would ever ditch Alista to pursue Dot. I knew she was way out of my league. She was the sun. I was a piece of space junk that would burn up if I got too close to her.

Sighing, I sat down on my bed. Our fight yesterday had been almost epic in proportion. I hadn't told anyone but Jimmy. Alista was packing to head back to Asheville for a few days. She'd been talking and I hadn't been paying much attention.

"Penny for your thoughts," she had asked quietly, sitting down next to me.

"Not thinking about much," I answered.

"Dot?"

"Yeah," I responded without thinking. I was a dumbass.

The fight that had ensued had almost made me want to throw up. Fighting, conflict, negative emotions...I didn't do well with them, and I hated to admit it, but Jimmy usually handled all those things *for* me. Sure, I could fight when I had to. Just not verbally.

The thing that bothered me most was people mistook my shy quietness for stupidity. I'd graduated every class I had ever taken with damn near perfect scores. I could have done so much more with my life than being a fireman, but…that's what Jimmy wanted to be when he grew up. He'd always been there for me, especially growing up. Mom had been human. Dad was a sperm donor. When my powers manifested, he never showed up. Jimmy knew in an instant, and he and his family had raised me instead of my drunk of a mother. Where Jimmy went, I would follow. I didn't *owe* it to him. I wanted to. He was more than a friend, or a brother. Half the time it felt like he was the missing piece of me. My twin.

Are we okay?

I nodded at my phone. *Of course. I love you,* I answered.

Love you, too. Be back in a few days.

K. Night.

Night. <3

I tossed my phone on the bed and figured I'd try being social before going to bed. If I tried right then, I'd be tossing and turning for a few hours. Opening my bedroom door, I stepped out into the living room and I smiled at Dot, who grinned at me when I walked out and sat down on the recliner.

"Where's Alista?"

My heart broke a little. "She flew back to Virginia to start moving and getting everything ready."

"When she coming back?"

I shrugged, not really knowing the answer myself. Alista hadn't been sure, and we weren't exactly on speaking terms when she left. We'd patched things up over the phone, or at least threw a bandaid on the wound. How it played out when she got back was another story.

Jimmy elbowed Dot in the ribs. He knew the whole story and I was grateful for the interference. Dot was a million things, but she knew when something was wrong just by looking at you. She had a natural instinct to want to

251

mother everybody and solve all of their problems for them. She meant well, but it was her one true fault. At least in my eyes. People needed to figure shit out on their own.

"Don't know," I told her.

"Oh, sweetie. I'm sorry. Do you want to talk about it?"

"Thanks, Dot. No. It will work out or it won't."

I ignored them as they began whispering to each other quietly. Eventually their conversation got loud enough for me to hear. "That she cared more about her brother than him," Jimmy said at almost normal volume.

It hadn't been my proudest moment. When Alista told me I loved Dot more than her, it had been the first thing that popped in my head and flew out of my mouth. They *were* twins. It was natural that they were closer than normal siblings. I knew that. But I still said it.

"Dennis, you moron," Dot said exasperatedly, mirroring my thoughts. She even shot me a stern look.

Heat crept up my cheeks. "I know." I did. I wasn't lying.

Dot got up and walked around the table, throwing her arms around me. *Fuck. Why does she have to smell so damn good?*

If Jimmy told Dot what I said to Alista, he had to have told her what prompted it. What she said to me. I felt the need to defend her, even if it was true and my screw up. "She was pissed when she said it, and instead of denying it, I just told her she was too close to her brother. I'm a fucking idiot."

"Yes. You are. But, look at the bright side. You have all the time in the world to tell her that you're stupid." She squatted down beside me and stared into my eyes. "Just take things slow. I'm sure they'll work out the way they were meant to."

Meant to. Not that everything would be all right between Alista and I. "I know. Thanks, Dot."

"And for future reference, if anybody else accuses you of being in love with a crazy bitch like me, just tell them you're not into insane." She stood up, kissed me on the forehead, and walked back over to Jimmy.

But I am. I sighed.

"Awww," Jimmy said with a chuckle.

He was just being Jimmy and it actually made me smile. I grabbed the cushion next to me and launched it at his grinning face. Time slowed as the pillow sailed through the air. The edge of it had slipped from my fingers a fraction of an instant too soon. It didn't sail at Jimmy. It flew at Dot. I screeched as it connected solidly with her face and slid down, nestling itself in the focal point of the universe, her lap.

There was complete silence for a moment until Jimmy started chuckling evilly. "Somebody's in trouble!"

"They are," Dot said cooly, picking up the pillow and shoving it in Jimmy's smug looking face. "He wouldn't have thrown it if you weren't such a shit!"

Jimmy just laughed harder. Until Dot used her pleasure spell on his thigh and his ass lifted off the couch. His body convulsed in the throes of ecstasy until he finally screamed, "Holy shit!"

"Did you learn your lesson?" She cocked an eyebrow at him.

"No. Do it again," Jimmy practically begged.

"There is something wrong with you."

"Yeah, but you love me."

I smiled as she froze for a moment while she stared at Jimmy. "Yeah. I do."

It was my turn. "Awww," I said and meant it. It really was a sweet moment. It could only have been sweeter if she'd said it to me.

It was the tears in my eyes that blurred the pillow as it raced toward my face. I didn't see it until it smacked me squarely on my forehead and nose. When I could see again, Jimmy was kissing Dot and she was holding up her hand in case I retaliated.

"Did you like that?" She inquired of her answer to him.

"Bet your ass, I did. Say it again?" His grin was almost infectious, and I found a matching one on my face.

"I do," she answered.

"No, say it, say it." He gave her puppy dog eyes.

"What?"

"Please?" He gave up the eyes and went for the full pout. There was no way she would be able to resist him.

"Fine. I love you. Happy *now*?"

"You have no idea." His grin came back ten-fold.

"Yeah. I think I do." She sat there, waiting. Staring at him intently. She wanted him to say it, too. Jimmy just smiled at her, teasingly. She lifted a finger and I sat back as sparks arced across it. "This one is set to stun…"

"Well, if I say it under duress, it doesn't really mean anything, now does it?"

"Jimmy…" I heard the warning in her voice. I half hoped he kept teasing her. Seeing him get finger-tazed might have been the highlight of my week.

"I love you, Dorothea Blackwell. I love you with all my heart." He leaned in and kissed her. I could feel the heat in it from across the room.

He leaned back and pulled her on top of him. I could almost feel his need. I knew, if she were kissing me, I'd need more, too. That was the most dangerous thing about Dorothea Blackwell…enough could never be had. Whatever she gave you, you'd want more. I didn't know how he could stand it.

His hands slid up her sweatshirt, fumbling with her bra. I wanted to get up and leave them alone. They'd just shared one of the most tender moments I'd ever witnessed, and I didn't want to be a burden. That's what I wanted. My body, however, refused to quit.

She pulled away and shook her head to clear it a little. "Take this into the bedroom?" I was almost grateful for her decision, taking away my inability to move.

"Why?" Jimmy tilted his head in confusion. The fucker.

"Dennis?" She asked without looking at me, too embarrassed it looked like. There was a flush on her cheeks that had nothing to do with the heat of their kiss.

"You don't want him to watch?"

I almost jammed my fingers in my ears and wiggled them around to make sure I wasn't hearing shit. *He wouldn't... She wouldn't...*

She twitched in what looked like pleasure as the words left his mouth. "Somebody likes that idea," Jimmy said with an evil, horny chuckle.

"I think two somebodies do. Maybe three," Dot said and looked over at me. I grabbed the TV remote and started flipping channels, pretending miserably to not have been watching. I don't think I'd ever been *more* embarrassed at any point in my life than right then. Being best friends with Jimmy for so long, that said a *lot*.

Out of the corner of my eye, I saw Jimmy squeeze her breasts as her back arched. "Take off your sweatshirt."

It was the motion of my hands that made me give up the pretext of the television. My head turned slowly as she lifted her own sweatshirt over her head, exposing herself to both of us.

Holy fuck, she is perfect.

I'd seen her breasts before. Everyone in the coven had at one point or another. In ritual, they were glorious. In the heat of passion, the feeling in my stomach when I saw them increased exponentially. Jimmy was staring at her as hard as I was.

She got up and Jimmy lifted off his shirt. She pushed down her jeans, leaving herself only in her panties. A shiver ran through me as my blood pressure dropped as it was diverted to my rapidly hardening cock.

"Holy fuck," I whispered simultaneously with Jimmy, his voice covering mine, as she straddled him in front of me.

"I don't' know if I'll go that far," she said to him with a grin.

I couldn't tear my eyes from her, not if a pack of velociraptors ran across the living room between us. Then she reached down and started unbuckling his belt and jeans. He reached out and stroked the front of her panties. How he had the willpower not to lift her off him and resettle her on his face, I didn't have a clue. That would be the first thing I would have gone for. I wouldn't have been able to stop myself from tasting her, feasting on her, pleasing her.

Jimmy stopped teasing her pussy and finished unbuttoning his jeans for her. It was cute watching her struggle, but I didn't blame him. I'd want to be in her, too.

"Thanks," she said, smiling at him.

"My pleasure."

"I'm sure it will be," she answered him.

She unzipped him, pulling him out with her fingers. It wasn't the first time I'd seen Jimmy's cock, but it was the first time I *wanted* to see Jimmy's cock. Picturing what her hands would feel like stroking me, was much easier to imagine while actually seeing her do it. Even if it was with Jimmy. I almost groaned when she started rubbing it across the front of her panties. How the hell he didn't explode all over was one of the great mysteries of the world. I probably would have shot the ceiling.

I could see his cock, so I didn't give two shits if he saw mine. It needed release from it's confines, and maybe even release in general. She wasn't focusing on me, so I unzipped myself and pulled it out. Picturing her hand on me, I slowly stroked myself in time with the movements of her hand. It was almost too much, too fast, so I slowed my pace.

"Put it in you," Jimmy whispered to her.

She shook her head.

"You know you want to," he said with a little grin. The smug bastard.

"Are you sure?" It almost sounded like she was begging.

He nodded.

She reached down and pulled her panties to the side. I wanted nothing more than to stand, walk over to them, and get a much better view. Watching her lift herself off him, part her lips, and impale herself was more than enough though. Watching the ecstasy on her face as he filled her. My cock started leaking with the heat of the moment. I ran my hand through my precum for lubrication, spreading it all around my cock, pretending it was the juice from her pussy instead. Picturing my hand as her soft walls as it opened up around me. I couldn't help it. I groaned.

It was enough to shift Jimmy's attention to me. He smiled as he saw me jerking myself off while they fucked. Before she opened her eyes, he looked back at her.

"You feel so fucking incredible," he told her, and I could hear the truth in his words. He wasn't teasing me, he was telling me what it felt like to be inside her.

"So...do you," she stammered as she began grinding on his dick, pleasure making her mewl little gasps of satisfaction as he filled her. She rode him for all she was worth, trying to get every last inch of him inside her and lowering her face to his neck, exposing more of her ass to me. My strokes picked up their pace. I was going to come soon.

"You should turn around," Jimmy said to her.

I almost panicked and stuffed my cock back into my pants, horrified at the thought of her watching me pleasure myself. But she heard what I heard in Jimmy's voice. He wanted her to watch me. He wanted her to expose herself to me. He wanted this to be between us, too. But most importantly, he wanted her to be happy and to do what she wanted.

That's when I knew. Dot wanted me to see her. The start of my orgasm was almost too much to stop. I quickly let go as a spurt slowly seeped from the tip, flooding my hand. The old familiar smell not bothering me in the least as I used all of it to wet my cock. With as wet as Dot's pussy had to have been right then, it was probable closer to what Jimmy was feeling, anyway.

She got up and turned around. Her eyes were closed as she used her hands to guide him back into her velvety smoothness. She cried out as he filled her again. I edged my orgasm, not wanting to finish before they did. I needed better access to my cock. Throwing my leg over the arm, I spread my legs and unbuttoned my pants, pulling more out through the front of my boxers and then reaching back in to free my balls. Fully exposed to her, I began stroking myself again. It was so much easier because her eyes were closed.

And then she opened them, focusing on me and my pleasure.

Heat raced through me as I was unable to stop myself, stroking my cock while she watched me. I almost whispered her name.

She smiled at me and let her eyes travel over my body before staring at my cock with what looked almost like hunger in her eyes.

"Oh, goddess," she cried out, an orgasm wracking her body as she rode Jimmy when his body arched on the couch, filling her pussy with his seed.

I'd reached my limit. My cock burst with a torrent of come and it splashed all over my chest, just as she wound down from her throes of ecstasy, Jimmy's cock splatting wetly against his stomach as *his* come slipped from her and pooled all over him. Jet after jet wetted my shirt, one shot splashing hotly against my shirt as I managed not to cry out as I came.

Dot looked at me and smiled. Embarrassed beyond anything I had ever imagined, I blushed as I got up and ran into my room, closing the door behind me and leaning against it as my come slipped slowly down over my shirt.

I needed a shower.

And a cigarette.

Author's Note

Reviews are important for new authors and I greatly appreciate everyone who takes a moment to leave one, even a line or two! Thank you so much for reading my reverse harem series! I'm writing away and more books will be out soon!

Follow me on Amazon to be sent updates on my new releases!

Come join my Readers Group on Facebook for news, fun, games, teasers for upcoming books, and naughty shenanigans! 18+ recommended.

Coven of the First Moon

About the Author

A late comer to the writing game, Jacquelyn had always been a fan of romance novels and lately become addicted to the reverse harem category. I mean seriously, who wouldn't? Sitting alone one night she flipped open her laptop and said, "I'm going to give this a whirl." And thus, the Lovin' the Coven series was given life. She has designs on other series as well, but only time shall tell.

As for her, she is five-foot-something, with graying hair, wicked eyes, an eager smile, and an annoying laugh. She lives at home with her dog, a cat, and that is about all she is comfortable sharing.

Other Works

Lovin' the Coven Series
(Reverse Harem- 7 book series)

First Moon
Second Blood
Third Charm
Fourth Rite
Fifth Essence
Sixth Sense
Seventh Seal

The Fox and the Hounds
(Reverse Harem – trilogy)

A Tail of Woah
A Tail of Two Kitties
The Tell Tail Heart

www.ingramcontent.com/pod-product-compliance
Lightning Source LLC
Chambersburg PA
CBHW070907180626
46817CB00003B/955